WINKIE

Also by Clifford Chase:

The Hurry-Up Song: A Memoir of Losing My Brother

*Queer 13: Lesbian and Gay Writers
Recall Seventh Grade*

CLIFFORD CHASE

WINKIE

Grove Press
New York

Printed in the United States of America
Published simultaneously in Canada

FIRST EDITION

Library of Congress Cataloging-in-Publication Data

Chase, Clifford.
Winkie / Clifford Chase.
p. cm.
ISBN-10: 0-8021-1830-5
ISBN-13: 978-0-8021-1830-1
1. Teddy bears—Fiction. 2. Terrorists—Fiction. I. Title.
PS3603.H3793W56 2005
813'.6—dc22   2006041145

Grove Press
an imprint of Grove/Atlantic, Inc.
841 Broadway
New York, NY 10003

Distributed by Publishers Group West
www.groveatlantic.com

06 07 08   09 10   10 9 8 7 6 5 4 3 2 1

For John

Winkie

Part One

"*The books we read in childhood don't exist anymore; they sailed off with the wind, leaving bare skeletons behind. Whoever still has in him the memory and marrow of childhood should rewrite these books as he experienced them.*"

—*Bruno Schulz, from a 1936 letter to a friend*

Please state your name.

Clifford Chase.

And what was your relationship to the defendant?

He was my teddy bear.

How long have you known him?

Since I was born, really. Because first he was my mother's, and then she passed him on to her kids. There were five of us, and I'm the youngest, so he was very old by the time he came to me.

What are your earliest memories of him?

I can remember, or I can imagine, I'm not sure which, lying in my crib and holding him.

And that would that have been when, Mr. Chase?

I slept in a crib until I was almost five, so this could have been as late as 1963. I can remember, or almost remember, how his small body felt in my arms—small and plump. I can remember the comfort I felt in his being smaller than myself.

Was there any indication, back then, that he was anything other than a normal toy?

No. Though, of course, to me he always *seemed* alive.

Why is that?

The way all toys seem alive to children, I guess. But there was something else . . . I think it was because his eyes opened and closed. They fell shut when you laid him down, and they opened again when he sat upright.

Why that in particular?

It made it seem like he could see me.

("Objection," says the prosecutor. "Speculation." "Sustained," says the judge. "The witness will please stick to facts, not feelings.")

Yes, sir.

Now Mr. Chase . . . You said the bear belonged to your mother first.

Yes. She got him when she was nine or ten, for Christmas. She called him Marie.

Marie?

He was a girl then.

(The courtroom begins to murmur. "Order," cries the judge. More murmuring. "Order!" Gavel blows. Silence.)

Where and when did the bear come into your mother's possession?

That would have been in 1924 or '25, in Chicago. She remembers that her parents bought him—or her—at Marshall Field's.

So during all that time, from 1925 until quite recently, the defendant remained, to the best of your knowledge, in the custody of someone in your family?

Yes—Oh, except once they left him in a motel room and had to go back for him. My brother cried and cried. That was before I was born.

("Your honor," says the prosecutor, "this so-called testimony . . ." He throws up his hands, as if helpless. "Sustained," says the judge. "The defense will please get to the point.")

Of course, your honor, of course . . . Mr. Chase, how can you be sure the defendant is the same bear that you grew up with?

I recognized him immediately—on the news, I mean.

But isn't one teddy bear the same as another?

Oh, no, as anyone can see, Winkie is quite distinctive. I've never seen another bear with eyes like that, and his ears are much bigger than other bears' ears. Besides, he's so worn out, and he's been mended so many times, that his face has become completely his own. I looked into that face many times as a child, and so, as I said, I recognized his photo immediately. And then I made the connection to his disappearance from my parents' house, which was about two years ago.

But no one reported this disappearance?

Normally one wouldn't report a missing teddy bear. Now, of course, I would.

(General laughter.)

Mr. Chase, what do you remember most about the defendant?

I was a strange and lonely little boy, and it seemed like Winkie understood that. Because *he* looked strange and lonely, too.

(The prosecutor shakes his head theatrically but makes no formal objection.)

So your memories of him are ones of love and comfort?

Yes.

Can you recall anything, anything at all, to indicate that the defendant would ever commit the serious crimes of which he has been accused?

No. He was a strange bear, but I think he was a good bear, and I still believe that. No matter what anyone says about him. Which is why I came forward.

Thank you. No further questions.

1' 9"

1' 6"

1' 3"

1'

0' 9"

0' 6"

SHERIFF'S DEPARTMENT
APD 11 30 00

"He was a strange bear, but I think he was a good bear."

Winkie

in

Captivity

I.

Some months earlier, outside a moonlit shack in the forest, dozens of helmeted figures crept into position. Pantomimed orders; crouched runs from tree to tree; a relay of nods; stillness again. It wasn't long before daybreak. Whitish strands of fog gathered and dispersed. Twigs dripped dew. The men blew quietly into their cold, cupped fingers, waiting.

Inside the shack, on an old mattress as worn as himself, the little bear lay wide-awake, thinking. But it wasn't the authorities who had roused him. In fact, he was completely unaware of them. Rather, he was sleepless with grief.

The past, the past. How it came toward you, Winkie thought. How it moved you without even touching you. And what did it mean—to remember and to feel? What was the point in feeling it all again?

Here in the forest he had been granted a child of his own, and she had been his joy. But before even a year had passed, she had died. In the weeks since then, alone in the cabin or wandering just as alone in the woods, Winkie had tried to understand this simple, unyielding fact.

Late one night he fell asleep with the TV going and, a few minutes later, seemed to awaken to its flickering—though he knew he was still dreaming, and next he saw that the flickering wasn't the TV but his little cub. She was floating there. She didn't say so, but he understood this was the only time he'd see her. She radiated something, perhaps comfort. Gazing at each other shyly, they basked in the present moment. A flickering infinity. Then the little one said, "Think back," and faded from view like any memory.

That was three nights ago. Since then Winkie had gone over his life again and again, searching for the right thing to remember, even one moment that could give him hope. Of course this meant remembering all of it anyway, in snatches, all the children he'd loved and what he'd been to them; then the desolate years up on the shelf, loved by no one; and finally, by a sudden miracle he would never understand, what he'd always wished for, the gifts of life and movement—

But what good had running away done? Even here, far from humanity, he'd lost everything.

"Lost, lost, lost," the stuffed bear murmured. Outside his dirty window, the horizon was just beginning to glow. Animals—the real animals—had begun to stir in their sticks and leaves. Winkie clicked shut his two glass eyes, and in that somber quiet not yet tipping into morning, his mind was drawn to earliest memories. He had never been smaller than he was now—his body was his body—but he had once been like a baby just the same. It was a time when he wasn't even Winkie yet, when he wore a white blouse and a black velvet dress, and he belonged to the little girl Ruth. He could almost hear her calling to him, across time, "*I love you, Marie*"—

A rhythmic chopping in his ears, roving flashes of light. He cradled his head in his paws, but the racket only grew worse. Recollection had been too much for him. The noise ratcheted to a merciless howl, the lights white-blue and blinding. Was he dying? All at once he realized the nightmare wasn't inside him. Shielding his eyes with one paw, blinking, the bear peered up through the window to see a large metallic object, greenish and whirring, hovering above the cabin.

Neither rising nor falling, the helicopter seemed suspended in time. But it rocked to and fro in the flashing air, as if impatient, and all around it the trees were swaying madly.

It shone a spotlight directly on the little bear's upturned face. Then Winkie saw other lights coming at him, from all directions in the woods.

"You're completely surrounded," said the hovering craft. Its deep, metallic voice was even more piercing than the thumping of its motor. "Come out with your hands up!"

Paws in air, Winkie stood in the doorway of the cabin, squinting in the floodlights and the helicopter wind. This must be what they do to toys that run away, he thought. He glimpsed red and blue revolving lights now, too, out in the woods, and silhouettes running between the vehicles, some carrying flashlights, some guns. They were yelling. Above the din of the aircraft he couldn't hear what they were saying, but they seemed confused. Their guns and flashlights pointed this way and that. Even the helicopter began to buck and sway. Winkie felt sorry for it, because it had no room to land between the trees.

"Don't move!" the copter said, but Winkie wasn't moving. Its voice had grown agitated. Winkie almost wanted to comfort it. "What the *hell?*—no, don't—"

A single shot rang out. Winkie felt the bullet whizz past his right ear. He flinched but didn't dare budge. He couldn't tell where the shot had come from. His soft arms were getting tired of being held in the air.

"Men!" shouted the helicopter. Though the craft's own voice was distinctly male, it seemed disgusted with the whole of the gender. "Hold—hold your fire! Hold everything!"

All the shouting stopped, and the silhouettes came to a halt under the trees. There was only the whir of the copter. Moths flitted in the floodlight beams. Already frightened, Winkie began to tremble.

"All right, now," the copter yelled. "Move *in!*"

The bear saw all the helmeted figures advancing toward him, guns drawn, rifles aimed. Though unexpected, the attack made sense to him as yet another misfortune, of a piece with his grief. The men stalked very, very slowly through the underbrush. It seemed they'd never get here. Even though the bear held perfectly still, bored as well as terrified, they kept yelling things like "Stay where you are!" and "Hold it!" or "Don't you dare move, you little cocksucker!"

Winkie felt faint. After everything he'd suffered, why should he care what they did to him now? But his two legs nearly trembled out from under him. The men drew closer. "I'll shootcha!" one kept muttering. "I swear, I'll shootcha! Ya think I won't?" The man was almost sobbing now. "Asshole, I will!"

Winkie thought, That one needs a hug. He saw a tiny burst of light. One of the subsequent thirty-nine shots knocked him over.

A blur of creation and not-yet-consciousness. In that long instant of falling, all at once Winkie recalled his life before Ruth. Why yes, now that he thought of it, he did have memories of the factory, the box he was placed in, a fresh pine smell, the lid coming down and then darkness . . . Time passing . . . Men's voices calling, jostling, a series of chuggings and whirrings, first with sharp bumps, then rocking, then bumps again . . . More jostling, more voices calling, and silence; then, all of a sudden: the lid lifted and there was the ceiling of the department store, ornate and aglow with Christmas sparkles—

"*He's down!*"

"*Fockin' A!*"

Footfalls . . .

"*Come on, come on!*"

Rustling. The voices drew nearer . . .

Day after day his staring eyes met those of the pink-faced children down below the glass case in which he'd been placed. These were the beams of hopeful light that etched themselves, faintly, on his blank, sawdust heart and fed his soul.

To be an appealing object. To be invested with Christmas feeling. To be *on display*, which was to be a part of an important story—

"*Damn it!*"

"*It wasn't 'dead or alive,' dipshit—*"

One voice sounded remorseful, the other angry. Winkie's eyes squeaked half-open to glimpse a wall of blue uniforms, their pink and brown young faces peering down at him. They were barely more than children. His eyes fell closed again.

"*That's one weird lookin'—*"

"*He dead?*"

The cold point of a rifle prodding him. Winkie drifted off again.

. . . And previously, in the factory, yes, as he was stuffed and sewn—and then the tiny, tired eyes of the seamstress who stopped to admire her work for just a moment. She laid him down and his eyes closed—dark. She lifted him up and they opened—light.

He wanted both, and the delicious difference between the two. It was his first inkling of knowledge and mystery. And of wanting.

Chop, chop, chop, said the helicopter.

"Call the chief."

"You call 'im, asshole."

Winkie ignored them. His mind had grown pleasantly methodical. He wanted to trace the thread of his life back even further, but soon he got lost literally in threads—in cloth, stuffing, the spool of what was to hold him together—in these his thoughts faded into smaller and smaller filaments. His soul seemed to have been gathered together along with these minute fibers. Was this abnormal? Was it magic? It seemed quite natural to him and inevitable—that there was now a will where there had been no will. For whatever reason, here had been everything necessary to create a soul.

"Hey. Hey, wake up—"

The point of a gun prodding him again. He willed it to stop. He wanted to keep thinking.

"Hey, whatever you are—"

Nervous laughter.

What *were* the threads of a soul? Winkie supposed only God knew, or the soul itself that wished to create itself—

"Is it real?"

". . . motorized . . . remote control maybe . . ."

"Mhm."

This roused the wounded bear. With effort he opened his eyes fully and blinked twice, click-click, click-click, to prove he was indeed alive and real. In unison the wall of faces blinked, too. Above them the helicopter circled, searchlights roving and crossing, as if weaving Winkie's fate.

2.

Wearily the chief detective peered down from the copter through his field glasses, trying for a better look. After that first shot, he couldn't see anything. In a way, he didn't want to see. The moment a criminal was apprehended always saddened him. He never understood why. He rubbed his eyes and squinted into the field glasses again. He could see only the helmets of his men and, between them, lying in the dirt—that weird midget? Yes, with the huge ears. So he hadn't been mistaken. But the men—why were they just standing there? First they fired, against orders, and now—

The chopper wobbled and he saw only trees. "Keep 'er steady!" he yelled.

The chief detective had been tracking the mad bomber for seventeen years now. At last the trail had led to this cabin. They were sure. They closed in. Descriptions of the suspect had been scarce and contradictory, but a baby-size madman was hardly what he'd expected. Could be a master of disguise, he mused; maybe wore masks, walked around on stilts or something to seem taller; maybe they were trained for that, in the Near East, the Far East, Africa, wherever terrorists were bred . . . But when the chief had first glimpsed the little one's face, peering up from the window of the cabin, he'd been flooded with an unusual feeling of—of what? Sympathy—overwhelming sympathy. As if he knew that little criminal's whole story from start to finish. As if he *was* that fuzzy, big-eared midget, peering up into the light, caught yet wondering, terrified yet hopeful . . .

"Take 'er down," he ordered.

The craft tilted and the tops of trees began reassuringly speeding by. He'd been chasing this one too long, he thought. "Whacking me out," he muttered. Normally such explanations were comforting, but now tears pressed against his eyes. Were the men using tear gas? Just then the copter alighted in a small clearing. He jumped out. He had never been so grateful to feel hard ground beneath his feet.

He was quickly surrounded by reporters, photographers, cameramen. They demanded to be allowed nearer the cabin. "No comment," he said importantly. He saw one of his men running toward him, waving a riot helmet.

"Chief, Chief!" The young officer nearly crashed right into him.

"Take it easy," said the detective sternly, but the officer paid no attention. He was breathing hard and yammering something about a "talking bear." The chief glanced uneasily at the journalists, who were filming, taking photographs, writing on notepads. It would only make matters worse now to order them away. ". . . then the little critter blinked," the young officer was saying. He had to lean over onto his knees to catch his breath, but he kept jabbering. ". . . and I thought, What the? . . ." As the cameras flashed, the chief stared down at the top of the young man's bare head, shaved to dark nubs. ". . . at first we thought he was dead . . ." They all shaved their heads nowadays, the chief thought, to look tough. But then they just fell apart in a crisis. They spoke gibberish. ". . . so I'm saying, 'I didn't *mean* to shoot 'im,' when I hear this little high voice, kinda raspy, and I look and it's him—the bear, I mean—and he says, I don't know, he says he *forgives* me . . ."

Actually Winkie didn't forgive him. Rather, the bear had said, "OK, OK," and he only said that to make him be quiet. Apparently it worked, because the young officer ran off. Winkie's middle hurt. He guessed that he had been shot. He wasn't sure if he couldn't move or if he just didn't feel like it. He didn't know if he was in great pain or just annoyed. He moaned experimentally but it didn't make things any more clear.

The officers didn't seem to know what to do. One said, "You ain't such a bigshot bomber now, huh, motherfuck?" Winkie had no idea what he was talking about. The others told the man to shut up. Their radios squawked. "Chief's coming," said someone. It was half warning, half reassurance.

There was a tramping sound, a murmuring of the men; the wall of uniforms parted, and the chief marched through. He stood there a moment looking down at Winkie. He was handsome with a big square gray head that Winkie liked immediately. Abruptly the chief turned to his men. "Well, what are you doing just standing there?" It was the same voice that had come from the helicopter, and it spoke with the same miraculous authority, as if from on high.

On his way from the helicopter to the cabin, the chief had once again composed himself. The contrast of the overexcited young officer had actually helped. He enunciated his next command carefully: "This suspect is no different from any other criminal."

As if a button had been pressed, the crowd of policemen suddenly began speaking and acting with perfect conviction, and each knew his duty. "You have the right to remain silent," began one. Another roughly placed Winkie's paws together and handcuffed them, not seeming to notice that the silver rings were too big. Winkie played along and kept his paws together. Several men had charged into the cabin, yelling, guns drawn. After some scuffling and more yelling, a voice called out, "All clear in here." Winkie rolled his eyes. Another called, very efficiently, "Don't touch anything." Still others had busily repositioned their floodlights even closer to the cabin, so that it was now bright as daylight. More men arrived wearing suits and carrying huge brief-cases. "Coming through," they said. They put on white gloves and blue paper slippers and entered the cabin. No one gave the bear a second glance now. Shortly an ambulance arrived in the woods, and two hefty men in white came running with a stretcher. "Shot," said one of Winkie's guards. "Stomach, we think." By his calm, professional manner the two emergency workers understood their own roles, too.

"Pulse: zero," said one, letting go the bear's cotton paw.

"Blood pressure: zero over zero," said the other, as the puffy black cuff wooshed out its air.

The first one shone a small flashlight in each of Winkie's glass eyes, each of which went click-click. "Pupils abnormal but reactive—what's yer name?"

"Winkie," said the bear, automatically. He almost added, "Marie underneath," but that was too hard to explain.

"Sex?" asked the other emergency worker.

Also too hard to explain. Winkie didn't answer.

"*Sex?*" the man repeated, annoyed.

The first worker gruffly moved the bear's handcuffed paws aside to reveal the place where Winkie's legs came together: a flat seam across worn blond fur. "Female," he said flatly and definitively.

If Winkie could have blushed, he would have.

"Sign here," said the second one. He handed Winkie a clipboard and pen. The bear made a large W.

"No, *here*." The worker pointed.

Winkie made another W.

Now each man took an end of the bear. "One, two, three—lift!" they said, and Winkie was on the stretcher. They tightened the white straps as far as they would go. "OK," said one, and the bear was upraised and carried along the overgrown path, one policeman trotting in front, one behind. Winkie began to like the jostling, but it ended quickly. As he was loaded into the ambulance, he turned and saw that a huge yellow forklift had been maneuvered into position behind the cabin. With a metallic whine, it lifted the little godforsaken shack right off the ground, and the men in slippers jumped out one by one like mice.

* * *

In the big gray hospital, the doctors could only play at treating Winkie. They huddled around X-rays that showed only his metal parts—eye sockets, joints, squeaker. They murmured strings of complicated words. The nurses pretended to draw blood and the lab sent back readings of air. It reminded everyone pleasantly of their medical training, when they practiced only on dolls and cadavers, and nothing much was at stake. The bear was carted around on gurneys and "hooked up" to various tubes and machines. At least once a day, detecting no breath and no pulse, they administered CPR, then electric shocks. "Clear!" they yelled, and Winkie got the jolt. "No response. Clear!"

The shocks were thrilling, but the bear tried not to make a peep. Just when the doctors and nurses seemed to have lost all hope, when they were about to pronounce the time of death, Winkie would begin quietly singing, "Beep . . . beep . . . beep . . ."

His imitation of a heart monitor was poor, but that wasn't the point. One by one the medical personnel lifted their heads in joy. Winkie liked this part of the game best. "You've done it again, doctor!" a pretty nurse might say. "Saving lives is my job," a handsome doctor would reply.

Actually it was the cleaning woman, Françoise, who had discovered the two bullet holes in Winkie, one in front, one in back, and she had had the good sense simply to sew them up with a needle and thread that she kept with her cleaning supplies. This was during Winkie's second or third night here, while his police guard was asleep. Françoise had tiptoed in after hearing the bear moan. Her face was unlined and light brown like Winkie's, her hair clipped short as brown fur, and even her heavily made-up eyes were the same light tan color as his. She looked at him with calm, open curiosity, and Winkie felt his intuition of trust kick

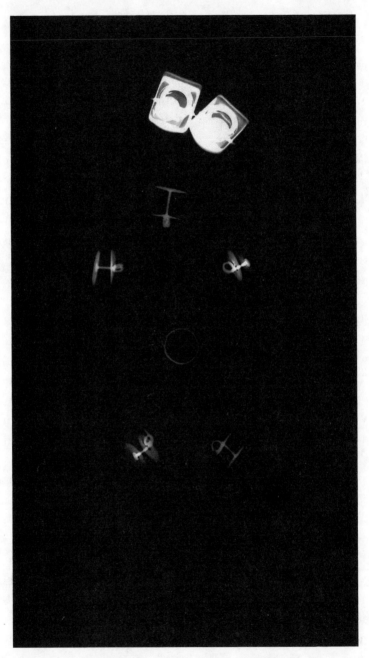

X-rays showed only his metal parts.

in for the first time in ages. He lifted his child's hospital gown and pointed with a loosely cuffed paw to where it hurt, on the left side of his fur-worn belly. There, too, where bits of sawdust leaked out, the cleaning woman turned her lovely brown-on-brown gaze.

The point of the needle hurt a little each time it went in, but Françoise was a gentle seamstress. "Ever since I was a little girl, I loved to clean. I don't know why," she said softly, so as not to wake the officer. Though her name was French, her accent was something else. "But last year the new bosses, they buy the hospital—for nothing. Now I do two people's jobs . . ." She laughed conspiratorially. "I'll be in big trouble for taking a break like this . . . OK, little bear, show me your backside." Happily Winkie turned over and Françoise started on the second wound. "I have come to this country from Egypt, in 1967. It was because my girlfriend, Mariana, she left me, on my eighteenth birthday. She said, 'Françoise, it's very wrong what we do.' So I decided that same day, 'Shit, I'm going to America.'" She giggled. "I never wanted to see her again. And what happens but Mariana comes here too, two months later. We are together ever since." Françoise tied off the last thread, which was hot pink like her uniform. She said musically with another chuckle, "So you never know about fate, do you, little bear?"

3.

Over the next few days Winkie began to feel better. He lost no more stuffing. He sat up in bed and watched television. When a distinguished physician noticed the pink stitching, the M.D. simply said to his resident, "It appears the surgery was successful." Winkie let them pretend that modern medicine had cured him. He had begun to eat, and the staff let him have all the Jell-O he wanted. Winkie offered stool samples as thanks.

To the police he offered nothing. When they had first said to him, "You have the right to remain silent," Winkie listened no further. He'd scarcely spoken to anyone but his cub, so silence sounded good to him now. Certainly he had no interest in defending himself.

Each day the chief detective came to question him, referring to such and such events in such and such places on such and such dates. Winkie no longer admired the detective's big gray head. "Now, Miss Winkie—if that *is* your real name," the chief would begin. The questions that followed were so confusing that it took the bear several days to understand even vaguely what he was charged with. "We found the old man, buried in a shallow grave next to the cabin—right where you left him," said the chief in outrage. "He found out what you were doing, and he tried to stop you—so you killed him, didn't you? DIDN'T YOU?!"

The bear winced—not at the accusation, but at the mention of the very man who had kidnapped his child.

Winkie wanted to cry out, but he could only look out the window and sigh—inwardly, for a real sigh would only bring queries about the sigh. It was sunny out. He could hear the chief detective breathing. He was beginning to dislike policemen as a group, though he knew it was wrong to generalize.

"Winkie, Hinkie, Slinkie, Stinkie—I don't care," said the chief. "Don't think, Miss or Mrs. Whoever-You-Are, that you're going to get away with what you've done."

Winkie almost perked up at "Stinkie." Miss Stinkie, he thought. Miss Stinkie.

The detective followed the bear's gaze out the barred window and saw nothing but sky. He tried to collect his thoughts. More and more now, they ran wild. Winkie—winking at us. Hinkie—flaunting her weirdness. Slinkie—she'll try to slink away, like one of those toys hopping down the stairs. Stinkie—like her crimes!

"Who do you work for?" the chief shouted.

Winkie yawned. It would almost be worth it to say he'd been lying before, that Stinkie was his real name.

Each night the chief tossed in bed.

Some kind of alien, he mused. Some kind of demon. Some kind of ghost. Some kind of antimatter. Some kind of deformity, the horrible physical result of unspeakable depravity. Some botched creation, a mad experiment gone wrong. Some sort of human-animal hybrid. Some sort of ultimate weapon. Some sort of government cover-up. Some sort of mutant, the product of chemical waste, global warming, nerve gas, radiation. Some freak of nature. Some advance in evolution that we can't even begin to understand. Some sort of dinosaur, reawakened after aeons. Some sort of time traveler. Some being from another reality or dimension. Some creature previously thought to be mythical. Some rare configuration of energy, a kind of quantum lightning. Some kind of message from the universe ("He said he forgives me"). Some kind of punishment sent by God . . .

The chief looked at the clock's glowing squared-off numbers: 3:15 A.M. "Piece of shit," he muttered. He put the pillow over his head. The phone began to ring, but he barely noticed.

Maybe it's innocent. Maybe it's the last of its kind. Maybe it's a renegade. Maybe it's a ringleader. Maybe it's just one of a whole race of them, thriving near Chernobyl . . .

"I saw an article about you," whispered Françoise, seating herself on the edge of Winkie's bed. She came by almost every night now, because the police guard always fell asleep at exactly 3 A.M. "Little bear, they say you make *bombs!*" She could barely contain her laughter.

Even with Françoise, Winkie hadn't yet chosen to speak, but he did often smile at her and now he let himself chuckle a little. He hadn't chuckled in a long time.

"And they say you are a girl?" Françoise made an expression of exaggerated surprise. "I was *sure* you were a boy! Because you remind me of my brother."

Winkie shrugged significantly.

"Ahh, OK," said Françoise, comprehending immediately. She ran her hand over her crew cut. "*That's* why you remind me of my brother."

Françoise had never mentioned her brother before, but Winkie, too, understood immediately more or less what she meant. As she took out the newspaper, the bear let himself enjoy his inclusion in Françoise's special circle of comprehension and similarities.

She cleared her throat and read aloud from the front page: "'According to sources close to the investigation, Ms. Winkie is very possibly the head of one of the most massive terrorist operations ever discovered in this country.'" The newspaper went on to list the many bombs the suspect had mailed to various locations over the past several years. "As to Ms. Winkie's extremely small stature and unusual appearance," the article continued, "police sources attribute it to a rare medical disorder that may actually be common in some parts of the world, such as Asia or the Middle East. 'Not coincidentally,' said one senior investigator, 'these same areas are breeding grounds for terrorism.' The investigator declined to name the disorder."

By now Françoise and Winkie were giggling so loudly that the guard woke up. The chief was called. Françoise was driven to the station and questioned through the night. Winkie was taken from the hospital to jail.

Violin

I.

The jail was no more than a block from the hospital, but the plain white sedan sped down streets and highways for hours. The FBI agents stopped to refuel again and again at the same Mobil station, making no attempt to hide the fact that they were driving in circles, and not even big circles. Winkie assumed they wanted him to know they could do this sort of thing to him if they wanted. The agents, one male, one female, one in a gray business suit, the other in navy, shared a single bag of potato chips at each Mobil stop but offered nothing to the prisoner, whom they left shackled to the armrest with a set of plastic cuffs. Occasionally the car screeched to a stop by the side of the highway, and not even bothering to unhook him, the female agent jerked the door ajar and commanded, "Go." It took Winkie a moment, the first time, to realize she meant for him to relieve himself.

As he lifted his hospital gown and squatted out the door, shivering, while car after car whooshed past in the weak sunlight, a memory came to him suddenly of being shaken and shaken until his eyes throbbed, by the first child he knew, Ruth. Then she ordered the sick bear to lie down and repeat such curative phrases as, "There is no power in matter," and, "Rely on God's allness and love"—

There was another jerk on the handcuffs, and Winkie had only an instant to pull in his behind before the car door slammed shut. His hospital gown caught in the door, so now he was tethered even more tightly. He supposed the journey could go on indefinitely. He was thirsty. Watching the same arrangement of trees flick by for the seventeenth time, he wondered why he'd never thought about Ruth while he was in the hospital, where he'd undergone so many play treatments and had even become a girl again, as he had been so long ago, for Ruth. Now that he did think of her, it made perfect sense that he should.

"*Because matter has no consciousness or Ego, it cannot act,*" he could remember Papa reading aloud from *Science and Health*. The three children listened, but Ruth, the youngest, listened most intently. In her lap sat the teddy bear she had named Marie. It was Sunday afternoon. "*Admit the existence of matter,*" Papa continued, his voice nasal and quavering, "*and you admit that mortality has a foundation in fact.*" A draft stirred the collar of Marie's blouse, and she wondered what matter was. And mortality. She was pretty sure she herself was dead matter, yet she could also think and feel . . .

As the wires rose and fell in the car window, Winkie realized he couldn't even count the number of years that had passed since that moment on Ruth's lap. His eyes clicked shut in pain. Yet something had opened within him—here, of all places. He was ready to remember more.

Marie's fur was thick and even, she had never been mended, and her eyes rolled open and closed with the satisfying action of freshly oiled machinery. She knew almost nothing.

Marie was neither boy nor girl, so it was both a privilege and yet an insult to be called "she" or "her." For wasn't it good to be a "she" and not an "it," and she definitely was not an "it," but neither was "she" who Marie was. Sometimes she hated herself for perking up at the sound of her name being called. There was a part of her that was deep and unnamed, and then there was that other part, located in the brightness of her polished glass eyes, that acquiesced and betrayed the self so easily, saying eagerly, "I'm yours," as if that were someone.

Marie was barely someone at all, and often for hours she stared ahead thinking nothing at all, even if the telephone jangled or the big Victrola began its tinny bleating down in the front parlor. She was no one until Ruth came into the room, and sometimes not even then, not until Ruth spoke to her.

"Hi, Marie," was all the girl needed to say, and the little bear's eyes were flooded with a jumble of color, her ears with the distant tinkling of the knife sharpener's bell, and her body with a smiling combined with excruciating sadness and regret combined with gratefulness combined with wanting to die again.

"You're the berries," Ruth might say, rubbing her nose against the bear's, and indeed the words were like sweet fruit falling down and down onto Marie's imaginary tongue. Then if Ruth hugged her tightly, Marie let out a squeak. She couldn't help it. She squeaked whenever she was hugged.

She seemed to draw her very life from Ruth's gray blue eyes and long lashes, and sometimes Marie loved the girl with such intensity that it dizzied her and made her own eyes flutter as Ruth laid her down to bed and the world flickered out like a power failure. The girl would speak for her then, out of the blackness, saying, "I love you, Ruth," and the accuracy of those words, heard from outside herself, would seem to strike Marie like blows to the head, igniting another wave of color and flashing lights.

"I love you, too," Ruth would say then, pressing on her belly and making her squeak—and again it was almost too much, it seemed to Marie she couldn't contain so much painful joy and she had to let out another short squeak.

"Father-Mother God, loving me, guard me while I sleep, guide my little feet up to thee," prayed Ruth and her sister, Helen, together, eyes shut, each in their cozy bed. Once Mama had pushed the black button that switched off the light, Marie was free to sit there in the dark near her beloved and, as the winter room grew cold, to watch colors streak past or swirl or march by in rows of dots all night long.

In the morning Marie was exhausted and haggard, and when Ruth hugged her and said, "I love you," again, the bear was startled by her own squeak.

"Marie, Marie, Marie," Ruth might sing, trying to distract herself from the morning chill, lifting the bear by the arms, swinging her around.

And the bear would say to herself, *"Who?"*

In the midst of such riddles Marie was evolving as quickly as a real little cub might grow in the wild. But to her it seemed like nothing was happening at all, since no one else could see the changes inside her, and nothing else about her ever changed.

2.

"All right for *you*," Ruth's sister replied, when Ruth had refused to do the dusting for her. Marie watched with some amazement as these magic words transformed Ruth's expression from defiance to regret. Thus Ruth relented and Helen went off roller-skating.

Gingerly Ruth lifted objects in the parlor and wiped the wood under them with her hand. She hadn't been able to find a dust rag, and she was too timid to disturb her mother for it. The house was silent. It was Saturday but her father worked Saturdays. Her brother, John, was at his clarinet lesson. Her mother was in the kitchen reading *Science and Health* to relieve a headache, for headaches aren't real. Sometimes Ruth shut her eyes and blew into the corners of the shelves. "There," she kept whispering, with satisfaction.

Marie had been annoyed with Ruth for capitulating to her sister, but now she watched from the piano with contentment. She enjoyed seeing things done incorrectly. It was her little protest against the world. At first Ruth had sighed with frustration not to have a rag, but soon she had become absorbed and the sunlit room grew hazy with floating particles.

Then Marie saw Papa standing in the wide, arched doorway, as straight and silent as a sentry. He watched his daughter a moment before asking, in his sardonic way, "Ruth, what do you think you're doing?"

Startled, the girl hid her sooty fingers behind her back. "Dusting," she answered.

Marie knew the kinds of questions that would follow and wished she could scream, or even squeak, to interrupt them. Where is the dust cloth, why are you doing your sister's chores, where is your sister . . . "Did you knock the card down from the windowsill?" Papa asked, and Ruth guiltily shrugged. "What if the iceman had come early today and didn't see the card? Then your mother wouldn't have any ice."

Papa bent to pick up the card and placed it safely in the window again. Marie tried willing it to fall. Ruth had begun to sniffle. Papa evenly told her to go find her sister but first to go wash her hands and then . . . Marie refused to listen further. The girl ran upstairs to wash and the bear was left alone with Papa. He of course thought he was completely alone. Marie watched him gaze out the parlor window looking worried and grave.

Ruth put Marie in the red wagon and tugged her along. The bear read over and over the headline of the yellowed newspaper lining the slats of the wagon: "Scopes Guilty in 'Monkey' Trial." She wondered what the monkey had done wrong. It was one of the first warmish days of the year and the sun was out. Ruth seemed slightly less dejected, maybe because Mama had asked her to buy some thread, so she felt useful again. They found Helen and her friend Eleanor near 107th Street, skating lazily on the fresh, smooth pavement. Helen wore her navy blue sailor dress with its striped white collar that Ruth coveted. Eleanor, too, wore navy.

"Father says you're to come home *right now*," Ruth said.

Marie knew Ruth could never question her father's rules, but she didn't have to relish them either.

"Oh, applesauce," said Helen.

Marie thought that was a good answer, but Ruth looked shocked. "I'll tell Father."

Helen ignored her. With exaggerated poise she said, "Good-bye, Eleanor, I have to go now," and skated off toward home.

Earlier Helen had hinted that Ruth herself might join in the skating today when the dusting was finished. Therefore Ruth informed Eleanor, "I can't come skating now, because I have to go buy some darning thread for my mother, on 103rd Street."

Eleanor only shrugged and began skating in tight circles.

Ruth pulled the wagon down the hill alone. Here and there a bush bloomed bright yellow, but most were a tangle of sticks. Marie felt sad for Ruth. She also knew she herself was Ruth's second

choice as a companion and so she, too, felt lonely and useless. She
watched the cracked sidewalk slope downward.

Ruth said to Marie, "When I was little, I was running down this
hill one day, and I didn't know you were supposed to lean back
when you run downhill, so I leaned forward. Boom! I fell right
down and skinned both knees."

Marie looked with trepidation down the steep sidewalk.

"There was a paddy wagon sitting right there at the foot of the
hill. I sat there rubbing my knee, and I didn't think I could get up.
Then a policeman leaned his head out the window of the paddy
wagon and said, 'Little girl, are you all right? I can give you a ride
home.'

"'No, I'm fine!' I cried. And I got right up and ran back up the
hill. I could just imagine what Mama would think if she saw a paddy
wagon drive up to the house!"

Marie had noticed how Ruth often pretended to be fine when
she wasn't. It was like a game she played with the world, so that
true and untrue changed places. Marie liked all kinds of pretend,
but this kind made her feel queasy, and worse, like even the queasy
feeling wasn't true either. It made her feel like everything was her
fault. Because if you could make anything true, if only you wanted
to, then everything really was your fault.

Soon a massive white building came into view, with four heavy
columns above a row of wide, white steps.

"That's the Church of Christ, Scientist," said Ruth. "Founded
by Mary Baker Eddy. But you can't go in there, Marie. It's not for
toys. It's for worship."

Marie wanted to know why toys couldn't go to church. She tried
to imagine what went on inside. *Father-Mother God, loving me . . .*
Was that what they all prayed in church, too? That ball of words at

the beginning—Father, Mother, God—always confounded Marie.
Who was Ruth praying to—Papa, Mama, God, or all three?

Just around the corner was the five-and-dime. The fat, cheer-
ful proprietor made much of Marie, sitting her up on the counter
and complimenting her black velvet skirt and ruffled white blouse,
which Mama had sewn. Usually Marie didn't think about it, but
suddenly she was abashed by the girly dress and her brown, furry
legs sticking out of it. "She's a pretty little thing," the man was
saying to Ruth. "Quite the lady." Torn between delight and doubt,
Marie wanted to wiggle out of these clothes and whoever it was
that she must appear to be.

From one of dozens of little gray drawers with brass handles the
shopkeeper extracted a glossy, neat spool of brown thread. "Here
we are," he said, turning back to Ruth—

"No!" he suddenly barked, toward the front of the store. "No
coloreds!"

Ruth turned to look, but of course Marie couldn't. She only
heard the door bang shut, then footsteps on the sidewalk. Ruth
seemed agitated.

"I don't want 'em in here," the man explained, not quite in his
nice voice again. "Except for you," he added, to Marie.

Now Ruth chuckled. "She's not colored, she's a bear!"

Marie wondered who the coloreds were and what they looked
like. She'd heard Mama and Papa speak of them before. Papa had
said colored people continued going places where they weren't
wanted. If so, Marie thought now, she wanted to meet them.

Out on the sidewalk she perceived no one who might fit their
description, just regular people. The young bear began to brood.
The shopkeeper's outburst was her first exposure to a wider world
of hurt and hindrance beyond the family. Already that world was
invisible again as Ruth rounded the corner and they made their

way once more among trees and houses. Suddenly the frustration of not being able to speak, to ask, or to participate drove Marie nearly mad. Ruth marched ahead, humming and daydreaming, as if nothing out of the ordinary had happened. Birds chirped. The sun shone even more brightly than before.

Ruth took a different way home and they passed through a small park. There, by the greening lawn, as the girl stopped to inspect a daffodil, Marie saw a young cripple in a wooden chair with four wheels like a pram, a dark blanket on her knees, and beside her a nurse and an old man, apparently the invalid's father. Marie couldn't tell for sure if the cripple was a boy or a girl, so slumped was he or she in the chair with wheels. As the father and the nurse chatted, Marie could see the eyes of the invalid widen and flutter. *As if she wished her eyes were mouths,* Marie said to herself. *As if those two eye-mouths could speak.* The father and the nurse began to chuckle over something, the invalid began to drool, and Marie felt a tug on the wagon.

Shortly they were toiling up the same hill and Ruth began telling stories again. "When Grandpa was only a little baby," she said, "he was riding in the back of a covered wagon with his parents through Kansas—and there was an Indian attack! Grandpa's father was killed by an arrow." Marie was still facing backward and continued watching the crooked sidewalk and the trees and houses receding and receding down the hill. "He was only a baby," Ruth said, "and he was lucky to survive. Of course his mother couldn't take care of her children on her own. Grandpa's sisters went to relatives' and Grandpa was raised by friends of the family, the Severances." Ruth sighed. "Those were pioneer times."

Marie felt the small rubber wheels bump over an especially big crack in the sidewalk. Again Ruth seemed quite satisfied with her story, as if she'd just given the right answer on a quiz, but it made

Marie feel even more lonely and blank. They turned onto their own block, and the bear glanced up wearily at the familiar trees above her head, the intertwining of twigs. Just a few houses down was their own, with its humbly blunted roof peak. Pioneer times. Marie, too, was riding in a wagon and trying to survive. In the lull and momentum of the wheels, she understood that as much as she was trapped in a lifeless body, she was also caught in a time and place. So was Ruth, so was her family. And they were all simply trying to survive. But did they have to like it?

A black automobile ticked by in its black canvas bonnet. Cries of hopscotch rose from down the block.

3.

"Yes, yes, Marie is going to the symphony too!" John sang, making Ruth and Helen laugh even more.

"No, we can't!" Ruth cried, but her tone was devilish, thrilling Marie.

The boy continued dancing the bear around the girls' room, singing the Charleston. Marie was transfixed by the black-and-white checks of John's sweater vest, which unlike the twirling room remained fixed before her eyes. She felt the forces of swoop and swirl. Ruth never played with her this way. Ruth was as careful with her things as her careful parents could ever hope her to be, though as everything wheeled by, Marie glimpsed even her dancing a little, too. Soon Mama could be heard calling from below, but the fun continued just a little longer, for with a jazzy flourish John placed the bear in Ruth's arms and they all clumped down the stairs together giggling. "Marie! Marie!" John cheered.

They came to a halt in the foyer, where Mama stood waiting in her best shawl. With tired, deep-set eyes she glared at Marie, sigh-

Caught in a time and place

ing loudly, but Ruth only hugged the bear tighter. Marie had never been so grateful. Now Mama glared at John, who straightened his bow tie.

"Ruth wanted to bring her bear," he said, shrugging.

Helen tittered.

Marie wasn't surprised by this betrayal, but her eyes ached at the thought of missing the concert after all. She wasn't even sure what a concert was. Mama seemed just about to speak—and Ruth's hold on the bear was already beginning to loosen—when Papa called from the front yard, with some irritation, that they were going to miss their train. By this fluke Marie remained in Ruth's grasp, and the family bustled down the hill to the station. As they waited for the train, the bear hoped they had entered a new era in which Ruth flouted the rules and Marie got to go new places. Beneath a billow of soot the chugging machine arrived, roiling Marie's heavy skirt. Inside, well-dressed strangers sat in maroon velvet seats, waiting only to arrive.

As if she could do otherwise, the bear tried to keep very still under Ruth's arm, in order to avoid Mama's notice. But as soon as Papa had found them places and the children had sat down facing their parents, Mama's disapproval resumed. "Really, Ruth, to a concert," she said, shaking her head.

Ruth, who hated to be reprimanded, immediately began to cry. "You didn't say I couldn't," she protested.

"I shouldn't *have* to."

"But—"

"And I shouldn't have to tell you not to talk back to your mother," Papa added.

Marie flinched to see Papa join in, too. He and Mama sat upright wearing identical expressions of weary reproach.

"I'm sorry," the girl whined, tears of shame wetting the top of Marie's head, whose own eyes now burned with shiny outrage.

"Ruth, you are too *old* for this sort of thing," said Mama. Ruth had turned nine the month before, but Marie didn't see what that had to do with anything. "You cannot possibly be so upset about that *bear*."

Still crying, Ruth hugged Marie closer, and she let out a squeak. John and Helen snickered.

"Ruth, if you keep this up, then you and I will get off at the next stop and take the train home," said Mama. "Your father and John and Helen will go, and I will have to miss the concert, too."

Ruth paused, evidently at the thought of her mother making such a sacrifice.

"All right then," said Mama.

Ruth was silent as the train rattled along.

The orchestra warming up and the crowd's murmuring together made an enlarging chaos, and then there was applause and a hush. From Ruth's lap Marie could see only the backs of the next row of folding chairs, the well-dressed concertgoers, hat after hat, and above them the mild sky. The violin struck a single note, and the orchestra joined in, first with one note, then a chord that grew and changed. More applause, another silence—what was happening? Marie could hear distant birds, a lifting breeze—then at last the piece began.

Five soft strokes like heartbeats. The notes that followed were quiet yet sure, just a few instruments, and seemed to be preparing the way. Marie had heard the family's gramophone as well as Mama's piano and John's clarinet, but these noises tickled her ears in new ways. Soon came a sad melody that somehow hid determination in softness, like Ruth marching up the hill pulling her wagon. A storm of possibilities followed, hundreds of trees seemed to shudder in wind, then a calm. What else could there be?—

Marie was almost ripped in two by the sudden, forceful stroke of a single violin—ringing, smoky, gorgeous, and alone. It was like a spotlight on a dark world. "Here I am!" it seemed to say, and it didn't care what the consequences were.

She might have expected it to snatch up the softly determined melody as its own, but instead the others kept their tune and the violin danced in and around it. When at last it did join in, it was only to complete the last few phrases, as if it could hardly be bothered with finishing a sentence that was already known, even a beautiful one. Marie lost the world at hand. Gravity let go. She seemed to be walking freely and happily through empty space. And not just walking but dancing, and not just dancing but dancing on a high wire, while the taut line quivered itself like a violin string beneath her stubby feet, which were light and sure of themselves, as if they always had been. The violin trilled and continued to trill, and all at once Marie saw the hats and chairs and Ruth herself wheel past as she tumbled out of the girl's lap, the trunk of her body a-spin. For that moment before landing she was a creature in motion, untouched, her own being, apart from Ruth, a planet twirling in its own galaxy.

With a short squeak the bear rolled twice in the grass before Mama whispered irritated shushes and Ruth whisked her up into her lap again. The violin had stopped trilling by now and the orchestra had taken over. Marie lay there dazed, her eyes fallen shut. So far in her life she'd been carried and towed and occasionally shaken—today she'd even been danced—but none of it was anything like this whirl in slow motion through empty space. She was convinced she'd somehow done it on her own—tossed herself out of Ruth's lap and onto the grass by the strength of her own swoon.

With an almost stabbing determination the violin rose up again. Every phrase was different now: furious, sad, petulant, defiant, pleading. Marie had felt these things many times, and she'd seen Ruth get in trouble for them, yet here they all were, one after the other, all part of the same music to which even Mama and Papa submitted willingly. The orchestra halted, and for many minutes the violin wailed its beautiful tantrum. It was the scratchy woodiness beneath the sweetness that thrilled the young bear most. She could hear it clearly, the very real, mundane substance of the instrument itself, and she could have wept, if her glass eyes had let her, to be witnessing its brave struggle to be more than it was— more than wood, strings, varnish, matter.

Marie lay there across Ruth's knees, sniffing the grass and the lake, paying no attention to the rest of the concert. If she moved just a little more each day, eventually or even soon enough she would be walking. She could learn to talk, too, first by willing herself to squeak, next by squeaking almost words, then actual words, and finally whole sentences. "Ruth, I'm going outside now"—imagine the girl's surprise.

Just then Ruth stirred at what turned out to be the last notes of the last piece, and there seemed to emanate from her a new vibration that reminded Marie of the girl's small rebellion earlier today. As she let out a series of furious, sharp sounds with her two palms, Marie was sure the music had held something new and significant for Ruth, too.

The family bustled back to the station. Ruth followed closely behind her father, as if she wanted to ask him something. Marie stared at his heels lifting and falling to the pavement again. On the train Ruth sat once again between Helen and John, but she paid no attention to them, not even when John teased her for it. "All aboard," was called, a whistle blew, but the train didn't yet move, and in that tense, hushed moment, Ruth suddenly blurted out, "Papa? I would like to play the violin."

Everyone laughed. The railway carriage jerked foward.

"Oh, you would?" said Papa.

"She never wanted one before today," said John.

"Violins are expensive," Mama warned. "And we already have a piano."

"I know," Ruth murmured.

The train clacked. Marie wanted to bury her head in Ruth's shoulder. It was true that the girl sometimes asked for things she didn't want very much or forgot about a day or even an hour later—so how could Ruth convince them?

Papa said, "Of course you all know the story about Ikey and the carriage."

It was a very old joke—older than automobiles—and a family favorite. Even Marie, who had been with the family only since Christmas, already knew it. Evidently Ruth's grandfather, the orphan, used to tell it.

It was a funny story about what could happen when people got carried away by their wishes.

"One fine Sunday morning a very silly family was walking to church," said Papa, "because the wheel of their carriage was broken and they couldn't afford to have it repaired. It was a long way to church, and the road was muddy, so they began talking about how grand it would be to have a new carriage.

"'I can see us riding in it now,' said the mother. 'It will be such a beautiful, shiny carriage.'"

Mama, Helen, and John were already laughing to hear Papa speak in falsetto. Normally a quiet man, he could tell a good story when he wanted to.

"'We'll get to church in no time,' said the father. 'We'll glide along like the wind.'

"'And everyone in town will see me riding right up in front,' said the little girl.

"'Me, too,' said her little brother, Ikey. 'I'll be riding in front, too!'

"'No, Ikey, there won't be enough room next to Father,' the girl scolded.

"So Father said, 'Ikey, be a good boy and ride in back with Mother.'

"'I don't want to!' cried Ikey.

"'You have to,' said his sister."

Even Ruth was laughing now, and Papa himself chuckled in anticipation of the punch line.

"Then Ikey started jumping up and down in the mud, hollering, 'No! No! I don't *like* it in back! I want to ride in front—*in front!'*

"And the little boy was making such a fuss that finally his father shouted, 'Ikey, get right out of the carriage!'"

4.

Winkie sighed. Undulating telephone wires had given way to darkness and the occasional play of headlights across the car's beige ceiling full of tiny holes. He saw himself as Marie, hoping and surviving, growing up, as it were, and he knew not only how long she'd have to wait for what she longed for, but how it all ended— here in the back of a white sedan, driving in circles.

Once upon a time, Marie could change nothing, not in Ruth's life, not in her own, just as Winkie could change nothing of his own story. There was Ruth the girl, and there were her parents, and before them her parents' parents, et cetera. Later there would be Ruth the mother, and her own children. These were all facts. Even now, Winkie wanted to rebel against them, refuse them, yet they continued reeling out before the tired eyes of his memory.

It could be said that the whole of the bear's life as a toy formed one long incantation that produced, at last, the miracle of his coming to life. Winkie half hoped to understand that incantation through recollection, maybe even to reproduce its magic and thus regain his freedom.

For the eighty-seventh time the car turned left, tires squealing. Winkie tugged idly at the handcuffs, letting the rough plastic cut into his paw. He didn't want to remember his life with fondness; he didn't want to love only in retrospect. Yet he did love Ruth, even now. It was yet another thing he couldn't change.

5.

Outside Ruth's window, the huge cottonwood tree creaked and rustled.

"*You command the situation if you understand that mortal existence is a state of self-deception and not the truth of being,*" Ruth read out, laboring over the bigger words. At breakfast she'd announced she was going to read *Science and Health* every day from now on. Marie was annoyed at such an obvious attempt to win the parents' favor, but she had to admit it might help the girl get a violin after all. "*Mentally contradict every complaint . . . master fear through divine Mind. . . .*"

Marie's own mind made her glass pupils go cloudy with boredom. In the middle of the night she had decided to rename herself Mouth. Every time Ruth said, "Marie," the bear yelled, Mouth, in her mind, to blot out the name of that poor bear that couldn't answer. "*. . . master the propensities . . .*" Mouth, Mouth, Mouth, she thought now, trying to feel what it would be like for her stitched mouth to actually make that sound. For a second she could almost believe it had, but in fact she was already getting bored with the game. "*Choke these errors in their early stages . . . destroy error. . . .*"

Marie herself was beginning to feel choked and destroyed. These teachings were like the wallpaper of this house, and all at once Marie seemed to glimpse in that ornate pattern a monstrous face, livid and forbidding, with Mama's mousy hair and Papa's sad, deep-set eyes—the Father-Mother God—

Fortunately Ruth put the book aside just then and the image dissipated. "Just a little each day," Ruth said, much to the bear's relief. Then she picked up Marie and began whispering plans for playing in an orchestra when she grew up and the many marvelous experiences she would have. Her breath tickled Marie's ear almost the way the music had. It worked the bear into a fever of anticipation, not only for Ruth's future but for her own. "But it's no use pestering him about it," the girl suddenly warned, meaning her father. "You'd better just sit here quietly," she added, putting Marie down again. It didn't calm the bear one bit. Ruth went out to play, while Marie listened for every word and movement in the house. The concert had made her large ears even more sensitive; she found that she could hear a lot, if she concentrated. Water sloshing from the icebox tray as John carried it to the sink. The stray words of a practitioner who had come to see Mama about her headaches—"*mental malpractice . . . mental contagion . . . mental miasma . . .*"

That night when Papa arrived home from work, Marie doubted Ruth would be able to restrain herself from bringing up her big wish. She didn't right away, but in the middle of dinner, the girl blurted out, "Papa, may I have a violin?"

Upstairs, Marie winced. The leaves of the cottonwood were dark as velvet in the window.

"We'll see," said Papa slowly.

Marie had heard this reply from him before. Maybe this time it really did mean he would think about it—Marie couldn't tell. Her anticipation only grew. It seemed her own fate and her own desires were toying with her, too, refusing to answer.

Tines clicking on plates.

"If I had a violin," Ruth said, in a dreamy way, "I'd play Beethoven, Mozart, and also Haydn."

"Ah, *mm-hmm*," said Papa.

His tone remained the same, but Ruth couldn't seem to stop herself. "I'll play with the Chicago Symphony, and I'll sit with all the other violins, and—"

"Sure, Ikey," said her brother, and everyone laughed.

Marie felt the usual outrage, but when Ruth came upstairs after dinner, she didn't seem at all upset. In fact, she was unusually serene. The bear watched her carefully as she took out crayons and began drawing a violin. Marie wanted to know how Ruth went about wishing. If someone wished in a particular way, or with a particular intensity, would she get what she wanted?

The next morning, after reading from *Science and Health*, Ruth took Marie with her down to the basement, intent on something. The bear had never been down there before. The light was dim. Holding up the ceiling were two medium-size tree trunks, bark and all, as if the house were sprouting from them like branches and leaves. Ruth set Marie down on the worktable and went to rummage in a dark, fertile corner. She returned with an old cigar box, two paint stirrers, a hammer, and some other things. Immediately she set to work gluing the cigar box shut, then nailing the end of one of the paint stirrers to the box. The object now had a body and a neck. Marie wanted to cheer, but in fact Ruth needed no encouragement. "Good," the girl said to herself. She'd hit the nails in crookedly, bending them over, but she didn't seem to mind these imperfections. Usually such things bothered her a lot. Marie continued watching her carefully. Four thumbtacks at either end, long rubber bands hooked around the thumbtacks—and the project was done. Ruth plucked one of the rubber bands and it made a dull noise of a certain pitch.

Marie's ears tingled. The object that had taken shape before her eyes was better than a real violin. Cobbled from scraps, square instead of curved, it was only the idea of a violin; that is, the essence of a desire. Ruth strummed the rubber bands and to Marie's delight they made a series of twangs bearing almost no relation to music.

"Listen, Marie!" she said, and taking the violin by its neck, she pushed its square body awkwardly under her chin and with her other hand raised a second paint stirrer high. She paused theatrically, and then in one masterful-looking stroke drew the stirrer down across the rubber bands.

The makeshift strings pulled, twanged loosely, and the wood of the homemade bow scraped against the box.

Again! thought Marie. Again!

Ruth tried once more, with equal force. The assuredness of her strokes, the disappointing sounds it made—they sent an electrical thrill right between Marie's eyes. *Skggh! Twoog! Fshp!*

But then Ruth put her creation down, frowning, the spell broken. She wasn't crying, but she was obviously disappointed. Marie didn't understand. Had Ruth expected the violin to *work?*

Ruth frowned again, though now it was a crooked frown. She placed the violin under her chin and began playing again, but moving the stirrer very lightly this time so that it barely made a sound, and bobbing up and down, smiling wanly as if in ecstasy. She was making fun of her own creation. This saddened Marie a little, but soon Ruth began to twirl, pretending to play, her eyes closed. She was humming the tune now, and it was no longer a joke, after all.

"What is *that?*" said Helen with disdain.

In anticipation of dinner, Ruth had taken the cigar box up to her room.

"Nothing," she said, placing her handiwork on her dresser and Marie beside it.

Helen put her book down and came over to the dresser wearing a malicious smile. "Is that what you've been doing *all day?*"

"No," said Ruth sullenly.

Helen plucked at one of the rubber bands. "John!" she called out, running to get her brother. "Look what Ruth made—a vio-*lin!*"

"So what?" John called back. Today he was above it all, too old to be bothered with his sisters' affairs.

So many forces at work in this house, Marie thought, and sometimes they worked to Ruth's advantage. Helen returned, smirking "Vio-*lin,*" but without John to witness the teasing she quickly gave up. She flopped down on her bed and resumed reading *Wuthering Heights*.

Ruth sat on her own bed to read *Science and Health*. "*. . . for Mind can impart purity instead of impurity,*" she murmured, "*strength instead of weakness . . .*" Marie didn't understand how Ruth could submit to it just now. Her own head was still spinning from the music of the basement, but she had to agree the book was an unassailable way to ignore Helen. After a little while the bear heard Mama's step on the stairs. She appeared in the doorway.

"I need one of you girls to set the table. I shouldn't have to ask you every time."

It was Helen's turn, so Helen said, "Look what Ruth was doing in the basement today."

Marie was afraid Ruth might get in trouble—for using the hammer, perhaps, or the glue. She watched Mama pick up the homemade object.

"It's my violin," said Ruth, shrugging, yet the tone of her voice was like opening both her palms in supplication.

"Ah," said Mama in her distant, inscrutable way. "I can see you worked very hard on it." But at least Ruth didn't seem to be in trouble. Mama went out and Helen followed.

Ruth continued reading until their footsteps receded down the stairs. Now that the girl was alone, the bear stared ahead more intently, hoping that Ruth would play with her violin some more. Marie wanted to see her make those wild virtuoso strokes again.

"No, Marie, you can't have my violin," Ruth said suddenly. "You're only a bear. Bears can't play the violin!"

Marie was startled and annoyed. She didn't want to play the violin, did she? That was what Ruth wanted. And Marie had wanted it for her.

"Silly bear!" said Ruth. She came and picked up Marie and began shaking her up and down, making her eyes click open and shut. "Silly bear! Silly bear!"

It was sort of like their headache game, but worse, because Marie doubted there would be a calm, healing part. She wished for a return to the more placid, careful Ruth. The girl kept saying, "Silly!" over and over, shaking Marie up and down and side to side, making her big lifeless head wobble on its weak cloth neck. "Vio-*lin*," Ruth said disdainfully, exactly as Helen had said it. "I want a vio-*lin!*" she made Marie say, while she also made the bear dance sideways in weird loops. "Vio-*lin!*" The awkward pirouettes were a harsh parody of the high-wire movements Marie had performed in her concert vision, and it was as if wanting itself—wanting anything—were only a weird, ridiculous, painful dance. Between flickers of her eyes, Marie glimpsed an entranced hatred in Ruth's face. She kept repeating "Stupid bear!" and "Vio-*lin!*" and making Marie dance like an idiot in the air. The bear tried to summon her will to move, to tumble out of Ruth's grasp once more. Everything started going dark around the edges. Then the feeling pushed a step further and Marie began almost to enjoy her neck flopping sharply back and forth, the way her eyes seemed about to crack with the jerking open and shut. "Harder!" she wanted to cry. "More!"

But just as suddenly it stopped, like a storm that never was, and Ruth was calmly setting Marie down on the pillow of the bed, smoothing out the bear's black velvet skirt. Ruth's face had a busy, pinched look of concentration, like Mama when she was carefully sewing a seam shut. Marie could only stare, dark and dizzy from the shaking, trying to pierce that mesmerized intention. Ruth kept smoothing and smoothing the velvet, saying nothing, seeming to think nothing at all.

"Ruth," said Papa. Marie started. Ruth turned around quickly, embarrassed.

Marie's vision was still cloudy around the edges. Just now it was hard to believe there was anyone else in the world besides herself and Ruth. But here was this man, standing in the frame of the doorway, very tall and thin, looking as worried and sad as usual. The sight was even stranger because Papa never came up to the girls' room; it wasn't his realm.

He nodded toward the dresser. "Is that the violin you made today?"

"Yes," said Ruth uneasily.

Was he angry or just curious? Because of what Ruth had just done to her, Marie actually hoped the girl was about to be punished. She ticked off in her mind again all the rules Ruth might have broken today. But the girl couldn't have looked more innocent. Her side of the room was, as usual, perfectly neat, in contrast to Helen's, and despite rummaging in the basement she'd managed to keep her white dress and white socks perfectly clean.

Papa picked up the homemade instrument. "That's quite a violin," he said wryly.

So intensely did Marie hate the object at this moment that she took pleasure in his little joke.

"And you've been reading *Science and Health?*" said Papa, nodding toward the little volume that lay on Ruth's bed.

"Uh-huh," the girl answered.

"That's a very grown-up book for a nine-year-old to be reading."

"I know . . ."

Marie was hoping he might disapprove, but he began examining the violin again.

"It doesn't really play," Ruth admitted. Maybe she thought that showing she knew the truth might win her points, for surely she was in trouble. Then she joked, "Marie helped me make it."

"Oh, well, that's why it doesn't work," Papa said, laughing.

Marie thought she might burst into yellow flames of fury and frustration. That would get their attention. For she already understood, by Papa's tone, what he was about to say next—she could see how everything was suddenly turning around and how Ruth was going to get her way after all.

Papa knit his brow. "I think, Ruth," he said, tapping the thin wood of the cigar box lid, "we will get you a real violin."

It appeared to the miserable bear that undeserved candy was falling down from the ceiling in colorful waves. Ruth seemed to dare not move or speak, and Marie watched a moment as this bounty fell and fell on the girl and her father.

Why should Ruth get her wish, and never Marie?

Even so, the bear couldn't help but see how extraordinary it was—a violin for Ruth. The bear felt a sharp pain behind the eyes. How could she begrudge the miracle? Against the odds, Ruth had known what she wanted, she had persevered, and she had gotten it.

"I may?" said Ruth meekly. She didn't leap up or hug her father, knowing he didn't like that sort of thing. She only looked up at him with not too much excitement.

Marie marveled at this timid little girl's canny resilience. Marie had to admit it served Ruth well. This house was like a maze, and somehow the girl kept finding her way through it.

Papa spoke of when they would buy the violin, how they would find Ruth a teacher. Already he was backing out of the room, as if he'd overstayed his allotted time. On his way out he warned that supper was nearly ready.

"I'll just finish reading one more verse," Ruth said.

She and Marie were left alone. The rain of goodness had subsided. Ruth didn't seem to know what to do. She picked Marie up and hugged her tightly; Marie was scarcely less angry but she squeaked anyway, she couldn't help it, and Ruth, in her happiness, mimicked her: "*Eehkth.*"

In Ruth's arms Marie was neither yielding nor resisting. Nor was Winkie, in the arms of memory. Though Ruth's childhood would continue for some time, that evening his own had come to an end. For Marie had realized then that she hadn't pitched from Ruth's lap on her own power. She remained only what she was. Would she always? She felt Ruth's tears soak through her blouse. Soon she would acquire new illusions, but for now she was free of them. She wasn't such a bad bear as to forsake her duties—to listen, to comfort, to cuddle. As Ruth squeezed her tighter, Marie squeaked once more. Over the girl's shoulder, in the narrow window, she could see the summer evening light between the leaves. It was her first look at such light, yellow gold behind a lattice of green. So many summers to come, and each would bring back this first one, of sloping ceiling and narrow window, of having and losing at the same time, of eyes wide-open in a hug.

Prisoner
Winkie

The plain sedan screeched short in front of a large, windowless building with a square white roof like the lid of a shoebox. "OK, miss, let's go now, c'mon, c'mon, let's go, let's go, miss, come *on*," said the two agents, though Winkie offered no resistance as they threw open the back door, yanked him out of the car, and pulled him forward so quickly that his two legs dangled above the ground.

Weee, thought the bear angrily.

Inside, it reeked of disinfectant. The agents exchanged gruff hellos with two jailers sitting at a desk behind a thick window— "Al." "Joe." "Mike." "Mary Sue." Everyone seemed to know one another. They spoke in fragments and finished one another's sentences. "The two two seven?" "Yep." "Area—?" "B. Sure." "You need the—?" "Yeah. Thanks." Above their heads a big plain round clock read exactly 4:00, seeming to define this particular world— as if the jail and the jailers could only exist at this precise moment in the middle of the night.

The little bear was dragged swiftly down numerous concrete-block hallways and buzzed through numerous gates and doors, arriving finally at a large white room where a row of greenish video monitors displayed still more concrete hallways lined with barred cells or solid doors. The same terse hellos had been exchanged along the way, and now again with the two hefty jailers standing at a large console full of buttons and more screens as if they were piloting a spaceship. "Bill." "Cindy." "Mike." "Mary Sue." Winkie had thus deduced the useless information that Mike and Mary Sue were the names of his two agents. "Two two sev—" "Yep." "B?" "Thanks."

A button was pushed, there was the same sharp buzzing sound, and Agent Mary Sue shoved Winkie into a small side room. Before he could even turn to see her go, the door shut behind him with a loud click, and the bear was alone. He turned to the good-sized window expecting to look out at the monitors and guards in the central chamber, but instead beheld only himself in a dim mirror, handcuffed and bewildered, still in his hospital gown. He watched himself sigh.

At 9 A.M. the next morning, in a federal courthouse nearby, the judge, a large, round man in black robes, was handed a list of attorneys available to serve as counsel to the indigent defendant Miss Winkie. He began to read:

Bane
Chafe
Choke
Fear
Fink
Flamer
Guilloton
Lies
Monstrosky . . .

The judge stroked his chin. "Hm. Curious . . ." He looked up at the small, neat clerk who had brought him the list, but she said nothing. She was definitely prettier than any of his own assistants. He asked, "You're new here, aren't you?"

The clerk shrugged. The judge continued reading:

Murk

Rattle

Roach

Sleeper

Slutsky

Smagula

Snakey . . .

He turned the paper over but there was nothing on the other side. "These aren't exactly the county's most successful attorneys," he said musingly. "Murk, for instance—I don't believe he's practiced in several years now."

The clerk rolled her eyes. "Sir, *these* are the *names*."

Her pert, blond ponytail twitched with every word, and the judge felt suddenly very, very tired. He sighed. Three deputy attorneys general had called that morning to remind him that this was the kind of high-profile case that could end a judicial career. He was tired of his career. He said to himself now, as lately he had taken to saying to himself many times a day, to soothe himself, Sometimes ya just can't win. And his weary eyes settled on a name near the bottom of the list.

"Unwin?" he said, tentatively.

The clerk nodded. "That would be Charles Unwin the Fourth, Esquire," she said, snatching the list out of his hand. "Of Unwin, Grimble, and Slyz. I'll contact him immediately."

The white concrete walls were nearly soundproof, but sometimes Winkie could hear snickering or swearing on the other side of the door.

". . . disgusting . . . ," he thought he heard someone say, maybe Agent Mary Sue.

Despite the haste with which they had brought him here, the authorities now left him in the small room for hours at a time. The little bear began to worry about Françoise—where they had taken her, whether she, too, was in jail simply for her kindness to him. He doubted any of his captors would tell him, even if he had the chance to ask. Sometimes it sounded like someone was about to come in, but then nothing happened. Winkie fell into a fitful doze. He dreamed of Ruth and of her five children, each of whom was a playing card in the bear's hand. Ruth sat across from him, intent on her own cards. Half waking, knowing he'd spoil the game by doing so, Winkie placed each one faceup on the felt table—Carol, Helen, Paul, Ken, and Cliff. It was the end of the game now; there were no more chances to be drawn or played. "That was Ruth's family," he murmured sadly, waking a little more. It was as if he had summed up every finality both before and since, including and especially the hopes and losses of the forest, which hadn't even figured in the dream.

The door of the cell clicked open and a plump female jailer entered, complaining to Agent Mike that the jail had no clothing on hand that would fit a traitor and murderer as puny as this one, and that something had to be specially ordered, which took most of the goddamn day and which the little piece of shit didn't deserve. "Put it on!" she shouted, throwing a set of gray baby clothes at the bear. The outfit fell from his grasp to the floor. "Pick it up!" she shouted now.

It seemed to take an excruciatingly long time for him to remove his hospital gown and pull on the little T-shirt and pants, and indeed Agent Mike grumbled, "Christ—finally," when Winkie was done. Glancing down at the baby outfit, the bear didn't think he could be any more humiliated than this. A row of figures was stenciled on the front.

"That's *yer number*," said the jailer, enunciating angrily as if the suspect might not understand, or might pretend not to understand, these simple words. "From *now on*. Don't *forgit* it."

Then she and Agent Mike dragged the bear down yet another long hallway to be photographed and fingerprinted. Shoved up against the white wall marked with heights, waiting for the camera to be ready, Winkie cleared his throat, getting up the courage to ask about Françoise—

"Shut up and smile!" Mike yelled, and then came the flash.

The spots in Winkie's eyes must have looked like dapples of sunlight, because as he stood there blinking, he was suddenly overtaken by a forest memory, one as complete and unbidden as a dream. Together, he and his cub descended into a shady bowl of ferns, between which a stream swished and gurgled. The little one let out a sigh of pleasure at the prospect of a drink. "Ye-e-s," Winkie crooned, as he did every day; for they came here every day, and every day she sighed halfway down the hill, first as he carried her and now as they walked side by side between the new, bright green fronds. "And after?" Winkie asked next, like always, meaning after their drink, and the toddler answered, like always, "Violins," her playful name for fiddleheads, because Winkie had once carefully explained to her that a fiddle was a violin. Then the two of them chuckled, as they did each day at her jest, because of course the little cub had never seen either a fiddle or a violin, and probably never would see one, not here, deep in the woods—

"Hey!" Mike hollered, tugging Winkie's chain. "Move your fuzzy fuckass back to the holding area."

*   *   *

The slight man in a baggy gray suit was very nervous and spoke so quickly that the bear could scarcely understand him. "Hello, Miss Winkie, it's very late, we don't have much time, my name is Charles Unwin, I will be your court-appointed attorney, since I understand you are unable to afford one, nice to meet you, too, and let me tell you, I had a devil of a time getting in to see you today, oh, they had all kinds of excuses, first one and then another, and the assistant DAs were all laughing at me behind my back, I know they were, they always do, why would they stop now—but anyway, *ahem*, that's all in the past now, and I'm sure you and I will get along fine." Abruptly he sat down, opened a file folder, and became absorbed for several minutes in its many pieces of paper full of typewritten words, nodding to himself and grunting. After a few minutes Winkie cleared his throat once again to ask about Françoise, but the lawyer held up his hand, frowning severely and shutting his eyes as if being interrupted were the most painful thing to him in the world. He continued reading for several more minutes. Then, without even looking up, he began again just as quickly as before: "It took some doing, and really I don't know how I did it, ha-ha, but I managed to get the FBI to declassify at least *some* of the charges against you—as you can see"—he lifted the stack of papers and set them down again—"though my request for bail has been denied, so that's definitely out—but of course you already know that, otherwise we wouldn't be sitting here right now at the county jail, we'd be in my office, or a coffee shop or something, wouldn't we?" Unwin's cheeks turned a blotchy pink and he began rapidly shuffling first one and then another piece of paper to the front of the file folder. "I finally did also manage—again, I don't know how, but I did, though it took all day, and that's why we have so little time, which is unfortunate—but in any case I did finally manage to get in here to see you today, oh yes, I already said that, and anyway of course you can see me sitting right here in front of you now, so you know that I succeeded in getting in to see you, ha-ha, so, um, so, uh, so . . ." His face now bloomed a heated raspberry shade to the tips of his ears, his watery eyes darted from one corner of the little room to another, and his voice seemed about to give out. "As I was saying, *ahem,* the crimes you're accused of, as I'm sure you know, um, as I'm sure you're aware, are very grave—*very* grave indeed"—though the redness in his face began to die down, Unwin's eyes continued darting here and there, so that the bear didn't know where to look—"and indeed there are so *many* charges, they go on and on, page after page after page, that honestly I can scarcely make heads or tails of them—I mean, of course I can make *sense* of them, I mean, that's my *job*—so, so, so, so, so—oh yes—so, at this time I must tell you, Miss Winkie— now, defendants never want to hear this, and I'm never any good at telling them—oh well, what can you do?—at this juncture I must prepare you—now, don't shoot the messenger, and don't take this personally—*I* take everything personally, but *you* shouldn't— again, it's not that I'm saying you necessarily *will* get the death penalty, it's only one of many possible outcomes, but you must consider that, especially given public opinion at this time—and let me tell you, right now the name Winkie is about synonymous with 'radioactive dog shit floating in toxic—'"

Just then something on one of the closely typed papers caught Unwin's skittering eye and he started reading again, paging forward, then back, and as Winkie watched, all trace of distress departed as if by magic from the man's otherwise haggard face so that he appeared almost boyish, his straight graying hair falling in front of his eyes. "Now this . . . Now *this* . . . ," Unwin muttered, shaking his index finger in an imaginary courtroom. Then he was silent again, shuffling the papers quickly and reading with the greatest speed and absorption, so that Winkie breathed easier and after several minutes began to stumble into another busy, dream-filled sleep . . .

"So there's always hope, right?" said Unwin suddenly, quickly gathering his things. "That's what you have to tell yourself, over and over, don't worry, don't worry, don't worry, don't worry, just tell yourself that, and yes, by God, one way or another, I don't know how, I never know how, but some way, somehow, I *will* get you out of this!"

Winkie was glad that Mr. Unwin was feeling better, but he still needed to ask his one question. "Where . . . ?" he attempted to say and found his voice unwilling. He cleared his throat and tried again, but still nothing. The lawyer was about to leave. Grasping his ballpoint, Winkie scrawled across the Formica table: "WHERE IS FRANÇOISE?"

"Mr. Winkie, what are you doing, you're defacing public property, please give that back—"

The bear began pointing vigorously at the name of his friend.

"Françoise? Who's Françoise?" said Unwin. "I don't know anything about a Françoise." He waved one hand in the air.

"THE HOSPITAL," the bear wrote now.

Unwin remained puzzled for a moment but suddenly brightened. "Oh, you mean your *accomplice*."

Winkie didn't bother to correct this but simply handed back the ballpoint.

"Miss, Miss, Miss—let's see—yes, yes, yes, Miss Fouad, Miss Françoise Fouad," the lawyer muttered, paging through a thick folder. "Or Faoud. They have it both ways." He squinted at one of the papers, then flipped back to another. "Aiding and abetting . . . Accessory after the fact . . . Yes, it appears she remains in custody as well. OK?"

Unwin was more than ready to go now, but Winkie looked stricken.

"Don't *worry!*" said Unwin, hastily patting the bear's shoulder and heading toward the door. Winkie didn't know what to think or feel. "OK, well—" He knocked three times, the door opened, and Unwin disappeared down the hall, calling back over his shoulder, "Now, I *mean* it!"

In another grim room, on another floor, Françoise sat before the chief detective. She had been questioned several times over the past two days, to no avail, so the chief had decided to interrogate her personally.

Chief detective: *The thread that was used to sew up Miss Winkie's wounds is the same as the thread in your sewing kit. An exact match. Indisputable. There's no use denying it.*

Françoise Fouad: As I have already said again and again, yes, I mended him. And I want a lawyer.

"Him"? Who do you mean? You "mended" another terrorist as well? Where and when was that?

No, I mended only the little bear. He is a boy, and I already told you that, too.

(Laughs condescendingly) OK, have it your way, so who told you to "mend" "him"?

No one. I heard him moaning, and I wanted to—

Who trained you in the use of a needle and thread to treat battlefield wounds?

(Sighing) He is a stuffed animal.

So that's your story. That's still your story.

It isn't a story. He is a teddy bear!

Some teddy bear. Who told you to say that?

No one.

So that's your story.

(Sighing again) My story is that it is not a story.

Don't get smart. OK. Sure. And this "stuffed bear" can walk, and talk, and blow things up?

I do not believe he blows things up, but yes, he can walk and talk.

And how do you explain that?

I cannot explain that.

How many other stuffed bears can walk and talk?

(Pause) Mother Nature is mysterious.

We'll get to your extremist beliefs in a moment. You're a lesbian?

Yes.

It's OK, you can admit it.

I have already said several times that I am queer.

(Yells) *Queer enough to have sex with a twelve-inch terrorist?*

What?

We know for a fact that the two of you had sex, that Miss Winkie seduced you, and that's how you were drawn into this conspiracy. That's how she drew everyone in. It wasn't your fault. If only you would tell us the truth, we could help you.

I told you he is a boy, and I like girls, and besides, he is a stuffed animal.

To each his own.

(Silence.)

Doesn't Islam forbid such things?

Forbid what?

Sex with one-foot-tall freaks!

(Sighs) Sir, I am an agnostic and a feminist, and though I do still believe in many of the precepts of Islam, I do not believe in restrictions on sex between men, women, or, as you say, freaks.

That's convenient. So lesbian sex with terrorists is OK for agnostics?

I am telling you that we did not have sex, and he is not a terrorist. He is a good bear, and he is my friend. Not that having sex is bad—

(Rubs his eyes.) *This discussion is going nowhere.*

That is what I have been trying to tell you.

You make me sick.

I came to America to get away from people like you—but maybe I made a mistake!

Oh, you made a mistake, all right.

(Her voice breaking.) I said I want to see a lawyer.

Miss Fouad, as I'm sure it has already been explained to you, you are an immigrant, and you have not yet been charged with a crime, therefore—

I am an American citizen!

That's right, hide behind the very freedoms you seek to destroy.

Standing squarely in the doorway of Winkie's cell, the plump jailer read aloud a list of the facility's rules, beginning with, "I will respect myself, my fellow inmates, and, most of all, my jailers. . . ." Her headful of short, thin, purplish curls bobbed from side to side with the effort. Winkie looked at each of the four white walls as if there might be some escape, then at the jailer's badge, which said Deputy Wing. "And the Most Important Rule of All," she concluded, her small eyes a-twinkle with improvisation. "I'll be *watchin'* you!"

Deputy Finch, a large man whose shaved scalp formed a shadow cap on his round head, snickered in a sinister way. "We watch traitors and terrorists *speshly*," he added, kicking Winkie's feet out from under him so that he fell against the concrete slab of a bed. "Little fuck."

So this is how it's going to be, thought the bear, not without fear. He calculated that Deputy Finch was six times taller and thirty to forty times heavier than he was. Slowly he climbed up onto the unpadded platform, testing its hardness with his paws.

Wing said, "You might try to hang yourself or somethin'," apparently to account for the missing mattress, though she explained no further. As if conducting an English lesson she began pointing and naming everything in the cell. "Sink. Faucet. Bed. Other bed. Door. Food slot. Stool. Floor drain. Other stool. Counter. Terlet. Terlet paper."

Abruptly and without another word she and Finch exited, and the heavy cell door clicked shut. Winkie was about to allow himself at least a small sigh of relief, but then he saw the two of them standing in the door's wire-crossed window, smirking and waving at him. This went on for quite a while, and just when it seemed they had tired of the activity, an inmate also appeared in the window, and the door opened.

"Hey!" called the inmate, a skinny woman with gray-red hair and gentle-seeming granny glasses. Thus far she was the only prisoner Winkie had seen who was white. "Housewarming present!"

A heavy book whizzed past the bear's face.

Through the ensuing laughter Deputy Finch yelled something about "your kind" and the door clicked shut again. They watched the bear awhile longer, but soon Winkie could hear an authoritative voice calling from somewhere, and the window quickly cleared to the plain white of the hallway. In the sudden silence, Winkie went and picked up the book: the Koran.

"Oh, I inquired after Miss um, Miss, um um—Fouad," said Unwin a few days later, as he pulled papers out of an overstuffed briefcase.

Winkie brightened, just a little.

"I don't know, I think I might've made things worse."

Winkie was downcast.

"Well, not worse."

Winkie brightened.

"Well, maybe worse. I don't know . . ." Unwin pulled a large roll of silver duct tape from his briefcase and looked questioningly at it. "Huh—I'm surprised they didn't catch this when I came in. I mean, it must be contraband, nearly everything is." He held it out to Winkie. "Do you want it?"

The bear shook his head, furious.

"Yeah, I guess there's no reason you would." He blushed. "Um, anyway, anyway, anyway . . ."

Winkie stared at him.

"Oh, yes, Miss Fouad—Miss Fouad—um, so I think I may have made things worse. The assistant prosecutor said, 'You're awfully interested in this witness,' and I said, 'Uh, I'm not that interested,' and she said, 'Then why did you ask about her?' so I said, 'No special reason,' and she said. . . ." The story went on for many more sentences, as Unwin sifted absentmindedly through his papers. ". . . So finally I said, 'Um, so where is Miss Fouad now?' and she said, 'Well, actually we were just about to release her, but now I think we won't, I think we'll need to question her further,' and so on like that, with this little *smile* on her face—everyone says she and the chief prosecutor are having, um, you know—so um, anyway, I tried saying, 'Um, that would certainly be very unfair to Miss Fouad,' and she said, 'That's not my concern,' so I stormed out." He pulled a second role of tape from his briefcase, shrugged, and resumed sorting through his papers. "But now that I think of it, um, they must not have ever intended to release her. Yes, they must have just been taunting me. That must be it, because they like to do that . . ."

Winkie thought he might burst into tears of frustration and rage when suddenly Unwin looked up from his briefcase and his small blue darting eyes actually stood still for a moment. "I just hope I didn't make things any worse for your friend," he said simply.

Now the bear couldn't decide whether to forgive him or throttle him.

"Um, um, um, um," continued Unwin. "Anyway, anyway . . . So, anyway . . . So, so, so . . ."

In the name of God, the Compassionate, the Merciful . . .

As Winkie tried to read, Deputy Wing and her granny trusty stood in the cell window, their hands clasped in mock prayer.

"Towel head," sang the trusty, whose name was Randi.

This had been going on since he arrived. Whenever he picked up his book, it seemed, there they were in the window again, jeering, one or both of them, or some other guard and some other prisoner. Winkie turned away in disdain, but as usual Randi began tapping on the thick glass with her thickly painted fingernails, crooning, "Towel head," again and again.

The bear sighed. "So, my head is made of cloth," he thought. "So what?"

He flipped a few pages ahead and tried to concentrate. During their many interrogations the chief detective had often quoted the Koran, seeming to think the bear already knew all about it and had, moreover, misinterpreted it to justify his supposed crimes. Winkie had no interest in replying to such arguments, but he was curious about the book itself—the only reading material he was allowed, yet he was taunted every time he opened it. Unfortunately it was also a difficult book, and Winkie never seemed to get very far before bewilderment made his eyes droop.

Do you think you will enter the garden of bliss without the trials of those who have passed before you?

"Well, yes," muttered the bear, somewhat affronted. "Why shouldn't I?" Besides, he thought, what if you've already entered the garden of bliss—and lost it? Could you, through more trials, return to it? If so, why so *many* trials? Exasperated, Winkie flipped the pages again.

. . . and whenever God decrees anything, God says to it, "Be!" and it is.

Winkie shut his eyes and opened them again—the words seemed to cut through him. For if this really was true—if God had decreed his existence—then why? And why give a bear his freedom only to take it away? Wouldn't it have been better to have no hope at all?

"*Aka-maka ha-moogh!*" called Randi, in "Arabic." Deputy Wing barked laughter.

Winkie curled up into a ball around the book, so that his tormentors wouldn't see him crying.

With a satisfying rustle of his robe, the judge swept from his private chambers into the courtroom. "All rise!" The ceremony of his arrival—it was the one moment of the day the judge actually enjoyed. In the wonderful silence he climbed the three steps to his august seat—

"Your Honor, uh, Your Honor, let me assure you—" said Unwin.

"Assure me of what?" said the judge, thoroughly jangled. "Counselor, I have not yet even spoken." With showy annoyance he seated himself.

"Oh, of course, Judge, I apologize. It was—it was the expression on your face—I misinterpreted it as a statement—"

The prosecutor and his favorite assistant stifled laughter and the judge banged his gavel several times. "Counselor," he said to Unwin. "I will now speak. Then you will speak based on what I have said. Do you understand?"

"Yes, of course, Judge, yes, oh yes, naturally—"

The judge banged the gavel again. "Now, where were we?" Crossly he began rubbing his eyes, not to think but so as not to see the tall, thin, disheveled Unwin, who stood before him so miserably as if naked before God. It made the judge himself feel naked before God. Picturing how he must appear to everyone gathered in the courtroom—his face pink and fat and irritable above the black of his robe—he shuddered with sudden and unaccountable embarrassment.

"Suppression of evidence?" prompted the prosecutor, with a felicitous smile.

"Oh, yes," said the judge.

"Your Honor, Your Honor, Your Honor, Your Honor!" said Unwin. "May I . . . ?"

The judge tried not to look at him. "May you *what?*"

"Speak. I'd like to speak."

The judge decided he had never before seen anyone or anything as detestable as Charles Unwin the Fourth, Esquire. The pale man undulated there in his baggy gray suit, blushing. With greater keenness than usual, the judge felt sure that his whole life was a hideous fraud and he could no longer go on with it. *He—just— couldn't—go—on!* His black robe became unbearably heavy and warm. He began to prickle all over. What if I just tore it off and underneath I was wearing women's underwear, and then I ran out of the room screaming, "Fuck me!"? he thought, to soothe himself. It didn't soothe him, but it enabled him at least to motion with one hand for Unwin to proceed.

Still the defense attorney stood there frowning and not speaking, staring at the floor as if in suspended animation.

"Mr. Unwin?" boomed the judge. He hoped that by talking very loudly he could give himself a sense of purpose. It wasn't working.

"What?" said Unwin, a moment or two later, as if startled.

"You had something to say to this court?"

"Oh, I didn't know I could yet."

The judge looked at the ceiling full of white rectangles and lights. "I just *said* you could."

"Oh, oh, oh, I didn't hear you. Strange. Strange . . ." His eyes moving this way and that, Unwin looked as though he might never overcome his bafflement.

"I *gestured*," said the judge, hating himself for speaking to this hapless man on his own terms.

Relief spread like balm across Unwin's blotchy face. "Ah, that explains it," he muttered. "So. So. So. So . . ."

The judge wondered if he could get through the entire trial without looking at the defense attorney ever again.

Bedtime was called lights-out, but the fluorescent doughnut above Winkie's concrete bed shone all night long. The dingy light was somehow blue, green, and orange all at once, and it flickered hundreds of times a second like the wings of a moth. Next to it was the small surveillance camera, a single dead eye.

What time was it? The hours passed strangely in jail and most strangely at night. Somewhere way down the cell block a young woman began to scream, Randi yelled, "Stupid bitch!" and the screaming died down.

Winkie's numbered baby suit reeked of industrial detergent and made his mangy fur itch. It didn't bother him so much during the day, but at night, which was as bright as day, the insistent tickle, first here, then there, quickly grew intolerable and he began to claw at himself. What little fur he had left on his belly was wearing away, and even in his sleep he knew he should stop but couldn't. He scratched and scratched. It provided a weird kind of relief; when he was scratching he seemed to think nothing at all. Before bed he tried to reason with himself that if Wing or Finch found fur on the floor of his cell, he'd be punished, but to no avail. Every night he scratched himself raw.

Once early on he tried simply removing the clothes and indeed lay there with relief for several minutes, enjoying the air on his nakedness—but soon enough one of the night guards banged on the window and told the disgusting whore to put her fucking T-shirt back on *now*, before he (the guard) threw up all over the video monitor.

Winkie turned on his side and lay still, in a brief lull of scratching, staring at the harsh white wall. Cabin, hospital, jail: His life had entered into a series of nowheres, and what if that never ended? The thought made the lines and unforgiving planes of his cell seem that much more harsh, as if he were trying to bite down on the concrete blocks, the metal toilet bowl, the sink and counter molded of some extremely hard, speckled beige material. Idly he clicked his claws against it, knowing he'd leave no mark.

The screaming again, then "Stupid bitch!" and echoing silence.

In the corners of the cell the jail's noxious floor cleaner had dried in small grayish white pools. Sometimes the bear tried shutting his eyes and pretending he was in the forest by a lively stream, but that meant remembering his cub, which meant grief. He felt the first tickle and did not resist but began to claw his belly again, first slowly, then more rapidly, desperately. For weeks now he had been kept in isolation and wasn't even allowed to attend his own preliminary hearings, not that they interested him. He was given just fifteen minutes of outdoor recreation each day, in a concrete yard, by himself, and usually the privilege was revoked anyway, for infractions such as frowning at Wing. There was no further news of Françoise. The bear lapsed into worried vacancy. He scratched.

"Yes, oh yes, of course, oh yes, naturally," the judge muttered, dreaming fitfully. ". . . the expression on your face . . ." His large head went from side to side and his eyes raced beneath his eyelids. "Let me assure you . . . Let me . . . Let me . . . Your Honor, let me assure you . . ."

The chief buried his head under his pillow, sniffing its dankness. "There's got to be some way to make them *break!*" he muttered.

By now Misses Winkie and Fouad had each been interviewed dozens of times, but despite every threat and enticement, the little mastermind still refused to answer a word, and the lesbian continued with her maddening deceptions. "They were very well trained," mused the chief. The pair's network of evil continued to grow in his mind, to involve all manner of crimes, each carefully conceived and executed to undermine the nation in some special way. Their plot was most clear to him in the middle of the night. "Yes. It all connects. I see it now!" he said aloud, as if he were understanding for the first time. Indeed, the conspiracy was so huge and so complex that he had to persuade himself of it again and again, and each time he was astounded. He stared ahead into the darkness, picturing the little criminal and her Egyptian accomplice breaking every conceivable law of civilized society. "They thought we couldn't imagine it," he mused. "And in a way, that was the fucking genius of it. But we *can* imagine it." He kicked off the covers. "Whatever they can imagine, we can imagine *twenty times worse!*"

The chief rolled over and pounded his pillow. Its dust filled his nostrils. Crimes unsolved for years were finally beginning to make sense to him. He started planning which ethnic groups to round up, how many, what ages; which newscasters and high-level officials to alert; which agents he could trust to investigate those aspects of the conspiracy he'd only just now realized . . . "Yes, yes, no, hell no, yes," he murmured, going down his mental checklist.

But at times such as this the little terrorist's weird face would seem to appear out of the darkness, sadly gazing up at him, spot-lit and hunted, whipped by helicopter wind—yet somehow hopeful.

Forcibly the chief turned his mind back to the investigation. "'The attorney general has given me carte blanche,'" he practiced telling a frightened Miss Winkie. "Carte blanche, damn it. CARTE BLANCHE!"

"Miss Winkie, as your lawyer, I must, I really must insist, I really must," said Unwin one morning. Again he was trying to elicit the bear's own recollections from the months and days leading up to the arrest.

Winkie only shrugged.

"Miss Winkie, I cannot, I simply cannot help you, Miss Winkie, unless—" He blew his nose into a flowered Kleenex. "As your attorney, as your *sole advocate*, it is my duty, indeed my *solemn duty*, to ask you such questions, Miss Winkie, painful as they may *be* . . ."

The bear stared at the floor. He knew he was acting like a child, but he couldn't seem to help it, no more than he could help scratching himself each night.

"All right, all right, um, let's maybe try going back to, um, the beginning," Unwin said, sighing. "Where, that is to say, in what city, were you born?"

The sheer ignorance of this question riled the bear, and he shook his head vigorously. He wasn't born, he was made. Why should he have to explain that?

"No, you won't tell me where you were born?" Unwin asked.

The bear rolled his eyes and threw up his arms, but then Unwin, evidently out of sheer frustration, happened upon the right answer. "Well, and I suppose you mean you weren't born at all?"

Winkie looked at the man with surprise, then nodded.

"Um, but what do you mean?"

Winkie rolled his eyes again. He wasn't sure what angered him more—having to answer these ridiculous questions or having been brought into existence in the first place. He started to make fierce snipping and stitching motions, then indicated himself with a sort of "voilà" gesture.

"Scissors . . . Sewing . . . You were sewn together?" Unwin put his pen down. Looking more closely at the bear, apparently for the first time, his small blue eyes widened and he drew back his chin in surprise. "Oh, well, of course, of course, I knew that." He fiddled with the pen. "I, um, well then, well then—where were you *made?*" The bear didn't answer. "I suppose in a workshop or factory?"

Winkie nodded just once and Unwin wrote it down.

"OK. And can you tell me where the workshop was?"

Winkie couldn't help but call the place to mind, yet despite its vividness the image didn't offer anything like what Unwin seemed to want. The bear shrugged. Anyway, what did it matter where it was?

"Doesn't know," the attorney murmured as he wrote. "Uh . . . well, OK, how about after that? Perhaps I could name places, and then you could tell me if they ring a bell?" The bear sighed, but Unwin took no notice. His voice had grown surprisingly calm and patient. "London, Rio de Janeiro, Poughkeepsie, Bangkok, Chicago—"

Winkie nodded forcefully.

"Bangkok?"

The bear opened his eyes wide in frustration.

"Chicago?"

Again Winkie nodded.

"And when was that?"

The bear motioned toward very far behind him.

"Ah, a long time ago," said Unwin.

Winkie didn't want to feel any of it, but even at these few words his heart began to soften and the recollections poured forth.

"You must have been very young when you lived there," said the lawyer.

Sadly Winkie nodded yes.

And by this method, gradually over the next several days, Unwin was able to sketch out the bear's entire life story. Soon Winkie no longer minded his questions, for as Unwin learned more, the questions grew more interesting. This man was, it turned out, capable of remarkable concentration and empathy. By the end, it was as if their two minds were functioning as one.

"When you feel the urge to do something," asked Unwin, "is it like waking from sleep, or a sudden welling up of a fountain within you, or a letting go?"

Winkie pointed to the middle of the table, indicating the middle option, but hesitantly.

"Maybe like a welling up," said Unwin. "Got it. A flood or a trickle?"

The bear shrugged.

"Depends. OK. And is it a welling up of multicolored bubbly water in sunlight, or a welling up of a dark underground stream in a cave?"

Winkie gestured to his right.

"Ah. Cave," said Unwin with satisfaction, writing it all down.

Longer visits with his attorney were among several new privileges Winkie had been granted that week. Starting Monday he found either a peanut butter cookie or a small piece of frosted cake, albeit stale, on his tray for both lunch and dinner. Tuesday afternoon he was taken to the exercise yard even though it wasn't his day, and that night at bedtime the light actually went out in his cell. The bear actually slept. Strangest of all, both Wing and Finch had grown extraordinarily polite.

"Miss Winkie, by order of the warden I am happy to inform you that you are hereby released from solitary confinement," said Deputy Finch, smiling and unlocking the bear's cell Wednesday morning. "For good behavior."

Winkie could think of no recent change in his behavior, unless increasing despair counted. Between Finch's legs he could see the other prisoners gathered around several metal tables in the common area. Randi waved at him gaily.

"Go ahead," said Finch indulgently, motioning toward the tables. "May I introduce you to your fellow inmates?"

The week of marvels continued with two movie nights, a badminton tournament, homemade ice cream, and a performance in the common area by a local string quartet. During intermission, Randi leaned back to whisper to the bear, "I think it's really great that you're planning to destroy America." She grinned, scrunching up her nose with delight. Such attempts to engage

Winkie in incriminating conversation only reminded him to be on his guard. As usual, he said nothing.

However, he couldn't help being stirred by the music, and at the end of the concert he had to hold back tears as he helped put away the metal folding chairs. He'd just placed the fifth one in the rack when Deputy Wing called out, "Oh, Miss Winkie, there's someone here I think you'd definitely like to see!"

The bear turned and saw that Françoise had just been let into the cell block.

She looked worried and drawn, but then her eye caught Winkie's and she smiled. "Come, little bear," she said, kneeling down.

Winkie ran to her, climbed up into her lap, and began to sob.

"*Shh*," she said, stroking his ears. "Don't worry, little bear. Don't worry."

Winkie looked at her pleadingly.

"Yes, I am fine," she answered, adding that her girlfriend had secured a lawyer through the hospital workers union. "I will have a hearing next week. Everyone will be there—our friends from the gay and lesbian center, people from the union, other Egyptians we know. Some of them are going to protest, too, in front of the courthouse!" Winkie wasn't sure what all this meant but her voice reassured him. They sat down at one of the far tables, and Françoise remarked on her good fortune of being reassigned to this cell block. The other inmates circled nearby, listening in, but Winkie paid no attention.

"Friends are all I have," said Françoise. "Yesterday I received a letter from my sister in Cairo. My lawyer gave it to me and I wish he had not. She writes that she and my parents hope my arrest will convince me to change my ways." Françoise sighed. "The letter is very depressing."

Winkie nodded, placing his paw on top of her hand.

"Fifteen years ago my sister came to visit, from Cairo, and when she saw that my girlfriend and I had only one bed in our apartment, she said, 'But where does Mariana sleep?' And when I told her that Mariana and I sleep in the same bed, because we are lovers, my sister started crying. 'Oh, I cannot believe it! Oh no, Françoise, you must stop doing this! You must stop!' And I said, 'Go ahead and cry, honey, because it isn't going to change.'"

Winkie wished he knew just the right thing to say.

"But we must remember better times. You know, little bear, I have already gone to jail once before—because of the giant rat!" She burst out laughing, but Winkie looked puzzled. "You have not ever seen the rat? We share him with the other unions, to use when there is a strike—you know, as a protest. He is three or four meters tall and there is a machine that fills him with air. The hospital really hates the rat—he is our secret weapon!" She laughed again, and so now did Winkie. "So Mariana and I go to the hospital very early in the morning to make the rat, but the machine functions poorly and even after an hour the rat has only a little bit of air inside him. Again and again Mariana says to him, 'Stand up, stupid rat!' but he won't, still he lies there on his side—and we cannot stop laughing. Then the police come to arrest us, because they say the rat is lying on hospital property."

As they laughed together, Winkie felt a strange, thrilling pride in the giant rat—in a fellow half-creature's ability to both appall and amuse. Françoise's giggling gently rocked him, and for a moment he felt what it was like to be whole again.

Just then he saw Finch and the chief detective in the window of the cell block door. The deputy seemed to be having trouble opening it, and the chief was yelling at him to hurry up. Now Wing hurried over and swiped her own card through. The lock made its distinctive thunk, and the chief entered yelling.

"Fucking goddamn *coward*, fucking piece of *shit*, you are *outta* here, mother*fuck*, stinking little—"

He marched forward and snatched the frightened bear from the lap of his friend.

Françoise cried out and Winkie reached back for her. The detective held him up by the scruff of his neck as the bear's feet ran in the air. Finch locked the miniature shackles around his wrists, then his struggling ankles. All at once the bear went slack.

"Your little friend here thought he could get away with pretending he was a *woman*," said the chief, apparently to Françoise. He handed Winkie to Finch. "Thought you'd throw us off, huh, asshole? Thought things would be *easier* here? Ya like hanging out with the *ladies?*"

"Gross," muttered Finch, holding the bear away from his body. Wing snorted.

"Sir, I have told you again and again that this bear is a boy," said Françoise.

"Well, you're in luck. Forensic high-resolution microspectral analysis confirmed it," the detective replied. "Let's go."

As Winkie was carried away, he managed to glimpse Françoise one last time. She was crying. Shackled as he was, he could only lift his paw a little, in farewell.

"Hey," Randi called. "I heard them say something about a *secret weapon*."

The chief stopped short. "What?" He ordered Finch to take the bear and stayed behind to question the informer.

Winkie tried to comprehend how he could be arrested in jail, since he had already been arrested in the cabin. The arrests must

go down and down, he thought, so that wherever Finch was taking him now, he might, soon enough, be arrested from there as
well and taken down to the next level of punishment. The deputy
set him down roughly on the cold elevator floor and after perhaps
a ten-second ride, up or down, Winkie couldn't tell, the heavy
metal doors rumbled reluctantly open on what appeared to be the
very same white cinder-block lobby they had just left. Winkie
blinked. The only difference was that the distant yells and cat-
calls were of a deeper pitch.

More hallways, guards, locked doors. It was almost as if they were
all being created on the spot, for Winkie's benefit, and he wondered at the jail's ability to spin out this endless white labyrinth.
At last Finch led him to what appeared to be a destination, but a
cluster of men in black riot gear was just marching in ahead of
them.

"Whassup?" Finch asked.

"Lockdown," one called back. The door slammed shut behind
them, and Winkie could hear their heavy boots charging down
the passage.

"Shit," said Finch. He turned to the two officers standing at the
console, but they answered nothing. After a moment one of them
gestured with his chin, barely, toward another door.

"Hey, guys," Finch said, shrugging, "I can't help it."

He meant it wasn't his fault that he had to bring them so con-
temptible a prisoner. Finch was ashamed even to be guarding him,
Winkie realized. Without a word the two officers buzzed open the
second door and Finch shoved the bear through.

In the muffled distance Winkie could still hear yelling. He and
Finch had been waiting in a holding cell for some time now. The
door buzzed and Deputy Wing appeared.

"I heard you were stuck here with this little em-effer," she said.

"Yeah," the deputy said glumly. He had already complained several times that his shift was supposed to be over.

Wing gestured with her head toward the distant yelling. "Somebody throwin' feces again?"

"'Parently."

Winkie had heard this mentioned earlier but understood only now that it was meant literally. The raw, animal desperation of throwing crap at your captors made perfect sense to him, even as it filled him with raw, animal disgust. Which was, he supposed, the point. In the same instant he realized that Deputy Wing had a crush on Deputy Finch.

"So what've you and the little A-hole been doin' all afternoon?" she eagerly asked. "Did he switch back to girl again?"

Finch only grunted.

"Here, maybe this'll cheer ya up," said Wing, handing him a page from a small pile of papers and envelopes in her hand. "I got it from my friend over at the federal lockup. Read it."

Finch bent his head to the page.

"No—aloud," Wing ordered. "I want the *prisoner* to hear it, too."

He cleared his throat. "'What Is a Jail Officer?'" he began. "'A Jail Officer is a composite of what all people are, a mingling of saint and sinner, dust and deity. A Jail Officer, of all people, is at once the most needed and the most unwanted. A Jail Officer is a strangely nameless creature who is "Sir" or "Ma'am" to their face and "Fuzz" behind their back. . . .'" The essay went on for some minutes in this vein, and Finch read it all with great feeling. "'. . . The Jail Officer must be a minister, a social worker, a tough person and a gentle person. And, of course, they'll have to be a genius. For they'll have to feed a family on a Jail Officer's salary.'"

Finch shook his head and was silent for a moment. "That is so true."

Wing glared at the bear. "Now maybe you see how it is from *our* point of view," she said, as if her own days were spent caring too much for inmates. The strange thing was, Winkie *did* see it from Wing's point of view. His undying sympathy went forward, almost against his will, and for a moment he looked upon Deputies Wing and Finch with a new sadness.

"And look, I brought little Miss, Mister, *whatever* Winkie some letters!" Wing said, with sudden hilarity. "Can you believe it? The little he-she gets *mail!*" With a comic flourish she laid a small stack of envelopes on the Formica table.

The bear snapped back to hating her. At first he didn't move, refusing to take the bait—but quickly his curiosity overcame him. As soon as he reached for the envelopes, though, Wing snatched them away—however, not before he glimpsed the return address of the letter on top: Cliff Chase.

"Way-way-way-way-wait!" Wing said. "Deputy Finch and me gotta look these over first. Make sure there's no funny business."

Finch chuckled. The envelopes were torn open and clearly had been examined already by the authorities. Could one of them really be from Cliff, the boy he once knew? What would it say? Not being able to find out drove tears of frustration straight from Winkie's eyes.

"Aww, looka dat," said Wing. "Da wittle tewwowist is cwying!" Finch laughed harder, his small mouth making little Os. Wing selected a colorful envelope from the pile and read aloud: "'Dear Occupant'—I guess that's yew, Whiny. 'Don't miss this chance to win a luxurious trip around the world! Enter now!'"

Finch was in stitches, but Winkie could scarcely pay attention. He stared and stared at the stack of letters, willing them to move toward him.

"Kinda hard to take a trip," said Wing, stating the obvious, "when you're sittin' in the gas chamber! But what the hey." She

found the entry form and took out a pen. "Let's see. Name: Moham-
med Filthy Faggot Traitor Winkie the Third. Address: Care of
Department of Corrections, County of . . ."

Finch was howling. "Mail it! Mail it!" he cried.

"Oh, I will! And the lucky little midget is gonna win, too!"
Wing sealed the return envelope and gathered up all of Winkie's
letters, tapping them coquettishly against Finch's shoulder. "I'll
see *you* later."

She left and Winkie watched the mail go with her.

It was nearly midnight before Finch and an officer from the
men's jail escorted the prisoner to his new cell.

"That's Darryl," said the officer, referring to a large snoring mass
on the bottom bunk, wrapped up in blankets. "Don't worry—he's
been sedated."

Winkie watched as the heavy lump rasped in air and let it out
again. Then he peered up at his own bunk, wondering how he could
climb way up there without stepping on the person he wasn't supposed to worry about.

"I hear yer new *roomy* is quite a *character*," said Finch from the
doorway. He yawned. "Hey, Walter, can we hurry it up?"

Deputy Walter was carefully removing the bear's little shackles.
He was much older than Finch and seemed a lot nicer. His face was
tan red and full of lines. "Darryl's OK mosta the time," he whispered,
lifting Winkie up onto his bunk, "but we hadta calm him down quite
a bit today. He threw, um, something at the warden."

Once again the light never went out, and the jail's too-bright
hours seemed to go on forever as Darryl snuffled and snored. The
undelivered letters danced before the bear's mind. He began to
scratch. He thought of a morning long ago when he sat on the lap

of Ruth's youngest, Cliff, and together they watched Ruth make cookies. The girls were away at college and the other two boys wouldn't be home from school for hours. It was often this way, back then, the year that Cliff was four—just the mother, the boy, and Winkie at home. Humming, Ruth pulled another baking sheet from the cabinet and rubbed it with a dab of Crisco on a scrap of wax paper. The radio rehearsed a tinny symphony. Against the window above the sink, the last few drops of a rainstorm fell. Both then and now, the bear shivered pleasantly. Cold and wet outside, but in Ruth's kitchen it was warm with the cozy odor of cooked sugary dough.

"Winkie is going to make blue cookies," said Cliff.

"Blue cookies?" asked Ruth.

"Yep." The boy squirmed pleasantly.

"OK, now I remember him saying that," said Ruth.

Both then and now, the bear tried not to miss even the smallest nuance of this luscious scene of which he was the sudden, lucky center.

"Will Winkie eat the blue cookies?" Ruth asked, completing a neat row of dough tufts in the pan.

"No, sell them."

Ruth laughed. "Well, we could use the extra income." Through the thin walls Winkie had heard Ruth complaining about money to her husband, who had recently lost his job. But at the moment she was in a good mood, unaccountably, always unaccountably, for even after thirty years the bear could never plumb or predict Ruth's moods. "What's in Winkie's cookies?" she asked, finishing the last row of lumps. "Green peas?"

"No!" Cliff hooted. He hugged the bear closer.

"Hamburgers?"

"No!" The boy was giggling with delight. "Yes!"

The timer rang but it announced no end and no beginning to this perfect afternoon. Ruth pulled the sheet of finished cookies from the oven and replaced it with a fresh one. She reset the timer. Her expertise was amazing. She took the spatula and began swiftly moving the hot, tan disks from the pan to the wire rack. "And who does Winkie sell his blue hamburger cookies to?"

"The animals."

"Oh, yes, animals like blue hamburger cookies . . ." The pan was empty now, and she glazed it lightly with a fresh dab of Crisco. "Where does he sell them?"

"At the zoo."

"For how much?"

"A penny."

"I'm afraid a penny a cookie isn't going to be of much help," said Ruth, more to herself than to Cliff.

Idly the boy began tilting the bear forward and back, and his eyes clicked closed, open, closed, open, which always made him pleasantly groggy. Outside it had begun to pour again. As Ruth dropped glob after glob onto the flat, freshly greased pan, Winkie himself seemed to be baking the cookies, and they were blue, with hamburgers in them, and over at his concession stand at the zoo, all the animals were lining up two by two to buy them . . .

The little bear wept now to remember it, shaking his head no. Not because he was a prisoner now, but because he was a prisoner *then* as well—full of hope but a slave to others' whims, silent and watchful, stuck in the warm confines of Ruth's family, loved, yes, but only as a toy and only for a time, always longing for more, even when he was held, never quite satisfied, often lonely, ever fearful, soon to be rejected, betrayed, and cast out.

He cried as well because he knew that it was his duty to recollect it, not just a moment of it or the simple facts he'd recalled for Unwin, but as much of it as possible, so that he might begin to understand. What understanding would do for him, the bear didn't know, but he had to understand anyway. "Think back"—He'd been avoiding his dream's command for months now, but he realized he couldn't much longer. It was simply the work before him, the clear task that had to be done, no less than stowing away his acorns in the fall, or finding them again in winter.

"—I *said,* get up, goddamn it!"

The yell shattered the bear's ears, and in the next instant he had leapt to the far corner of the bunk, pressing his back to the wall. He imagined his two eyes glowing like a wild animal's.

"Oh no ya don't," said Agent Mike, reaching for him. "Little—" There was nowhere for Winkie to go, and the agent simply grabbed him by his collar. "Shit, I've seen canaries harder to catch than you." He held Winkie out to Deputy Walter, who stood ready with the shackles. The bear continued squirming angrily.

"Come on now, little fella," said Walter, very calmly, "you don' wanna miss yer plea hearing, do ya?"

Winkie had forgotten that he was going before the judge today. He ceased his struggle but continued staring resentfully at Walter.

"Now, ya know I hafta do this," he said, locking the shackles.

"And we don't want to wake *Junior,* now do we?" Mike snarled.

In fact Darryl kept snoring in the bottom bunk, just as he had last night, tangled up in his blankets. He seemed to be hibernating. Winkie had not yet seen his cell mate's face, and he wondered, for a sweet, hopeful second, if Darryl might be a bear, too.

* * *

A huge crowd shouted and jeered outside the courthouse, jerking their placards up and down like spears. "Holy shit," muttered Agent Mike, who was driving. Like angry Styrofoam peanuts they poured around the car, packing it tight, so the bear had to wait there with Mike and Mary Sue as the police tried to clear a path. With terrified wonder he watched the angry faces undulating in the bulletproof windows. Their yells were muffled, but their signs were professionally printed and all said the same thing:

KILL WINKIE
—Leviticus 20:25

Past the mob, through the doors, down the halls, up the stairs, and inside a small, oval anteroom, it was perfectly quiet, except for the voice of Charles Unwin.

"Um, OK, um, Mr. Winkie—is 'Mr.' all right?—OK, Mr. Winkie —wow, that's gonna take some getting used to—Mr. Winkie, Mr. Winkie, Mr. Winkie—OK, um, anyway, I am trying my best, my level best, I assure you, to get you your correspondence, they can't just do that, withhold your mail without any reason." Unwin had mentioned this before, but only now did Winkie understand its significance, and he looked at his lawyer eagerly. "—But of course that will be a separate hearing, I'm sure you understand that that has nothing to do with today, so let's just, let's just leave that aside, for now, I mean, just for now . . ."

They had been waiting here sometime, with Agents Mike and Mary Sue and two policemen, for the judge to call them. Winkie looked up at his attorney's worried face with something like hope. He was the only human being who knew the bear's life story. Somehow he had won his trust. So then, Winkie asked himself, was this the man to save him?

"I guess all we can do now is relax until the judge calls us. Sometimes that's all you can do. Can you, can you, can you do that?" Unwin was asking. "Well, OK then," he answered himself, planting his hands firmly on his knees. He said nothing for a few minutes. Then as if the bear had beckoned, Unwin nodded and bent to speak to him more privately. "I probably shouldn't tell you this," he whispered. Winkie glanced sideways at the others in the room. "But I have this terrible, uncontrollable fear of losing cases. Silly, isn't it? It's just plain silly, I know, I know, I know."

The two agents and the two officers gazed down at their too-shiny shoes, smirking, but Unwin didn't seem to notice. The air-conditioner ducts loudly wooshed. Winkie knit his brow.

"You see, it's my name," Unwin continued. "I'm afraid it's a jinx. I know it's stupid to think that, but I can't help it. I say to myself over and over, 'Don't think that!' And before I know it, what happens? I've lost another case." He looked troubled and his small, deep-set eyes ran this way and that. "In point of fact, I've never won a single case. Not one! I shouldn't be telling you this either." Unwin swallowed several times, cleared his throat, and coughed. Winkie looked down at his own shackled feet. "Um, the closest I've ever gotten was a hung jury," the lawyer continued. "Oh, but that was sweet! That was truly truly wonderful! When was that—five years ago? No, um, seven." He sighed. "But I remember it like, like, like yesterday. When that jury filed back into the courtroom and the foreman said they were hopelessly deadlocked, suddenly for one brief moment it seemed as though—!" He lifted up both hands gratefully and smiled. "I mean, I felt as light as air! It was, it was, it was amazing. But then—oh well, what can you do?—a month later the man was tried again, and he was sentenced to twenty years hard labor."

Unwin fell into silence, his brow appearing first hopeful and then devastated, again and again. Slowly Winkie let his head drop into his paws. The ducts continued whooshing. Now and then he jingled his chains.

"Hear ye, hear ye, the Honorable Judge . . ."

With a flourish of his robes the judge took his seat and looked gravely at the little bear. "Mr. Winkie," he said sternly, "you are hereby charged with the following crimes." He banged his gavel once for each charge. "Terrorism." Crack. "Treason." Crack. "Conspiring to overthrow the United States government." Crack. "Providing material support to a foreign terrorist organization." Crack. "Possession of components from which a destructive device such as a bomb can be readily assembled." Crack. "One hundred twenty-four counts of attempted murder." Crack, crack, crack, etc. The list in its entirety went on for five hours, fourteen minutes. The judge had to stop in the middle for lunch, resuming in the afternoon. "Impersonating a woman." Crack. "Fraud." Crack. "Resisting arrest." Crack. By now nearly everyone in the courtroom had fallen asleep, soothed by lunch and mesmerized by the judge's droning, nasal voice and thick, black, furrowed eyebrows that never budged. "Corrupting the youth of Athens." Crack. "Holding the false doctrine that the sun is the center of the world and the earth moves." Crack. "Blasphemy." Crack. But Winkie himself did not doze. He hung his head in shame, listening to every word, even the ones he didn't understand. "Witchcraft." Crack. "Teaching evolution in the schools." Crack. "Ritual satanic abuse." Crack. In the courtroom window, the sun had begun to set, casting a fiery glow upon the lonely little defendant. "The creation of immoral works of art." Crack. "Obscenity." Crack. "And lastly—" said the judge, grandly turning the final page and enunciating with special distaste—"acts of gross indecency with certain young men of London." Three extra loud cracks.

The courtroom awoke with an outraged jerk.

"Mr. Winkie, how do you plead?"

A perfect silence like the beginning of time.

"Um," said Unwin, straightening. "Um. Um. Not guilty. Not guilty on all counts!"

The courtroom burst into uproar. "Horrible!" they shouted, as Winkie was led away. "Vile!" "Filth!" He dared not lift his head. For them to say such things, Winkie thought, he must be a very very bad disgusting dirty bear indeed.

Hurricane

Tonight Cliff had gone right to sleep, as had his older brother Ken. The bear heard Ruth's footsteps in the hall, trudging down the stairs, then Cliff's father's voice in the living room. From the shelf, he watched Cliff's little shape under the dark blankets and wondered why things had to be the way they were.

Winkie had seen it happen five times and now a sixth: a child being formed. Sometimes it was wonderful and sometimes he could hardly bear to keep his glass eyes open.

The child was being formed and the child was also forming itself. There were these two forces at work, and one could never tell what the outcome might be. The child was what it was, and then things happened to it, and in this way, as Winkie watched, unblinking, because he couldn't blink, the child became what he or she was to be.

Sometimes it seemed to Winkie the world and the child were two trains on a collision course. So that what the child was to become might be a wreck. It had never been so for any of the children in this family; but it might have been, it could just as easily have been; for in small ways it definitely was the case, again and again—Winkie saw it, just as he saw and felt and tried to help each child put itself back together, in these small ways. And then that was what the child was to become, too, something mended, just as Winkie himself was mended, even if only in small ways.

"No, no—it's necessary. *Necessary*," the bear muttered to himself. "Surviving is necessary." But he wasn't convinced. Perhaps Cliff dreamed of monsters and surely he would survive dreaming of them, but why did he have to? In a little while, by the subtle change in his breathing, Winkie could tell that the boy was now half awake. A sour-sweet fart floated in the still night air. Cliff had to go to the bathroom, yet he lay motionless. He was trying to hold it and he would not succeed. It had already happened in just this way many times before.

Winkie wanted it to be otherwise, but he tried to understand that this was the way of the world and it was so for himself, as well. And though the five-year-old would awaken to shame and might try to hide the soiled underpants in the bottom of the hamper, he wouldn't or couldn't stop even though lately he was in trouble for it all the time.

Winkie also knew that these very things were, in turn, forming him, a bear, and he was forming himself. That was how it was when Cliff renamed him; the toddler chose "Winkie," but the little bear who became him, breathed the name into his soul, turned into a boy, remained a girl, Marie, inside, and was proud of all of it, for all of it was his fate. From then on he stared back at Cliff with glass eyes both more ancient and ever renewed.

As to whether such events were necessary or not—whether they were what the bear most needed—he didn't know, but being formed and forming oneself were necessary, so therefore the experiences must also be, as was whatever Winkie did with them.

Still, he wondered sometimes why he had to see this—the child growing in its world—so many times, again and again. First Ruth, then over a period of many years and many places, the next five. Like Ruth and Dave, he had thought Ken, born five years after Paul, was the last, and before Ken he'd even begun to think Paul was the last, so Winkie was already done—but now here was Cliff, who surely was the last, and why him?

Chance decreed that there were five, and each of these five played out chance as well: They were like five possible paths, branching off from Ruth, who was the first path Winkie had been destined to follow. Not since Ruth had anyone thought to name him, not in more than twenty years—so that now he had awakened wholly as Cliff's, just as he would also always be Ruth's. He supposed that was chance, too.

Branching and branching. You couldn't stop it. Cliff had drifted to sleep again and his breaths came now with perfect regularity. In the continuing darkness Winkie seemed to see the infinite growing tree of life budding and branching infinitely before him kaleidoscopically and full of light. Through the half-open window he faintly smelled the too-sweet Louisiana gardenias along the drive and wondered by what combination of steps A-not-B or B-not-A over and over (indefinitely back in time and down to the tiniest molecules) he, Winkie, had been chosen both to witness and to understand this. A car passed down in the street, and behind the closed drapes he saw the dim, brief flash of headlights. "A particular bear," he murmured, falling asleep himself, "sees a particular this."

2.

Cliff stood by the sliding glass door holding Winkie and twirling his legs around each other tightly, trying not to move. His brothers lay on the couch watching a game show. Upstairs Ruth's violin could be heard, scales quickly snaking up and down.

"Do you need to go to the bathroom?" asked Paul, who was in charge today.

"No," said Cliff indignantly, though Winkie knew otherwise. It wasn't long after the family had arrived in New Orleans that the boy began shitting his pants.

"Are you sure?"

"Yeah."

In fact, it happened at least once a week, usually more, sometimes at night, sometimes during the day, and it had been going on almost two months now. At first Ruth had simply ignored it. Then she spoke to Cliff seriously, reminding him that he was five, not three. Soon his brothers were enlisted in the cause of clean underpants.

"He's holding it!" sang Ken, who was eleven. "Holding it! Holding it!"

"Shut *up*," said Paul, trying in his lanky teenage way to be responsible, but already Winkie could feel the outrage bubbling up in Cliff's chest, where the bear was being clutched even more tightly.

"Am not!" he shouted, and ran out of the family room.

"Now look what you did," said Paul to Ken.

"So?"

As Cliff neared the top of the stairs, he slowed to a dawdle. Up here Ruth's scales were louder but still muffled behind the closed door of the master bedroom. Though no one dared disturb her, the whiny notes were a familiar and therefore comforting sound. All these years, wherever the family lived, she had played in community orchestras. She hit a wrong note now, muttered, "Darn it," and began again, just as she had done a thousand times before—so that

Winkie and the boy seemed to float, timelessly, in the never ending era called Ruth.

Cliff peered down through the spokes of the banister to see if anyone had come after him. There was no one, of course, but Winkie knew the boy had to save face by waiting a little while before he actually went and did what he needed to do.

After he had gone to the bathroom, Cliff took off his soiled underpants, dropped them in the yellow wicker hamper, and replaced them with fresh ones. That was that. Then he came back downstairs again.

"Why do you take that stupid bear everywhere you go?" asked Paul. "You should stop being such a baby. You're too old for that."

Cliff was holding Winkie under one arm. "I'm not a baby."

"You *act* like one," said Ken. "Look at the *baby* with his *bear*."

Winkie was about to feel outraged, but he sensed Cliff shift his weight and loosen his grasp on him just slightly, and in that instant the old bear understood, with the sad experience of so many years lived as a servant and a toy, that he had become a tainted object. The next thing he knew, Cliff had thrown him across the room. Winkie landed on the seedy brown couch with a muffled *wump*.

"Na-na-na, nah-nah, na-na-nah," said Cliff, imitating Ken's taunt. He stomped out and slammed the sliding glass door behind him.

"I'll call Mom," Paul warned idly.

Winkie stared down at nubby upholstery. He was still trying to focus his eyes when Ken picked him up and looked him square in the face. The bear scarcely had a chance to flinch. "Dope!" the eleven-year-old said. Then he punched him in the nose and let go at the same time, so that Winkie flew backward at the blow. He landed with a *wump* again. Paul snickered.

Winkie knew it was difficult to make an older brother laugh, so having succeeded once, Ken would undoubtedly try again.

"Dope!" Pow. *Wump.* "Dope!" Pow. *Wump.* After five or six times Paul's snickers waned, and Winkie hoped it was over. He lay there dazed and furious. Ruth was upstairs practicing, but where was Cliff? In the corner of his eye he saw the little boy wander in from the backyard again, closing the sliding door more carefully this time. He stood there near the TV not saying anything, not looking this way, playing a little game with the drapes, lifting them and letting them billow down to the linoleum again.

"Look what I'm *doing* to him," sang Ken, grinning, holding Winkie up and threatening with his fist. "Loo-ook. Loo-ook." He punched Winkie again, and the addled bear flew down to the couch once more.

Only yesterday Cliff would have cried out against this injustice, but today he just said, "So what?" and marched into the breakfast nook. Winkie could hear him opening the cabinets that held his art supplies.

Now Paul sighed with boredom and also left the room. "I need a Coke," he muttered. In a moment Ken shut off the TV and followed, and Winkie lay on the brown cushion, forgotten. One of his eyes had slammed shut, and the other was open, so he stared up at half the plain white ceiling. Above, Ruth flubbed a fast run once, twice, three times—"Darn it!" A bad feeling built and built in the bear's middle and it seemed he couldn't lie there one minute longer, but still Cliff didn't come. From the nook he heard only the faint, scratching sounds of crayons on heavy paper.

3.

Once during the long drive down to New Orleans, observing the telephone wires rise and fall while Cliff napped and Ken and Paul fought idly in the backseat, Winkie had wondered if he was this family's guardian angel. He doubted it. But then again, maybe that was why there was so much trouble in the world: All the angels were as ineffectual as he was.

In Illinois Winkie had seen the family go through two years of bad luck. He gleaned the facts by listening through the walls. They had just moved back to Chicago when Cliff's father lost his new job. He was unemployed for several months, and then the only work he could find was a low-paying position at a hairspray factory three hours away. The family couldn't afford to move again, so they saw Dave only on weekends. Ruth complained a lot—to Dave, to her older children—about bills to be paid and savings dwindling, about Dave's poor choices and his never being home. Ever since she was little, Ruth had always liked everything to be just so, and now things looked like they would never be just so. Afternoons in the kitchen, Winkie watched Ruth complain, and watched the toddler, Cliff, watching her. "Dad just shrugs," she told Carol, the oldest sister, "and I'm left holding the bag." The girls had to leave their private colleges and attend the cheaper public university nearby. Ruth went to work in Chicago as a Kelly girl, and on those days Cliff went to nursery school. On weekends when Dave was home, late at night, as Cliff slept, Winkie strained to hear the couple's whispered arguments. "Well, I don't see why you . . . What about the . . . ? And I'm supposed to just . . .?" "I understand that, darling, but . . . I know, but I can't . . . I'm forty-eight years old . . . But I have to . . ." A cloud of turmoil permeated everything, so that even the house began falling apart, always needing some repair that Ruth said they couldn't afford. Then one day Dave was almost killed in a car accident; he came home with his ribs taped. A few months later, he fell off a pier and nearly drowned. Maybe these events were a weird kind of good luck,

Winkie thought, for Dave had survived, and something in Ruth seemed to snap back in place. Or almost did. She complained a little less. At last Dave announced one Friday evening that he'd found a good job, and the family was moving to New Orleans. There, Ruth told the children repeatedly, everything was going to be better.

Soon Ruth finished practicing and arrived downstairs to tell Cliff to put his drawing things away, because it was almost dinnertime. "And Winkie, too," she added, which gave the abandoned bear a bitter thrill of self-righteousness. "I've told you not to leave your things lying around in the family room."

"Ken had him last," the boy complained, but soon enough he came in to retrieve the bear. "OK, let's go," he said with resignation, as if Winkie were his annoying little brother.

Still, as he was carried upstairs, the little bear thought maybe all was well again and he heaved an inward sigh to be once more in Cliff's possession. He hardly noticed that one eye had clicked open as usual but the other, his right, was now frozen shut.

In the bedroom Cliff gave him the usual shake to make his eyes close and open but, seeing that this had no effect on the right eye, shook him several times more. Each time the bear wanted to cry out in pain.

"Winkie," said the boy, "why aren't your eyes working right?" He spoke with miniature exasperation, as if the bear were simply being uncooperative. Was he? As Cliff shook him even more forcefully, Winkie tried to will the hurting eye open again.

Abruptly the shaking stopped, and with his good eye Winkie saw the boy's index finger coming toward him. It veered right and he felt it, moist and warm, on the problem eyeball. Then the finger

In New Orleans, everything was going to be better.

pushed. The sensation was almost unbearable, but now the frozen orb gave way and grindingly rolled open.

There, before both his eyes now, was Cliff's face, very close, very intent, gray eyes staring. "*Hmt*," he muttered, just as one of his brothers would. He frowned, then Winkie saw the finger coming at him again. Once more it pressed right on his eyeball so that the bear wanted to scream. Slowly the orb squeaked closed again. There was no satisfying click, only a sound and a pain like sandpaper. Cliff pushed the eye open and shut a few more times, and for a moment it seemed to get a little easier . . . but then not.

Suddenly the boy hugged Winkie very tightly, and whatever pain the bear had felt today seemed altogether worth it. "You'll be feeling better soon!" Cliff said, and it was like soothing balm spreading over his bad eye and all through him, so that despite his treatment earlier that afternoon, Winkie's heart began slowly and almost painfully to unfold—

"Talking to your *bear?*" Ken sneered.

Winkie had heard him clumping up the stairs, but he had pretended not to notice, as if that could hinder him.

"No," said Cliff, holding the bear suddenly at arm's length.

"Oh, *Winkie*, oh, *Winkie*, how are *you?*" said Ken in a baby voice.

Swiftly Cliff put the bear up on the shelf, careless of leaving him with one eye open and one closed. Then he ran out and down the stairs to dinner.

Later that night as Cliff changed into his pajamas, he gazed up at the bear, seeming almost to relent, but then with a distracted air, as if he couldn't remember what he'd meant to do just now, he simply climbed into bed. Downstairs the galloping theme to *Bonanza* began.

For the next few days Winkie watched and waited to be picked up and hugged tightly once more, but Cliff came and went, woke and slept, without even speaking to him. Yet the bear held out some hope, because even though Cliff was trying so hard to be a big boy, he continued shitting his pants.

4.

"They're protesting in———now," said Ruth one evening with disdain. From his perch up in the boys' room Winkie couldn't hear the place, couldn't tell if it was near or far. He stared ahead with his one good eye.

"What do the niggers *want?*" asked Cliff.

"Nothing," said Dave. "It's all a buncha nothing."

"They don't know *what* they want," added Ruth with finality.

Uneasily Winkie sniffed their dinner of corned beef and cabbage. Making fun of Negroes had become a family pastime in Louisiana. At breakfast Dave liked to read aloud newspaper accounts of how a Negro tried to steal something but then was caught, because he was stupid. Or maybe a group of Negroes was protesting something and the police chased them away or arrested them. Winkie doubted this was fair. The stories made him feel woozy, as though the shelf to which he'd been exiled were tilting little by little and he were about to fall.

As it happened, Paul's own high school had just been integrated that year. By some irrefutable logic that Winkie couldn't grasp, this meant that all the girls, white and colored, now went to the newer, nicer high school that had been built for the white teens, while Paul and all the other boys had to go to the run-down colored high school across town. Paul didn't like the school, and Ruth and Dave held the Negroes responsible for this.

"Those jigs'll just ruin that brand-new school," said Dave. "You'd think the politicians would learn."

"Ah wanna go to dat nice white school," said Ken, which made Cliff laugh.

Winkie disliked any joke that made fun of people. He listened to forks clink on plates.

Ruth said, "We had integration back when I was in high school, too—because they'd started moving into Morgan Hill. They *ruined* my high school. You should just see it now."

The soft tinkling sound of dinnerware continued, as if completing the irreversible process of destruction that Ruth had just described. Winkie's bad eye began to throb. At the same time he noted that Paul had remained oddly silent during this conversation about his school. Suddenly the bear understood why the teenager always smelled like stale candy and cigarettes: He had been cutting class. Not even Cliff and Ken had realized this. Winkie stared half at darkness, half at the younger boys' two bedspreads. It was strange knowing things that no one else knew. Sometimes Winkie was proud of it, and sometimes he wished he could just spit all those secrets out.

5.

Dots, thought the bear, staring into the dark of the boys' room with his good eye. He called this boredom, instead of not-love or not-joy, because boredom could be endured, and boredom could be relieved. Today the president had been shot—he knew that much because Cliff and Ken had been sent home early from school. Things happen, Winkie reminded himself, with the satisfaction, if nothing else, of fear fulfilled. He looked at Ken's map of the United States on the wall, shades of gray in the dark, and it looked to him like a huge misshapen crocodile, jagged and ravenous.

Cliff and Ken slept. What was meant to be and what wasn't, what might have happened and what might not, what was chosen, what was half chosen, and what was not chosen at all, what was hoped for yet not, what could and couldn't be changed, what was suffered and survived and what wasn't, and what, by a hairs breadth, might not have to be suffered after all.

Cliff had forsworn Winkie but his resolve was not firm. Sometimes he carried the bear around the house anyway, seeming to have forgotten his brothers' taunts, and sometimes Ken and Paul seemed to have forgotten, too—they saw him with Winkie under his arm but said nothing. Or they might even join in the Winkie play, saying things like "Winkie wants to watch TV" or "Winkie's bored" or "Winkie needs a snack." The bear hated Ken and Paul all the more for these whims, because he knew it could just as easily be "Winkie needs a spanking" or "Oops, Winkie fell down the stairs." It was never "Winkie needs a hug."

Whether Cliff might pick him up or even kiss him on any given day was a repeated question that nearly drove the bear mad. His problem eye was also unpredictable. Sometimes when Cliff jostled him, the right orb might fall open, shut, and open again, just as it should. More often than not, though, the eye remained stuck and hurting. Then Cliff would begin pushing and poking it with his finger, absently testing it again and again, like a loose baby tooth. "Poor Winkie," the boy murmured, as the bear tried to choose between the pain like sandpaper and the unbidden joy of being held again. "Poor eye."

6.

Soon Ruth's father came for a short visit to see New Orleans and Ruth's new home. In the glimpses Winkie caught of him, he appeared as tall and thin as ever but now entirely gray and a little stooped, like a jackknife bent slightly closed. He made very little noise because, as Winkie had overheard Ruth say with admiration to Dave, her father spent most of his day down in the living room reading the Bible and *Science and Health with the Key to Scriptures*.

Up here, the vacuum cleaner roared and whined, changing pitch as Ruth slowly made her way down the stairs. "Darn it," she said, under her breath. Apparently one of the boys had littered the beige carpet with the small, white circles of a hole punch before leaving for school. Winkie had overheard Ruth's father point them out to her a little while ago. The observation was made in that deceptively wry and reserved way of his, so that even Winkie couldn't tell if it was a joke or a hint, and in any case Ruth had gone to get the Eureka immediately.

Such uncertainties had made the whole house vibrate unpleasantly since her father's arrival. Winkie knew that Ruth's veneration for him was as irreducible as her very molecules, and there was no point in wishing otherwise, so with one eye open and one painfully closed the bear was given over to pondering with both wonder and sadness the unchanging bond between parent and child. At breakfast, lunch, and dinnertime Ruth's eager storytelling voice echoed through the new house and up the stairs to Winkie. She told how she had solved a bookkeeping problem at the dentist's office where she worked part-time or how she had given Helen sensible advice when she called, distraught, from college in Illinois. Upstairs, Winkie couldn't hear her father's quiet replies or the three boys' murmurings, only Dave, who spoke less than usual and said things like, "That's absolutely right." Every once in a while the bear heard Ruth's laughter, and he knew that her father must have exercised the dry sense of humor that Ruth so esteemed.

"*Someone* took my hole punch and dropped little holes up and down the stairs," said Ruth in the foyer when Cliff got home from kindergarten, "so this morning I had to vacuum them all over again."

The bear strained to hear more, as if he could detect Cliff trying not to attract further notice on his way up to his room. From long experience Winkie guessed Ruth wasn't in a bad mood yet, but she was about to be.

Cliff came into his room carrying drawing supplies, which meant he was about to make a present for someone, probably his grampa, as a surprise. Winkie breathed in the quiet. It would be a little while before Ken got home to bother them, and maybe Cliff would even take him down from the shelf for a minute. At his desk the boy placed his hand flat on the white paper and drew around it with a ballpoint pen, embellishing this with crayons until it became a turkey. Winkie smelled a fart and knew the boy had to go to the bathroom, but still Cliff kept working until he had finished the inscription, a large and small *T*, which presumably meant Thanksgiving or turkey. He stood up then and his face took on that perplexed, annoyed yet blank expression that he always got when he had just had an accident, as if he hoped he were wrong. He went out and soon Winkie heard the toilet flush—always a reassuring sound—but when Cliff returned, he shut the door and pulled down his navy corduroys and also his underpants, whose whiteness indeed was marred by a medium-size brown stain. As usual the boy threw them in the yellow wicker clothes hamper and hastily dropped the lid shut. Then he took a fresh pair of underpants from the drawer and put them on, along with his corduroys. After tucking in his shirt, he took his drawing and raced downstairs, apparently in search of Grampa.

Before long Ruth came trudging up the steps and rolled the laundry basket into the boys' room. Winkie braced himself. As she opened the yellow hamper she, too, displayed for just a moment that same perplexed, annoyed yet blank expression. But immediately it crumpled to outrage, the dark tops of her cat-eye glasses like angry cartoon eyebrows. She took the offending pair of underpants to the banister yelling, "Cliff! Come up here—right now!"

Winkie heard her go into the bathroom then, muttering with despair, "I just don't know what to do with him. I *just* don't *know* what to *do!*"

Washing sounds, and Cliff stepping lightly on the stairs, ascending slowly and reluctantly, almost tiptoeing.

"Come in here," Ruth said.

Winkie heard the slightest creak and rustle of the boy moving toward her. He heard Grampa's step as well, coming up the stairs, then pausing near the top.

"*Look* at this!" Ruth said. The swishing of water again. "Look where I have to wash them. They're too dirty for the sink."

The dripping sound of cloth being wrung out, then the shrill roar of the toilet flushing. The tank began to fill and the washing sounds resumed.

"See what I have to do?" said Ruth. She was almost crying. "*See?*"

And it was as if Winkie himself could see it, too: the brown-stained underpants and Ruth's hands in the toilet.

It was as clear as if it had been projected onto the back of the bear's one closed eye, which indeed had begun to throb. Then he saw the small boy standing there, his mother kneeling at the bowl, and nearby, her tall, thin father, paused at the top of the stairs. The three of them appeared to him as if in a diagram, each as stark and immutable as a circle, a square, and a triangle: the three of them, father, daughter, and daughter's son, three beings; that is, three facts. They seemed almost frozen there before his mind's eye, but he knew that was only the illusion of slowed time at the moment of disaster.

Intentions were one thing, but facts, Winkie knew, were quite another. Facts were incontrovertible, as was tragedy, and so in the sawdust of his mind he tried to cushion time and slow it down before anything more could happen.

Winkie thought he heard Grampa then lift his foot to the last carpeted step, and immediately, like a ricocheting eight ball, Cliff came running into his room from the bathroom, crying, and flung himself not onto his bed but on the floor between the wall and the bed, where even Winkie couldn't see him. In the reflection of the tilted Etch A Sketch, the bear glimpsed Grampa proceed quietly, even stealthily, down the hallway to the room he'd been given and carefully shut the door. In a moment the washing noises resumed at the toilet as if they were a continuation of normalcy, and after one last flush, Winkie heard Ruth go quickly, even stealthily, downstairs, presumably to the laundry room.

Also plain as day, the bear could foresee the agitated yet purposeful expression she would wear as she pretended to herself that her father had not witnessed what had just happened. Turning the washing machine dial to the left and pursing her lips, she would will the business of the day to proceed.

Even now Winkie wished Cliff might come and hug him tightly, like in the old days, but no one was to be consoled, and the boy's suppressed, irregular whimpering sounded almost like old, tan cloth sadly ripping.

7.

Staring, staring, listening, listening: How much longer could he stand to be alone? If only Cliff loved him like before, with the old fervor, Winkie could be happy being a toy forever. But the blankness and the waiting seemed to go on and on, and he never knew when it would stop. It might never stop. Or surely there would come a time when it would never stop, and even if this wasn't that time, it may as well be, because forever-alone was coming anyway.

Ratfinks were little plastic trolls that Cliff bought from gum machines. The bear watched Ken and Cliff build a large house for them on the floor next to their beds, using nearly all of the red plastic bricks and small white windows and doors. Winkie wanted to play, too, but Cliff only played with ratfinks now. Ken and Paul didn't seem to think they were the least bit babyish, and indeed here was Ken playing with them himself. Ratfinks were too hard and small to hug. They were ugly and felt nothing. Now they were Cliff's favorite toys.

Ken and Cliff even made furniture for them out of the little bricks—couches, beds, kitchen counters. Usually the two brothers fought, but today they were playing well together. They left off the roof so they could see inside and move the ratfinks around.

Ken rigged the back stairway to fall at the slightest touch. *"This'll fix 'em,"* he said, holding a white ratfink and making him wiggle and speak. *"Uh oh, here come the nigger ratfinks."*

Winkie's bad eye began to throb again. He had seen this game before, but still he wanted to cry out, outraged on behalf of the dark ratfinks, yet envying the lighter ones. Ken had positioned the four black and brown ratfinks in a model car over by the dresser. It was an open convertible, so the boys could put them in and take them out easily. Ken pushed the car quickly forward. *"Errrt!"* he said, like squealing rubber, and the convertible stopped short in front of the big brick house. Cliff giggled.

All the white, yellow, and blue ratfinks were hiding upstairs. *"They're here!"* said Cliff, placing one near a window.

Ken wiggled the black ratfink in the driver's seat. *"Oooh, looky dere—a mansion!"*

"*Ooh!*" said Cliff.

"*Let's steal somethin',*" said Ken. "*Better go roun' back, so we don't gets caught!*" He pushed the model car in a half circle around the house, making the chugging sounds of an old, run-down engine, which then sputtered to nothing. "*I gots to get dat fixed!*" Cliff giggled more. Ken lifted the driver from the car and made him approach the rickety staircase. "*Dum-de-dum,*" Ken hummed. "*Hello. Any white folks dere?*"

"*Nobody home!*" Ken answered himself, taking the part of the ratfinks inside.

"*Dat's good,*" said the black one, moving toward the house. "*Come on, let's get up dem stairs—AAGHGH!*"

As the boys laughed, the rigged stairs fell over.

"*AAGHGH!*" cried Cliff.

Winkie was so angry by now that it almost gladdened him when the two brothers began fighting again.

"OK, time to clean up," said Ken. There were red and white plastic bricks all over the floor of the bedroom.

"OK," said Cliff, beginning to gather pieces. But Ken simply headed for the door. It took the six-year-old a moment to realize. "Hey—"

"They're *your* bricks," Ken said. With a gloating smile he was already backing out of the room. He imitated a TV parent: "Put away your toys now, Little Cliffy."

"No!"

Winkie could tell Cliff was madder than usual, inflamed by the story of the trick staircase.

"I'm *giving* them to you," Ken sang. He was at the top of the stairs, out of Winkie's vision. "They're *all yours* now."

Then he stomped victoriously down the stairs, but Cliff ran out after him with the model car in his hand. He was crying wildly now.

"No!" he screamed, and there was a clattering sound. He must have thrown the car.

A moment of excruciating silence. Then Winkie could hear Ken whining, "Mom, Mom," on his way to the kitchen. Which meant that he was OK but also that Cliff would be in trouble.

In a moment Winkie heard Cliff run into the bathroom and slam the door.

8.

In a flickering like fog, time began to go more quickly. Christmas and birthdays were celebrated. Cliff learned to read, and he began writing stories, which he made into little construction-paper books. He stopped shitting his pants. Mardi Gras, Easter, Fourth of July, Halloween. Still Winkie longed to be held; rarely he was, and then more rarely still until it was almost never. Sometimes his eye bothered him, sometimes not; he heard noises—footsteps, doors slamming, cars coming and going—or he ignored them; sometimes and even for long periods he felt nothing, whether his bad eye was open or closed, stuck or free. Occasionally by some trick of the barometer or humidity, the painful orb might of its own accord suddenly ease itself open or shut, depending on whether he'd been left seated or prone, and for a moment the world almost seemed normal again, because his eyes were in unison, no longer straining, hardly hurting him. Then it was almost as if whatever he saw or didn't see made sense, and he seemed like himself again, if only for a moment, the self he'd always known. But soon enough if Cliff did happen to pick him up for a moment, perhaps to retrieve something else on the shelf, Winkie would realize in the jostling that his bad eye was stuck again—closed, open, or worse, uneven and in-between, so that he seemed to be at war with himself, offering the world what he knew to be a crazed, drunken look. He might hear Cliff giggle at the sight; for a moment it was sweet. Then came a sadness like terror: pounding all through him, because he didn't even have a real heart to hold it—there was only a fear and burning, the wish to cry out or weep. He knew he was a crazy bear then, a hopeless bear, even if Cliff happened at that moment to be holding him— an unlovable almost-creature alert to every bad thing in the world and himself. Then Winkie's mind began its rapid flickering until he blacked out. Or sometimes the oblivion part took a long time or maybe never came—everything just went sort of blank gray. The boy had put him down long ago. Winkie only half woke. Calm again but listening for every noise, sniffing every molecule that floated by—waxy crayons; the old blocks; his own ratty fur and stuffing; and down in the street, the bug spray pouring from the back of the mosquito truck . . .

In this way, nearly two years passed.

9.

TV commercials and Ken's taunting singsong down in the family room, Cliff screaming, "No!" then crying up the stairs, and soon here he was, at full volume, like so many times before— he stumbled in and curled up on his bed, and even now the bear's heart all but broke open for the boy who never touched him anymore.

"Seven," Winkie thought, gazing at him, trying to be objective. A boy of seven crying, then trying not to cry, succeeding, and soon simply breathing, but still curled up. His small, short breaths, his little head of straight, sandy hair. His little nose . . . Why couldn't the bear simply let him go—as he had first with Ruth and then with each of her children up till now?

"Too soon," he answered himself. Not that it was too soon for Winkie to let go—in fact, he knew it was already past the time. But Cliff's rejection of him had come too soon and too cruelly, so that each time Winkie encountered the boy he was filled once again with the injustice of it.

"A wall," he said to himself. "A wall between us, a wall there, a wall, a wall . . ." The words were almost like weeping, though they didn't satisfy. Did real weeping satisfy? Did curling up and breathing? Wall, wall, wall, the bear thought, and it seemed almost like he was getting through to himself, like finally he might understand that this child was indeed lost to him, like all the others, and he was truly alone: a fact, a simple fact.

But as if this were the magic thought—as if acceptance, through some paradox, also broke the spell—just then Cliff turned to him and sat up on the bed. "Hi, Winkie," he said. His gray blue eyes were huge, moist, and full of love. How long had it been? Cliff came over to the shelf and lifted the little bear down, holding him in his arms like a swaddled infant. Winkie's good eye had neatly clicked shut; the other was lodged open. How long had it been since he was held so tenderly?

"I never play with you anymore," Cliff said, solemnly gazing down at him.

True, the bear thought. He wanted to snuggle deeper and he wanted to squirm free. Half in ecstasy, half in rage, he could only gaze with his one bad eye back up at the boy who had spurned him. Yet as if that cockeyed gaze suddenly held some power of persuasion or even truth, the boy's face now crumpled into remorse.

"I'm sorry, Winkie!" he sobbed.

And the old bear was cuddled up tightly into Cliff's arms, which now shook with grief.

10.

No, no, no, it wasn't possible, a boy could not go back, nor a girl, nor any child, Winkie had never in all these years been returned to, in all these years a child's love had never resumed, never like it was before, no, it wasn't possible.

And what had caused Cliff's outburst? Winkie puzzled over it through the rest of the afternoon, the evening, and all night as Cliff slept, but he knew only that school had started that week, and that afternoon Ken had been teasing him (Winkie didn't even know why), so Cliff ran upstairs crying. Then he stopped crying, then he turned to Winkie . . . But the tearful reunion ended as abruptly and unaccountably as it had begun: Still sniffling, Cliff simply put Winkie back up on the shelf and went downstairs, apparently to watch TV again.

Neither could a bear go back, nor did Winkie want to, nor would it do any good even if he could, even though he had thought for so long that that was what he wanted; no, he shook it off, it was too late.

Yet the next afternoon, while Ken was still at band practice, Cliff came upstairs and lifted Winkie off the shelf once again. "I'm going to play with you every day now," he whispered. He gingerly pushed the bear's right eye open so the left and right agreed, and then he made him walk along the bed. Winkie didn't want to, and yet when Cliff hummed, "Doo-di-doo," the bear began to lose himself anyway, and it was as if he really were walking along the bed and humming a tune—a forgotten tune so beautiful that it seemed to have arisen from his very soul . . .

But just as quickly, as if by some mistake, Winkie was placed back up on his shelf without another word, and Cliff went out.

* * *

Now more than ever, and against his better judgment, Winkie watched and listened for his one companion, whose distant voice from the kitchen or the family room tickled the bear's huge ears and made him wince with longing. Not more than a week ago that very longing had seemed to summon Cliff to himself, yet now day after day the boy ignored him, apparently without remorse, without even a thought.

Early one afternoon Ken and Ruth came into the boys' room, and as Ruth stood by, the pudgy thirteen-year-old climbed on top of the dresser and began stretching masking tape from corner to corner of the large picture window.

"OK?" Ken asked.

"I think you'd better double this one, too," Ruth answered.

"OK . . ."

Winkie had heard their businesslike chatter and the crisp screeching of the masking tape from the other bedrooms and had wondered what they were doing. Ken traced a second **X** on the window, a few inches from the first.

"Thank you," said Ruth as Ken climbed down. "Of course *Dad* is away, so I have to take care of everything myself . . ."

Inwardly Winkie sighed at Ruth's favorite complaint. Dave was in New York this week, on business.

"Paul says we might have to 'evacuate,'" said Cliff, who had just appeared in the doorway. All three boys had been sent home from school early today.

"They don't even know for sure if it's really coming here," Ruth answered, annoyed with such tales. "It could veer off."

Indeed, past the **X**s in the window, the sky exhibited a pale, harmless blue. Winkie's right eye, still wedged open, was especially swollen and painful, as it always was in fine weather. He began to grow anxious anyway. Ruth and Ken moved on to the bathroom window and Cliff tagged along making wind noises. Now Winkie could hear the tape sound from downstairs as well, which must have been Paul at the same task.

As dusk approached Winkie noticed that the pain in his bad eye had not only lessened but disappeared altogether, for the first time in two years. Usually it felt better in the rain, but never this good, and just at that moment he felt the orb actually ease loose in its socket—he was sitting upright, so the eye remained open— but now it freely bobbed up and down just a little, as it should. For the first time in two years, neither eye nor eye socket was swollen. He wanted to say, Look! to someone, but everyone was downstairs at dinner and the bedroom was dark.

Outside, the sky had quickly clouded over and already it was night. Soon the wind began to blow and the rain to fall. The streetlight and the lights of the houses across the street grew blurry in the wet, and the silhouettes of the young trees began to thrash and strain against the slender poles they were tied to. The picture window rattled with each gust. Winkie could actually see the glass with its masking tape bulging slightly inward, snapping back as the wind suddenly dropped, bulging inward again with the next as- sault. It was raining hard now, and the drops hit the window like fistfuls of pebbles.

The bear began to shiver. He felt very small, even smaller than usual. He wished Cliff would come upstairs soon, if not to hug him, then at least to pick him up, if not to pick him up, then at least to talk to him, if not to talk to him, then at least to look at him, if not to look at him, then at least to turn on the light . . . And yet the pelting rain and the rattling window seemed almost to have been conjured out of the bear's own loneliness and wrath. Let the terrifying storm destroy this house and everyone in it. The evening wore on and still no one came. He heard someone on the stairs, but it turned out to be Paul; as on any ordinary weeknight, the teenager shut himself in his room and began playing "House of the Rising Sun" on his guitar. Between gusts of rain Winkie could just hear the TV going downstairs—music, actors' voices, a news bulletin. ". . . winds gusting to nearly . . . Hurricane Betsy . . . Residents are advised to . . . nearest evacuation center . . ."

"In this wind?" Ruth cried. "Carrying our food and bedding?"

Wind and rattle. The television said something else, and Ruth replied, "Why would we be any safer there—in some school, with a whole bunch of other people?"

Winkie puzzled anxiously over whether she was right or not. Paul sang another mournful verse, the warnings on the television continued, and then, out the rain-smeared window, the whole block went dark.

"Oh," said Ken and Cliff. Paul stopped strumming. "OK," said Ruth mildly, and Winkie felt almost reassured.

The only sound now was that of the rain and wind pummeling the bedroom window along with all the other windows of the house.

"Where did Dad put the flashlight?" Ruth complained. "It's supposed to be right on top of the refrigerator."

"Get out of the way," said Ken, evidently to Cliff.

"*Here* it is," Ruth sang at last, and Winkie could imagine the circle of light shining on the kitchen floor, the glow on Cliff's and Ken's faces. Here it was still pitch black.

Ruth called, "Paul!"

"Yeah," he called back manfully, and Winkie could hear him making his way down the stairs to the rest of them.

"Well, now what?" asked Ruth in her humorous way, as if this were any ordinary household emergency, but the rain and wind continued and in fact were growing worse.

Ruth said something about finding candles and the other flashlight in the trunk of the Falcon. Like some terrible weather instrument, Winkie's window was rattling even more wildly. In the blackness he imagined the two masking tape Xs shaking more and more frantically. Xs mark the spot . . .

"What if there's a flood?" Cliff asked.

"It's a two-story house, dope," said Ken. "We'll just go upstairs."

Winkie took some comfort in this, since he was already upstairs, but then Ruth warned, "Stay out of the living room. I'm afraid that window will go." The living room window faced the same direction as Winkie's.

"It's past your bedtimes," said Ruth to Ken and Cliff. Between the rattling, footfalls on the stairs.

In the purple Mardi Gras beads, the bear saw flickering light reflected, and Ruth entered the bedroom holding the flashlight. Winkie felt its weak, yellowish light pass over his worn-out face.

"This is the worst one," Ruth said, shining the beam on the window. "Just listen to that."

The storm gusted and the glass rattled again.

Paul had come in behind her with his own flashlight. "Wow, it could just blow in, *any second*," he said.

"Paul!" She sighed with annoyance. "Well, Ken and Cliff had better not sleep in here. Here, hold this."

She handed Paul her flashlight, and Winkie watched her pull the sheets and blankets off the mattresses and carry them into the hallway, where he could hear her shuffling about, making her usual irritable housework noises. "Can you hold the lights in one place, please?"

"Why can't they just sleep on the couch in the family room?" Paul asked.

"By the *sliding glass door*? There's already *water* coming in." She hurried in for the pillows and threw them down in the hall. "I'll be up all night *mopping* down there."

"OK, OK . . ."

"Go see if you can find your transistor radio."

He stalked off, and shortly tinny bulletins began wafting from Paul's room. ". . . Levees . . . Pontchartrain . . . sea level . . ." Evidently Ruth had gone downstairs, and before long Winkie heard Ken's and Cliff's voices ascending, along with Ruth's. "All right, let's go get your pajamas," she said, and for a moment Winkie felt almost safe, imagining bedclothes and the cozy blankets and pillows on the floor of the hall, like a sleepover. He seemed almost to be lying there already, snug and cared for . . .

"Is there going to be a flood?" Cliff asked, groggily. It was now well past his bedtime.

"Only in *nigger* neighborhoods," Ken corrected him. "They won't let it happen to our part of town."

Winkie wondered if this could be true. Probably.

Ruth's flashlight shown into the room again, and Cliff and Ken tiptoed in, as if hoping not to disturb the window that continued shaking loudly in the rain and wind. The pale Xs quivered and glowed. Ruth trained the fuzzy circle of light on the dresser so that Cliff could see—and it was then, just as the seven-year-old was pulling open the second drawer, that Winkie realized what should have been obvious: that Cliff intended to retrieve only his pajamas, not his bear, too.

The boy took what he'd come for, closed the drawer, and scurried out. Ken and Ruth followed, shutting the door behind them, leaving Winkie alone there with the darkness, the rattling glass, and the storm.

Rattle, rattle. A child had to live and a child had to grow and in growing he had to leave things behind, just as Winkie always had been left behind—and how could he think this time he wouldn't be?

Betrayal and wind and blackness and rain and rattle.

Stupid, stupid, stupid for dreaming it wouldn't be so with Cliff just like all the other times, this time which was also surely the last time and therefore final. Winkie was alone—stupid bear alone, stuffing and cloth alone, stupid hidden thoughts alone and fading to nothing in the storm—and that was what had to be and only a stupid bear would ever think it could be otherwise.

The glass shook, halted a moment, and shook again in the gale that blew straight toward the bear and was turned away only at the last minute by that single clear shaking pane.

But if, but what, but whether, but who, but nevertheless, but insofar, but why, but otherwise, but even if—

In gusts came also terror and a hundred times he pictured that dark pane bursting at last—shards, wind, wrath, splinters, all in a swirl, lifting up the bear and swirling him away, foul, furious, above the soaking trees, the flooded lawns, the pavement and the houses and the mud, away in the terrible windy rattling dark.

But even if he was to be left alone, even if that was what had to be, the bear had hoped at least—hoped at least—hoped at least . . . He couldn't grasp it—not then in the terrible room, not now, years later, in his cell—just what it was he had longed for, what he had hoped might not be lost this last time, nor why that unnameable whatever, if indeed it wasn't lost, would somehow save this boy from what must surely be the fate of all humanity, and maybe of every other creature, too, nor why he felt that saving Cliff, whatever "saving" was, could somehow also save himself, too.

Neither cruelty chosen nor innocence flown, neither lies believed nor wishes smashed, not rage returned, not knowledge lost, neither sadness borne nor shame endured. No, none of these had he meant to save the boy from, but something bigger—what?—nothing less than the Way of the World itself, and he had hoped against all reason and experience that maybe this one time it would not have to be the Way of the World after all.

"Just this one time," the bear said to himself, back then in the stormy dark, and now again in his too-bright cell, both to torture himself for wanting it and to want it again anyway. After all, after all. Stupid, stupid, stupid. How could the Way of the World be otherwise?

Winkie and the Way of the World. Winkie and the Way of the World. The rain pelting the glass. Winkie and the Way of the World. He stared ahead at the rain pelting the glass.

All night and in the dark, the window jiggled and creaked. It never did break.

Part Two

"*Ah, if children only had the means, what different histories*
they would form of themselves!"
—Frederic Tuten, Tintin in the New World

Winkie
on His
Own

How did the bear get from his shelf in a suburban bedroom to the shack in the woods where he was arrested? The extraordinary journey began with nothing more than an idea. It was one that Winkie had had many times before, but this time he also knew he could do it.

The house seemed to hum quietly with a new expectation. No one was home. All by himself, Winkie stood up, shook the dust off his snout, sauntered down the bookshelf, and jumped to the windowsill. The softness of his feet cushioned the landing and made him bounce up and down a little. He gazed through the clear pane. The neighborhood was sunny and absolutely quiet. A new tree had been planted by the sidewalk, and its few, pale leaves flickered in the wind. An elderly man pedaled by on a giant tricycle, and then there was no one.

Winkie knew well the stories that begin, "In the old times, when it was still of some use to wish for the thing one wanted . . ." Now he saw that the season for wishing was new as well as old and continued to this day. He picked up a large book from the windowsill and hurled it through the glass. The crashing sound did not startle him, so fixed was his intention. He crawled out the window between the jagged pieces.

Winkie stood on the plantless weathered window box looking around, blinking in the sunlight. He hadn't been outdoors in nearly forty years, when he was included in a puppet party on the lawn. The dimness of that memory made him doubt himself a moment. He looked down at his soft, round little bear's paw, the one that had thrown the book. There were no fingers or claws, no muscles or ligaments, only worn fuzzy cloth and stuffing. And yet this paw had picked up the book and thrown it. "Huh." Winkie shrugged. "There are lots of things I can do."

He stepped off the window box onto the hedge. He shuffled around a little on the clipped, prickly branches full of dark green leaves. The prickles poked but didn't pierce him. The hedge quivered and shivered under his cottony steps. "Huh," he said to himself. "So this is the world."

Sometimes in his cell, Winkie thought about this time and wondered, why, if he could come to life, couldn't he also now grow wings or turn himself into a stronger monster that could crash through the walls? Or even the kind of monster that didn't care?

Back in the quiet house, up on his shelf, Winkie had forgotten ever being loved. The family moved to a new state and he was placed on a new shelf. Nothing else changed. As the years went by and the dust swirled and settled and the room grew hot and cool and hot again, he had lost all hope of ever being picked up and cuddled. More years. By then he had lost hope so long before, and so completely, that at last he reached a final and transformative purity. He blinked just once, with new and terrible understanding, at the precise moment he reached this point. And in that blink—a simple falling and rising of his two glass eyes with a tandem click-click—he had exercised his new power for the first time, not even meaning to. For he had blinked all on his own, without being tipped forward or back by anyone or anything. It could almost have been an earthquake—and indeed it was that monumental in the bear's life—but Winkie knew what earthquakes felt like, and he knew there had been no such thing.

Exhausted, afraid to think another thought, he went to sleep for several days, his eyes still wide open. Dreaming countless dreams, each forgotten as soon as it was finished, Winkie groggily began to wake. He seemed to be sitting at the bottom of a pool of clear liquid, looking up at the flickering light of the sky. But then he saw that he was in his pastel room like always, leaning against the same old book, gazing sadly down at the two blue twin beds made neatly, perfectly still. Perhaps time itself had stopped. Then Winkie's three wishes came to him, which was the same as his knowing that they could come true.

First, he wanted to gain his freedom; second, to find something good to eat; and third, to learn to go doo-doo.

Now, out on top of the hedge, on his own for the first time, Winkie hesitated. He was frightened. From his customary perch on the shelf, he had glanced out the window longingly at this rectangle of green more times than he could count. And now, here it was, he was touching it, he was making it quiver. Colors seemed brighter. His eyes hurt. He looked up at the blue sky, down at the patchy green and yellow brown lawn, and across the street at the white, rusted pickup truck parked there. Something about the truck gave him courage. "OK," he said. "Let's try doing some more things." And with an "*Umf*" he leapt off the hedge. He let his arms fly up at his sides in the wind and felt his terry-cloth robe flapping at his waist. His eyes blinked open and shut as he dropped.

Winkie was enjoying gravity. But it was much farther from the hedge to the lawn than it had been from the shelf to the window-sill. Winkie had thought, given all the possibilities the day had already offered, that he wouldn't exactly fall but would glide down-ward to the lawn, guided evenly by the same unseen hand that had given him life and motion. But though his descent seemed to take a long time, the landing was fast and hard. Winkie tumbled over several times, coming to rest flat on his belly next to a dandelion, his stubby arms and legs outstretched.

He convulsed, gasped, found air. With a grunt he rolled him-self over and looked up at the sky, which was spinning somewhere past the tip of the bright, yellow dandelion. Oxygen elated him. He felt all sorts of strange sensations throughout his plump trunk and especially in his limbs: hidden movements, tingling, minute twitchings beyond him. Winkie became keenly aware of his white terry-cloth robe, sewn for him long ago. "This isn't me," he said slowly, with perfect conviction. He wanted only to be naked. The thought made him struggle to his feet. The robe was his past, old and done with, and he stripped it off and threw it down on the grass, where it lay in a heap. He would have liked it to have been somehow burned away as he leapt from the house to the lawn. He seemed to be traveling in time, whether backward to some prior, purer essence of himself, or forward to some more perfect incar-nation, he didn't know. With a dizzy pride he bent and inspected the exposed, light tan fur of his round belly, faded, patchy, and worn. "Mange," he said with satisfaction.

Woozily he fell back on his rump and sat looking around. The world, and his place in it, amazed him. In his head he drew fantas-tic mathematical triangles from himself to the newly planted tree to the peak of the neighbors' roof and back again; then to another tree with red spiny blooms or to the dull flat street or to the rusty

The world, and his place in it, amazed him.

white pickup truck perhaps and back—over and over. He saw that by the lovely, infinite, and specific combination of just such triangles, he was located in naked, ancient, mangy existence.

Winkie had almost forgotten about eating, but there on the grass, several yards away under the new tree, were a dozen or so long brown pods of some kind that had fallen. Not many days before, Winkie had looked out the window and seen an old Korean man and his wife bend and pick up these very pods, gathering them into a paper grocery bag. Then they hobbled down the block, on to the next little tree, and continued gathering. Winkie hadn't realized then that the pods were food. But now he understood: They looked delicious. Crawling delightedly on all fours, Winkie made his way down the fragrant lawn and huddled under the shade of the tree that made the pods. He picked one up, sat down, and began to gnaw on it. Quickly he broke it open and sucked on the large seed inside. It tasted like chocolate.

Soon Winkie had eaten every fat seed in every pod that had fallen under this particular tree. He peered up into the sparse new branches overhead and saw more, dangling enticingly, long and brown between small, pointy, gray green leaves. He was full but he enjoyed gazing at the minor abundance that he might climb up into if he so wanted. "They look sort of like turds," he said to himself with satisfaction, and then he remembered his third wish for the day.

Winkie had never actually gone doo-doo before, but he had pretended to many times. Now that he had eaten, like a real animal, it should be easy. He scampered to the edge of the lawn and squatted, waiting for something to happen—as he had seen dogs of all shapes and sizes do on countless occasions. He stared intently at the blades of grass just in front of his eyes. And when in his concentration it seemed that the multitude of crisp, new blade tips had become the entire world, and there was nothing to see ever but green and grass,

Winkie felt a slow yet irresistible churning deep within himself, down, down, more profound than he had ever felt before.

The sensation was heavy and slightly prickly, warm as fur, and seemed to glitter inside him. It was both gathering within him and pushing slowly and inevitably through him. It hurt but not too much. He felt some unknown inward part of himself solemnly making way. Then a small seam quietly opened, and for the first time, something that was inside him was now coming out. He shut his eyes. In the darkness the new not-quite-ecstasy flowed through him like a huge, rumbling truck in slow motion. Then it was done. Shivering once, he turned to see what he had made and beheld the brown shining mass nestled in the green. He sniffed it once and, detecting a hint of the brown pods he had just eaten, was proud. It was much better than make-believe. Then he raised on tiptoe and gazed up and down the block at all the little brown-pod trees in a row, and the yellow green rectangles of lawn, one after another. He wanted to make his special mark, again and again, on each and every plot.

Nearly everyone in this neighborhood was old, and during the heat of the day they stayed safely inside their houses or emerged from their automatic garage doors already locked inside plush, womblike, air-conditioned vehicles. Winkie had eaten the pods and done his business on twenty-five lawns before he saw anyone at all. It was late afternoon and hot, and Winkie was very tired but still determined to continue his newfound activities because he didn't know what he wanted next. The old woman made her way briskly down the sidewalk in a bright turquoise terry-cloth running suit. Winkie disdainfully paid no attention and continued peeling the layers from an especially juicy-looking pod. The turquoise figure advanced in the corner of his eye, the fresh cloth swishing loudly. "She really should take that off," Winkie said to himself contentedly, remembering with pleasure his own liberation from clothing just a few hours before.

The large chocolaty seed had just come loose and slipped onto his tongue when Winkie realized the old woman hadn't passed by him but was standing there, a few yards down the sidewalk, staring at him. Winkie turned and glared back angrily with his wide, medium brown eyes.

"What a, what a, what a cute, cute little, little," the woman cooed. Winkie was stirred immeasurably by her high singsong, which seemed a voice older than time itself. Her hair was bright white behind a thick turquoise band, and her face was as tan and old as Winkie's own. She peered at him through big, thick glasses. She didn't seem to see very well. "What kind of little-little boo-boo are you?" She began tisking and holding out her hand enticingly as if offering food. "Are you a little itty pet-pet? Baby pet? Now, who'd let such a cute, cute little boo-boo like you get out?"

Winkie felt keenly and painfully torn between two worlds, the human and the animal. The woman's crooning seemed to be pulling him backward. Forgotten memories of cribs and dolls and hugs and little cheeks crowded around his angry, staring eyes. He dropped his seedpod.

"What are you, what are you?" she sang, a white-haired siren. She was kneeling now on the grass, trying to see what Winkie was. "Who does a little furry-furry boo-boo belong to? Does a little furry-furry need a home-home?"

And even though Winkie knew exactly what he was, and what he was doing at that moment, and though he understood these facts in a way he never had before, he was filled with doubt and loneliness. He had gotten his three wishes and now what? He still belonged to no one. "Baby, baby, boo-boo?" cooed the voice. "What kind of baby boo-boo is it, now?" Winkie wanted to touch the bright white hair and nuzzle the tanned wrinkled face that resembled his own. Her milk blue eyes blinked behind the blurry glasses. Winkie understood that if she came too near, she would see he was neither quite beast nor toy but something frightening and strange that had never been seen before in the world—a protean creature always in the midst of change, ugly, self-invented, stitched together from the body and spirit and will that he'd been given.

The old woman edged forward cautiously on her knees, still crooning and tisking in her high singsong, and Winkie's fear or grief or anger boiled over: Involuntarily, he let out a series of high yelps like maniac laughter. He had never made nor heard such sounds before—but here they were:

"*Heenh! Heenh! Heenh!*"

The old woman jumped back in alarm. Winkie didn't move but kept staring, and she turned and began tiptoeing carefully away. He almost wanted to call her back but it was too late. She began a hobbling panicky run, disappearing around a corner. Sadly triumphant, Winkie made the sounds again.

Compelled by his new solitary destiny, Winkie made his way that night to the forest. He had spied it from one of the little sidewalk trees, which he had climbed to find out if the pods that dangled tasted different from the ones that lay on the ground. In this way he had hoped to distract himself from the memory of the enticing old woman. Hanging on to a branch, munching without much interest, he looked through the leaves and saw, above the red-tiled roof of a pink house, the faintest tip of a blue, wooded peak. The sun had dropped behind it, and the mountain looked cool and peaceful beneath a perfectly clear, even, yellow sky. Winkie knew that was where he had to go.

For hours he scampered from lawn to lawn, crossing one gray street after another, dodging cars, hiding from dogs and children. It seemed he was getting nowhere. He had gotten his three wishes that day: Were there to be no others? "I will go live in the mountains," he repeated to himself, half crawling and half walking, entranced. "Like a real bear."

Winkie had been old for so long that he had surpassed being either old or young. Or, in any case, he had no one to compare himself to. He had been the toy of one child and, years later, the toy of five more. Each had offered him a fresh life, a reprieve. But at last the chain had ended, and anyway, that was years and years ago. After that, Winkie had measured time in quantities of boredom. Ten little boredoms made a big boredom, and twenty big boredoms made a superboredom. After twenty or more superboredoms, he lost count. But his waiting had never become excruciating, for by then he had forgotten he was waiting for anything in particular. He lost track and thought about life. In this way he had acquired his own brand of wisdom.

It came to his aid as he made his way through neighborhood after neighborhood, thinking of that mountain peak and of the life he would have under the trees. He got bored with his journey but he didn't give up. At last the lawns began to grow wider, and sometimes there was nothing but trees and tall grass for many strides between the low-slung sprawling houses. He began to hear strange animal sounds, mysterious calls that both beckoned and frightened him. What if the wild animals didn't like Winkie? But even if he was to be torn to shreds by lions or tigers that very night, then that was his fate, and he would accept it.

Just then the lighted kitchen window of the last house passed out of view, and the darkness of the huge, magnificent night trees closed over Winkie's head. He heard the sound of a creek off to the left and nosed his way toward it through thick tangled luscious-smelling underbrush.

He broke out onto a small, rocky beach, and there in the moon-light, overhung by the trees, the water flowed by in ripples. Winkie stooped to sip and then to nibble a few dusky orange berries that clustered by his head. The taste was a wave of pleasure he'd never known, like stars exploding in his mouth. A desire for sleep over-came him sweetly in the heaviness of all his limbs. Winkie had arrived. Dozing off on a little mossy boulder in the last hours of night, he knew that his wishes were many more than three, that they would continue to come to him one after the other, and that sooner or later they would each be granted.

But when Winkie woke, only a few hours later, he was stricken with a wild, tearing pain in his middle. He turned onto his belly and began to press his soft hips into the stones of the beach. All night he had dreamed decapitations, which were each the culmi-nation of a series of actions and sensations that went forward of their own accord. He rolled over and over kicking until he was lying in dirt and leaves instead of rocks, but the pain was the same, and he began pressing himself into the earth again. It was as if the dirt itself radiated a keen excruciating suffering in warm waves, which arrived more quickly now, and his kicks were forced to follow them. It went on all morning and all afternoon. When the hot waves had reached the speed of vibration, they seemed to turn into light, there was an obliteration of vision, and Winkie felt as if all his seams would burst. The mass of pain passed through and through him and then out and out, seeming to take forever, so that inside and outside were the same. Then he fell back and it was over.

He was all wet and began to shiver. He blinked to try to wake himself up. He wished he hadn't eaten those berries the night before, and he turned to look at the terrible doo-doo he must have made.

But it wasn't doo-doo. There, nestled in the grass and leaves, was a baby Winkie.

All those years up on the shelf, and even during these last two days spent in the wide world, Winkie had never even hoped to find another creature such as himself. But here it was, only smaller and completely helpless, with a thick coat of fresh tan fur, looking back at him. So this had been his deepest wish, all along, without his even knowing it. Like a pearl or a diamond, the baby had been forming itself, also all along, little by little from the burr of loneliness, under the light pressure of Winkie's stuffing.

The creek flowed by, gurgling. The small one's drowsy eyes winked shut once, opened, and winked shut again with a metallic tandem click-click just like Winkie's own. Blindly it opened its tiny mouth, and Winkie pressed the baby's lips to the mangy nipple at his breast, where pearly drops of nourishing milk had already begun to seep out. The newborn went to sleep suckling.

Just as dreams and stories take on lives of their own, so Winkie came to life. And just as every meaning gives rise to a deeper meaning, so Winkie gave birth. He held his baby in his lap and quietly took in the world: the quivering high tree branches, the fluttering of thousands of bright green star-shaped leaves. As Winkie watched, the breeze intensified, and though still quite green, two or three leaves released themselves with soft clicks and tumbled down through the branches to the ground. Winkie was understanding everything now. He glanced across the shallow water pooling and then eddying past, wish after wish, and in the same instant he realized that some final transformation, even beyond the marvel of childbirth, had taken place in him. Something had happened to his winking glass eyes. They were wet and over-flowing. Drops fell. Winkie was crying.

It was growing dark. Above, between the trees, stars were coming out. Winkie's teardrops landed softly on the new baby's soft furry cheek, one by one. The little baby Winkie gently woke. It looked up wondering at the cool drops' source, into its mother-father's moist, knowing eyes, and saw galaxies reflected.

Remarkable
Lives

I.

Just down the hill glossy purple berries offered themselves darkly from between the pale leaves, and without prompting, Baby Winkie quietly began pulling each laden vine toward her and plucking the blackest fruit one by one with her mouth. Satisfied that his cub was getting nourishment, Winkie too began to feed. It was an ordinary summer day.

Yet nothing could be more extraordinary than these two creatures—Winkie, the come-to-life; and Baby Winkie, his miracle child, conceived of loneliness, longing, and newfound liberty. No human had ever caught more than a glimpse of them, and they were the only examples of their kind. That they had managed to survive the mountain winter was even more of a marvel, for Winkie had had to improvise his every animal instinct, from where to sleep to what to eat and including, most important, how to care for this perfect furry tan baby who depended on him so utterly.

Munching tartness, Winkie kept an eye out for danger. He didn't even know how long her childhood would last, since she was his first, but seeing that she was about half his size, he guessed she was about half grown. He began to wonder, as he often did, about what course her life would take.

"The world and fate, the world and fate," the trees above him seemed to sing.

He watched her spit out a stem and pluck another berry. Even though she still depended on him, she was her own little being and always had been. For instance, she was a girl (though Winkie used the term loosely). She was curious and remarked on things such as bugs and hilltops that Winkie, the busy parent, tended to ignore. She took in the world in her own way.

"And over there?" she asked now, done with these berries, inclining her head toward the next hill, where leaves of various kinds roiled.

"A hill of green," he said. It was a game they played about where they might go next, what they might find.

"And there?" she asked, gesturing toward a grove of pine trees. "Shade and coolness."

If she wanted to go someplace and Winkie didn't, the game alone used to appease her, but now she chuckled and set out with determination toward the pines.

Winkie nodded to himself, in answer to whether he should let her go. He refrained from following too closely. An invisible tether between them: She pretended to tug on it—another running joke they had—which meant she wanted to be left alone.

Slowing his pace, Winkie watched his child pass behind the complicated silhouette of a bush. When she was very little, and hunters with their guns came tramping through, he used to pick her up by the scruff of the neck and hurry back to the secret lair he'd concocted in a hollow tree. How she screamed! It drove Winkie nearly mad—he tried to explain—she was too young to understand.

Now she understood but often disagreed. "That's good," Winkie said to himself, "it's good to disagree." But the mere thought of hunters made him scamper past the bush and up the tangled hill to find his cub again, who was standing now in dreamy awe below the cool, tall pines.

Winkie breathed easier but Baby Winkie, catching sight of him, scowled to have her reverie interrupted. Winkie shrugged and half turned, feigning interest in the ferns and prickly red brown needles at his feet.

The bear who for so many years had helped care for others' children was now a parent himself. "A baby bear, a little baby bear," he used to murmur to himself before she was weaned, to spur himself on as he nibbled acorns so small and hard that even the squirrels had rejected them or as he scavenged through wet trash along the roadside, in the middle of the night, while Baby Winkie slept clinging to his back. When she was old enough to walk along beside him, Winkie had tried to teach her things, most of which he had only just figured out himself.

"This is how you do it," he'd said only this morning, regarding how to pick the purple berries.

"It is?" she'd answered, smiling wryly.

"It is," Winkie affirmed, but he was giggling.

Ever since her eyes had first clicked open, Baby Winkie's particular genius had been to see right through him. When Winkie had first run away, it had been his firm goal to live the life of a beast, not a plaything, apart from the wishes and constraints of humanity. He'd wanted the same for his cub, and for a time he'd almost forgotten that he'd ever worn a robe or sat in a rocking chair or pretended to sip from a miniature teacup. But somehow Baby Winkie knew better.

Late one night when the two of them came upon a remote vacation home, Winkie showed her how to push over the trash cans and strew the contents all around the property. It wasn't necessary to do so in order to find the spent jam jars or stale hamburger buns or whatever else might seem especially tasty, but Winkie wanted to make as big a mess as possible. It seemed to verify their brute nature, setting them apart from all houses and their inhabitants.

"There," he said, licking a candy wrapper.

"There," Baby Winkie replied, tossing a Dixie cup over her shoulder.

They both laughed to behold the paper plates and tinfoil and pink Kleenexes glowing in the moonlight. But just then a lone raccoon happened upon the scene and began mutely and ravenously tearing at a Styrofoam container, ignoring the stuffed bears and their snickering. Winkie needed only a single glance from his own child to realize the obvious: Truly wild things didn't joke about their own wildness. The animal realm couldn't encompass the two Winkies any more than could the human. They were, ever and always, something both in-between and beyond.

And so on this warm August day, as Baby Winkie gazed upward with wonder and Winkie tried not to watch, the very soughing of the pines, the silent streaks of cloud, and the rushing of a nearby stream seemed to call to them, almost moaning, "Who are you, anyway?"

The stillness then seemed to be waiting for an answer, with an intake of breath.

"Winkie?" piped the little one, turning to look at him.

"Baby Winkie," called the other.

"Winkie?" the one repeated.

"Baby Winkie," replied the other.

It was sort of a joke and sort of not. It was their oldest game, one they'd played since the child could first speak. In this way they could spend an afternoon simply calling each other's names, or each calling his or her own name, again and again.

2.

In another part of the forest there lived a mad professor who had recently become obsessed with Baby Winkie. No other human being had ever seen her—Winkie was ever vigilant, and the two of them hid at the slightest scent or sound—for Winkie, the former toy, knew well the human passion to clutch at anything so perfect and singular as his child.

The professor had moved to his secluded forest hut several years before, and until he spied Baby Winkie, he had believed he could never love anyone or anything ever again. He spent his days making bombs, which once a month he carried to the edge of the forest and mailed to one of his enemies. Then he'd return to his hut, wearily turn on the old TV, and wait to see what happened.

Invariably he was disappointed, for try as he might, his bombs refused to explode. The local bomb squad always had ample time to carry the package out to some faceless parking lot, run to a safe distance, and fire on it. Usually the device wouldn't go off even then.

No (the hermit often argued in his head), he was *not* merely an ersatz Unabomber. Granted, both of them had taught briefly at Berkeley and subsequently taken up residence in a remote cabin in the woods. And true, both of them hated the modern world—but then who didn't? And of course there was the superficial similarity of sending bombs to one's enemies. But unlike the Unabomber, this hermit had never been caught and, moreover, never would be (he told himself). Besides (he concluded), the Unabomber was a mathematician, while this professor had taught creative writing. (He was fired midsemester for certain comments he had made in the classroom in praise of *Mein Kampf*.)

His subsequent crusade against college administrators and all other forms of evil had once filled his brow with heady purpose, but lately the hermit had to admit that he no longer found terrorism fulfilling. He couldn't tell if this was because he had had so little success in the field or if he would have lost interest anyway.

As a child he used to enjoy killing salamanders and other small creatures easily caught. Hoping to revive youthful enthusiasms, he began directing more of his jittery attention toward hunting and fishing. He called this "Living off the Land," meaning not so much the lost arts of angling or marksmanship (for which he possessed no aptitude) but an elusive feeling of oneness with his natural surroundings—"Really *living* it!" he liked to say to himself, as he aimed his rifle or set his traps. Often the animals outsmarted him (which killed the feeling), so being an intellectual he vowed to learn more about them. To this end he built a complicated blind even deeper in the forest, from which he could observe birds and mammals for long periods without being detected. He recorded hundreds of minidiscs of them, each of which he labeled "Living off the Land." Though he chided himself that the DVD was a modern convenience, he argued back that it was potentially an effective means of getting his message out, for instance, on his own TV show. Usually this thought depressed him. Just what was his message? As the hermit berated himself exactly forty-seven times a day (once for each year of his life), he had never really come up with one. Despite thousands of pages of notes in the neatest handwriting, the manifesto itself eluded him.

Into this fevered uncertainty entered Baby Winkie.

It was a hazy day overhung by clouds, and the little bears were making their way along the brook's edge, frowning and not speaking, because Baby Winkie had wanted to continue eating olallie berries, while Winkie was of the firm opinion that any more of them today would make her sick. They were now seeking wild rosehips, but Baby Winkie did so only reluctantly.

The hermit heard a rustle to his right, and he peered out of his blind to behold two of the strangest creatures he'd ever encountered.

They looked like bears, but not like any he'd ever seen either in life or on television. They were no bigger than two small infants, and one was even tinier than the other. Sometimes they sauntered upright like dwarf human beings, deftly grasping the reddest rosehips with their forepaws. Sometimes they crawled on all fours and hungrily plucked the fruit with their mouths like common animals. Their brown eyes opened and shut with a click-click of satisfaction each time they swallowed. More curious, these eyes appeared to be composed of metal or glass, and the pads of the bears' paws looked to be faded cotton—he could see coarse stitching around the edges.

It cannot be overestimated, the effect of an actual marvel on a mind already unhinged by delusion. The professor watched as the two whatevers continued intently searching through the thorny bushes, like fugitive wishes in the foliage of a nightmare. Observing them filled the hermit with a fine, untenable sensation of forgotten yearning. He wanted to cry out, "Here I am!" from his secret place, like the smallest child in a game of hide-and-seek as he spies his older brother pass by unseeing. Then, to his even greater surprise, the smaller one of the two, the beautiful and perfect one, began to sing:

"*Happy talk*
Keep talkin' happy talk
Talk about things you'd like to do."

Like fugitive wishes in the foliage of a nightmare

The professor nearly fell back in his blind. The creature's voice was as high and mellifluous as a tiny oboe.

"You gotta have a dream
If you don't have a dream
How you gonna have a dream come true?"

When she had finished, the larger, mangy one's laughter sounded uncannily sophisticated—he could have been a department head at a cocktail party, and for a moment the professor thought the two creatures were mocking him. Had they known he was there all along? Were they putting on some kind of ridiculous show and laughing at his expense? Or worse, were the two creatures themselves some kind of cruel hoax—robots or holograms sent to drive him mad?

But then each of the bear-likes simply moved on to the next vine, and they appeared so innocent and unconcerned as they nibbled that the hermit was reassured. They did look to be genuine animals, despite their profound oddness; and no, they must not have detected him.

The two were quiet again, intent on the berries. Above, in the high crisscrossing branches, the breeze increased a moment and subsided into seemingly infinite silence.

"Winkie?" chirped the smaller one.

"Baby Winkie?" answered the other.

"Winkie?" repeated the one.

And as the other replied, the professor, too, mouthed the words *Baby Winkie* to himself. Indeed, it seemed to him that no more perfect name could have been given her. He nodded to himself, trying to steady his mind, but he was growing giddier by the instant. He told himself he was experiencing simply the thrill of scientific discovery, but it was more than that. As he continued to watch, the astonishing little being craned upward, and a patch of sun caught the golden tan of her intoxicatingly dense, short fur.

The hermit was dazzled. His face and arms exploded with a mist of the tiniest goose bumps—as if his own skin were suddenly furred, covered with millions of subtle and intricate follicles like velvet. He thought his heart might give out. Never had he wanted to possess anything so much in his life. Was it a hallucination? No, he knew he was truly witnessing something both extraordinary and real, and, not knowing what else to think, he told himself the sight had been granted him because of the mission he had undertaken here in the woods. This is the sort of thing everyone would see, he thought, if only they'd get back to the land. He switched on the camcorder.

At the click, the two creatures bounded away.

"Fuck!" The professor's cry echoed through the empty woods.

The camera caught only a rustle of leaves, which back at his cabin the hermit watched repeatedly, hypnotized. When he could bear it no longer, he set to work constructing several more observation blinds and waited in each for this rarest one, Baby Winkie, to appear again. But the crafty little bears were extra cautious and deftly avoided all of the professor's haunts. As the days and weeks passed without a sign of Baby Winkie, the hermit grew ever more agitated. His heart grew weak from its racing. He left off making bombs altogether and turned the full force of his madness upon the little pet he wanted for his own. How, how, how, he asked, could he relieve this terrible longing? Crouched behind his tangle of sticks, stroking his beard, he wrote neatly in his notebook: "Baby Winkie—Some Preliminary Notes."

He thought a moment, then began: "Baby Winkie appears like a jewel in the longest, most beautiful sentence you've ever read.

Baby Winkie surrounded and supported by density and beauty of language."

Just then he heard a rustle and, with an intake of breath, almost believed he'd conjured his love. He peered out of the blind— no, just a stupid deer. He continued writing.

"Baby Winkie crying in such a way and at such a moment as to make you cry too. You long to comfort her. 'Poor Baby Winkie!' you say. The moment is couched in such circumstances—danger, entrapment—as to make Baby Winkie's perfect cry excruciatingly piercing." The professor sweated. He paused, biting his pencil. But pausing was unbearable. He couldn't scribble fast enough.

"Baby Winkie crawls somewhere. Baby Winkie separated from the bigger one called Winkie. Baby Winkie imperiled in some way. Baby Winkie makes a new friend. (Me?) She appears momentarily safe. But then something happens, Baby Winkie *turns a corner* and finds the danger, after all—waiting, roaring! (Me?) Does Baby Winkie survive? If so, how? a) by learning from the ordeal and outsmarting her opponent? or b) by accident, unwittingly, so that the event only affirms her innocence and purity?

"It HAS to be b)." The professor had to restrain himself from leaping up out of the blind in excitement. His hand shook as he wrote. "She's the wild animal of the unconscious. She's like a little furry Buddha. She's in all your favorite books—books you haven't even thought about in years—*Walden, Orlando, Portrait of the Artist* . . . She has the timeless, irreducible poignancy of a 1930s cartoon character alone in the landscape: duck on a pond; rabbit in a hole; mouse on a riverboat. What will she encounter when she is no longer alone in the frame? That is, in what unexpected and hilarious way will she defeat and humiliate her hapless enemy?

"The wolf smashed flat?

"The cat chopped to bits?

"The hunter blown up by his own gun?—"

Before the hermit's eyes, the page was beginning to quiver and break into bits. His breath stumbled. He fainted.

This is a delicious evening, when the whole body is one sense and imbibes delight through every pore. Baby Winkie goes and comes with a strange liberty in nature . . .

The professor's head twitched from side to side. His heart pounded, ceased, pounded again.

The sea-reach of the Thames stretched before Baby Winkie like the beginning of an interminable waterway. In the offing the sea and the sky were welded together like a joint . . .

The sound of trumpets died away and Baby Winkie stood stark naked. No human being, since the world began, has ever looked more ravishing . . .

I give the name Baby Winkie to a boldness lying idle and enamoured of danger. It can be seen in a look, a walk, a smile, and it is in you that it creates an eddying . . .

A wild angel, Baby Winkie, had appeared to him, the angel of mortal youth and beauty, an envoy from the fair courts of life, to throw open before him in an instant of ecstasy the gates of all the ways of error and glory. On and on and on and on!

The professor awoke from his swoon to a musical rustling just outside the blind. Was he in a book, a vision, or the world? He peered through the sticks and leaves. There she was—Baby Winkie —not more than a few feet away, innocently drinking from the stream. She looked different than he had remembered her—larger ears, darker fur—but no, it could only be she. The other one, the male, was nowhere in sight.

The professor's heart pounded. He burst through the blind and snatched up his love.

"*Heenh! Heenh! Heenh!*" she cried out.

And, echoing down the creek bed: an answering, deeper cry.

3.

Winkie saw the bearded crazy disappearing down the ravine, Baby Winkie yelping over his shoulder. Winkie crashed through the underbrush after them. Each of his child's cries was like a crack in reality. Why had he let her out of his sight? He scampered madly. The brambles, the muddy ground, the abductor's baggy ass flashing between the foliage.

The baggy ass carried his life away. He mustn't lose sight of that shifting patch of khaki. Winkie brayed and trumpeted. Ground, more ground, snapping limbs. Was he catching up? He brayed again. Were his baby's screams closer? Leaves flickering past, branch tips. There, just ahead, the patch of khaki seemed to be stuck. "Damn, fuck!" cried the kidnapper, trying to catch his breath.

The little bear tunneled through the brambles and sprang. He bit at the blob of ass. The blob held his cub, and her cries were like pinpricks in his eyes. Winkie growled and chomped. He saw spots—something was hitting him. Could a blob grow a fist? But Winkie would burst the wiggling khaki thing with his bites and it would release his child. Winkie saw more spots. He bit down into an especially soft place. He bit hard. The monster roared and staggered.

The moment slowed. Winkie tasted something strange and wet trickling in his mouth. It was the monster's inner substance leaking out. The wicked creature would deflate like a two-legged water balloon now, it would grow pliant and bland, and Baby Winkie would float gently down on the billows.

"*Heenh! Heenh!*" the cub was still crying. Don't worry, Winkie wanted to tell her, but he had to bite. The blows continued on his head. It was only what he deserved for leaving his only one alone, for letting this happen. The spots grew colorful. Then he felt his skull squeezed tight, a firm tugging. He chomped down still more, but the monster's soft flesh gave way.

"Shit!" the man gasped. "Little fucker!"

Winkie was held aloft a moment. He spit fluid. He glimpsed his baby's yawling head next to the monster's, held tight. Winkie snarled and brayed, twisting, wriggling.

The madman shouted: "Fuck—*off!*"

Then Winkie was flying through the air, the trees spiraling past. Behind him, his one child's piercing cries Dopplered down the scale. Winkie hit the ground with a squeak. He lifted his head once, tried to moan, but his eyes double-clicked shut.

The professor tied Baby Winkie with twine to his desk and offered her a wide variety of foods, of which she would eat only cheese balls and chocolate-covered ants. He had had to walk a dozen miles to procure these for her, and he placed them before her each morning and afternoon in two gold-leaf bowls. But Baby Winkie's whimpering didn't cease.

For many days she sat on top of the desk staring out the dirty window at the woods, murmuring, "Papa, Mama, Papa," as she used to call Winkie when she was helpless and tiny, when he nursed her night and day with his own breast. She kept waiting for Winkie's face—the one face like her own—to appear in the underbrush.

Instead, the professor's plaintive eyes and neat gray beard loomed over her night and day. "*Shh. Shh,*" he'd whisper. Occasionally, though she knew it was useless, she bit him.

"Now, now," he'd mutter, rapping her smartly on the nose. "No!"

Baby Winkie despised these attempts to "train" her, especially since the stinging blow was a relief compared to her bereavement.

Three times a day she squatted over the side of his desk and let
the shit drop to the floor, and three times a day he slapped her for
it, shoving her toward the litter box he'd purchased and shouting,
"In the *box*! Go in the *box*!" as if she hadn't yet understood. After
maybe the hundredth time she turned to the professor and said,
quite distinctly:

"The cycle of prohibition: Thou shalt not go near, thou shalt
not touch, thou shalt not consume, thou shalt not experience pleasure, thou shalt not speak, thou shalt not show thyself; ultimately
thou shalt not exist, except in darkness and secrecy."

Unknown to her captor, when the cub wasn't grieving for her
lost parent, she was reading. She had taught herself in a day; desperation had made learning easy. She read by moonlight while the
professor slept. Within a few weeks she had skimmed through all
his notebooks, hoping to discover some news of Winkie, and then
gone on to assimilate all the knowledge contained in the hermit's
jam-packed bookshelves.

It wasn't that she hoped to reason with him—she understood
this was impossible—but that her despair, which had grown day
after day, simply required utterance. Her own words being too good
for him, she chose others'; playful even in misery, the child simply said the first thing that came to mind. "Foucault," she added
now, in weary parody of proper citation.

This last touch startled her captor, but only for a moment, and
then her unexpected venture into speech was swallowed by his many
theories about her. These continued to fever his mind, perhaps even
more so now that he possessed her. He took out a fresh notebook
and sat down to observe his pet, as he did each morning. He wrote:
"Cloth and stuffing—vegetable. Metal and glass—mineral. Biting
and defecation—animal. Speaking and singing—human. Existence
—impossible!"

Seeing what he'd written, and his evident satisfaction with it, Baby Winkie rolled her eyes. "Do you think that anything that is not beautiful is necessarily ugly? And that anything that is not wisdom is ignorance? Don't you know that there is a state of mind halfway between wisdom and ignorance? Socrates, as reported by Plato. Why is there more craving than there is in a mountain. Why is there. Stein."

The professor experienced slight discomfort at this last utterance, but shook it off. He noticed only that her eyes looked sad and ancient. "Old, yet young," he noted. "Compelling, yet scary. Cute, yet grotesque . . ."

"Your tale, sir, would cure deafness," said his obsession coldly. "What seest thou else in the dark backward and abysm of time? Shakespeare, *The Tempest*."

Now the hermit frowned. "Disturbing," he wrote. "Sometimes B. W. seems to mimic with an intention—as if she *meant* what she said, choosing enigma. It's as if she's joking with me, *at my expense*."

Baby Winkie went to her dish and disdainfully ate an ant. "He made a collection of butterflies and asked his mother for arsenic in order to kill them," she said. "On one occasion a moth flew around the room for a long time with a pin through its body." She sat down glumly. "Freud. The dream is made witty because the straight and nearest way to express its thoughts is barred to it. Ibid. Song of the bleeding throat! Whitman."

The professor had expected the little creature to be a pure voice of innocence in his life, yet she spoke in his own language, that of books, which echoed back to him across a vast sadness. He continued uneasily: "Her choice of food, for instance: a genuine preference, contempt—or both?"

For a moment Baby Winkie tried to empathize with the hermit's complete inability to empathize. Peering into his soul, she saw a wall, behind which things seethed. It made her head hurt. "For free association really is a labor," she whispered, "so much so that some have gone so far as to say that it requires an apprenticeship. Lacan."

Deciding he'd simply discovered his captive's potential, the hermit set out to tutor her in the arts and sciences, explaining to her that it would be like the end of *Wuthering Heights*, when the refined girl is seen teaching the uneducated boy to read—the professor had forgotten the two characters' names, which was unimportant—and the student-teacher relationship makes the boy and girl both more suitable for each other, by equalizing their level of education, and brings them closer together, for they are described as leaning their heads intimately over the same book—

Baby Winkie thought bitterly that she would have laughed if she weren't also unspeakably bereft. She thought of all the times she had once called her parent's name and he had answered—but no more. What had the world come to? Staring up into the hermit's gray nose hairs, she said, "Hobbesian man roams the streets, quite risible, with glitter in his hair—"

The professor gave her a rap on the nose and began the day's lesson.

It was around this time, the thirteenth week of her captivity, that Baby Winkie decided to disappear. The idea came to her in the middle of the night, with sudden and almost peaceful certainty, along with the understanding that disappearing was a skill she'd always possessed. It had always been there, at her disposal.

Her normal expression must have altered profoundly, for the next morning the madman suddenly interrupted his lesson and blurted out: "You've given up on that other, bigger bear. You've let go, haven't you?" He knew he was speaking too eagerly, but he couldn't help himself. "You have! I can see it in your eyes."

He meant she would be willing to be his pet now, but that wasn't it at all. Beginning to whimper as she hadn't in weeks, Baby Winkie said, more to herself than to him, "I wanted to eat of the fruit of all the trees in the garden of the world. Wilde." She sighed, turning away to the dingy window and to the scene of the empty, Winkie-less forest she had beheld for so long now like a yellowed, heavily varnished painting. She hid her face. "And yet what purple hours one can snatch from that gray slow moving thing we call Time."

This was her last regret. She calculated that her disappearance would take a few days at most. This would allow her to pass through the necessary layers of acceptance, though not to turn back. She began to glow slightly. The sweet ants and sour cheese began to collect in her two bowls. She peered out the window as longingly as before, hoping to see her parent not in the forest but in the next world, whatever that world was, past or present, and in whatever forms the two of them might take.

Sometimes she was already there, either remembering or anticipating, she wasn't sure. The not-here and not-now presented itself to her in thousands of intricate episodes and eras, story after story, and it wasn't simply that each was possible, but that each already existed in all its fullness.

It was a while before the hermit noticed her glowing, because it didn't at first outshine the slight halo of light that had always surrounded his pet from the first moment he saw her. He continued tutoring her, and he assumed that her less frequent replies were a sign of acquiescence to the new way of life he had provided. He even looked forward to the day when he could untether her.

But one evening as he set out a bowl of fresh ants, having emptied out the previous, mostly uneaten bowl, he was startled by a golden-sunset effulgence upon the many tiny dull brown chocolate shapes. He looked to the illumination's source and saw only his little bear-love. Even though her glass eyes remained sad and downcast, revealing nothing of her plan, he understood—with the terrible, almost prophetic insight of hopeless longing—that she was leaving, she was as good as gone.

In all the world she was the only one as rare and strange as he was. He had hoped they could come together as fellow anomalies but this was not to be. She couldn't survive in captivity. She was wilting like a wildflower and her wilting was a glowing. Far from making the cuddly cloth creature his own, he had simply presided over a wilting flower.

Or was he the one wilting away? His heart thumped up and down a crooked scale. Indeed, it had been ready to quit for sometime; this was just one more thing he had scarcely noticed. Lost, enraptured—the professor dropped to his knees. "I beg you—" he entreated.

The miracle child said: "It is in the analysis of such a case that one sees clearly that the realization of perfect love is a fruit not of nature but of grace."

The hermit fell over dead.

Either she, or her very glowing, had begun to emit a hum that carried through the forest, seeming to radiate from every twig. Soon this fundamental music reached the sleeping Winkie.

His eyes clicked open with a start. He had been lying there for months and vines had begun to grow around him. He had nearly returned to toy.

But even in that immovable blackness, as he lay there in the thick woods unable to either know or act, Winkie could hear his precious child's cries. Now it was as if they had reached a crescendo that woke him, but, upon his waking, all that was left was a persistent ringing, like the organ's echo in a cathedral.

With difficulty he rose and began staggering through the leaves, the broken branches, the ferns, the old tires, the mud, the plastic six-pack holders, the wildflowers, the heaps of dirt, the ashes of spent campfires, the brambles—oblivious to his cuts and bruises, drawn to the sound of his dying child. The whistling-ringing-hum grew louder and he burst into a clearing.

There, in the cabin's dirty window, he saw Baby Winkie, bright furry gold as a flame and burning still brighter—an exquisite explosion that was almost all light.

His only child turned, and seeing that her parent had at last come for her, she realized that, all along, her disappearance was no solitary act but a wild performance for the source of her to behold. It was like doing the most ridiculous dance she could think of. Within her glowing, she half shrugged, as if to say, wryly, "Look. Another miracle."

Did Winkie understand her? Gazing at his child aflame, he knew only that it was a question of what could be taken away and what could not. As it turned out, he had given birth to a saint. Her small martyrdom couldn't redeem anything or anyone, though it was emblematic, as all suffering was, of all suffering, and therefore of all absurdity. Tears in his eyes, Winkie cocked his head quizzically. As he watched, like a firefly she suddenly went out, glowed once more, and was gone.

* * *

Before her disappearance, Baby Winkie had begun writing her memoirs, by moonlight, on a legal pad she had discovered in the drawer of the desk to which she had been tied. Winkie came upon it sometime later, hidden behind the desk. Though her short life had been so cruelly impeded, the child apparently had found much to remember. The pad was filled both back and front with hundreds of notes and fragments—people, places, incidents. And though Winkie knew nothing of these people or places or incidents, some-how he also understood perfectly. The pages concluded:

Upon our arrival that day we received news of Oscar Wilde's death. My one companion, Gabrielle, was even more devastated than me. We wandered the port city in a broken daze. And yet as we made our way up from the sea, along the narrow, winding streets, we noted all the changes taking place there—the new bars and cafés never before seen in that neighborhood, the fanciful holiday bistros including a min-iature white castle with four faux turrets—all of which seemed to mark a new spirit that was to come. The sun was beaming brightly. We went into one of these new eating establishments and sat down overlooking a small patio.

Knowing this was a day to grasp life in all its fullness, Gabrielle an-swered without hesitation the waiter's call to participate in the butterfly auction. With pride I watched my lover of more than fifteen years glide out through the glass doors in her black velvet gown and stand regally at the little folding table on the patio. As I watched, tears in my eyes, Gabrielle, smiling for the crowd, reached down into one of the three large, orange jars before her, and there, brilliant against her black, honey-soaked sleeve as it reemerged from the earthenware: a cunningly gor-geous butterfly.

She did so again and again, and each time a new iridescent creature appeared on her sleeve, attracted by the honey and the velvet. Its wings flapped gently—intricate blue against flame orange; or gold surrounded by smooth white; or chartreuse with scarlet on black. I broke down then because, even on that day when persecution and imprisonment seemed to have triumphed once and for all, I knew that now was indeed a turning point for the better—which would, soon enough, change for the worse once more, perhaps unimaginably worse, and later, for the better still again, maybe even unimaginably better—over and over. Gabrielle, my dear friend, stood in the sunshine of a new century.

Nice, 1900

W i n k i e
G r i e v i n g

The even grayness of the evenly clouded sky made softness everywhere. Many of the leaves had fallen, so that the trees appeared
both decimated and plushly fuzzy with little branches when seen
from a distance. In tracts of dead yet impossibly yellow leaves, light
glowed upward. Between the barest trees, others still not at all
denuded quietly bonfired chartreuse or pale salmon or browny red.

It had been several weeks since Baby Winkie's disappearance.
Remembering the lost child's last brightness in the window,
Winkie saw light everywhere and its myriad effects.

A round, tangled tree of tiny crab apples seemed to have pul-
verized bright orange into pinpoints that the tree could then more
easily disperse into the calm, gray light of the afternoon forest.
Every bush and branch seemed to be getting rid of something,
namely the light of each painfully dazzling leaf or berry, which
registered on the eye as if on a Geiger counter. Before the leaves
could fall, they had to give off all those penetrating rays; it was
the light, not the leaves themselves, that had to be gotten rid of.

The gray light fell from the rumply clouds but also seemed to
be sopped back up into the cottonlike softness, which Winkie

imagined was like his own soft stuffing. The bear had to somehow absorb and absorb the stark and lonesome facts all around him, including his own despair. He looked up into a lattice of dark gold and greenish maple leaves, whose huge branches twisted in Medusa-like but harmless poses. The tree seemed to be trying in vain and with too much fanfare to wave him off. It was like the gesture of a half-crazy person, greatly alarmed but for no apparent reason, warning him ridiculously too late that something terrible was about to happen.

If only he hadn't left her alone that day. She wanted to go upstream, he let her go, and then—

Winkie walked under the autumn trees. Dull brown leaves fell around him on the path. Whereas before there had been two walking under the trees, now there was only one. Winkie walked alone under the autumn trees.

He returned to the hermit's cabin, where he had remained for more than a month now, watching for some sign that his child might return. The hermit was dead and Winkie had removed him. Deciding to stay reflected a choice between two evils: the forest without Baby Winkie or the cabin without Baby Winkie. Yet his instinct to remain in the terrible place where she had vanished was as fundamental as digging or burying.

It was with a dazed curiosity, in the first moments following his child's flight from the earth, that Winkie had ventured to examine the lifeless body of her tormentor. It lay on the floor of the cabin, whose interior no longer glowed but appeared simply as a collection of mundane particulars—wood, dust, and old cooking smells. The hermit was no longer exactly a monster. In repose he seemed almost nice—the kind of quiet, bearded old man who might feed little animals and let them sit on his shoulder. Not that

Winkie would have liked that, but he could see how it might ap-
peal to a certain kind of animal, like a chipmunk or a robin.

It wouldn't have appealed in the least to Baby Winkie, even if
the hermit had indeed been a nice man, and this thought made
the living bear wince. He pretended that he hadn't had the
thought, because he knew it was a grieving thought and he wasn't
ready to admit he had to grieve. He kicked the mad professor to
make sure he really was dead. The thud was the very particular
thud that only a dead thing could make.

Winkie already knew in his heart of hearts that Baby Winkie
was forever gone, but he affirmed to himself that she still might
come back and, if there was any chance of her doing so, he must
remove the evil hermit from sight so that the frightened child
wouldn't be scared away any longer. In a burst of anguished energy, Winkie grasped the dead man's dirty flannel collar with his
teeth and began jerkily dragging him toward the open door. The
difficulty and slowness of the project made its futility apparent and
so the bear began to cry, yet he knew he couldn't give up, which
only made him cry more.

The professor's clothing made a distinctive, short scraping-
whooshing noise against the cabin's wooden floor each time
Winkie lurched him forward a few inches. It was the necessary
sound of the moment. Winkie knew that he might have chosen
another necessary sound, perhaps that of shredding the hermit with
his teeth and spitting him out and then chewing up every last bit
of the cabin and spitting that out, too. But he had decided on this
course of action, dragging, and therefore this was his fate, and the
dragging noise was his contribution to the awful stillness of the
forest twilight in which there was now no Baby Winkie. A crow
cawed somewhere. Crickets were beginning. Drag, drag, drag.
Winkie could barely see through his tears but it was important to

follow through. The next sound would be that of furious digging and then burying and then stamping on the earth, which would be a little like stamping on the tormentor himself. None of it would satisfy, so in this sense it didn't matter what Winkie did, and yet in another sense this was the bear's essential task now, to rid the world of the big dead blob that he was now rolling down the three concrete steps of the cabin.

Early fall turned to middle fall and then late fall. Each morning Winkie would look out the dirty window at all the cute animals performing their cute activities—bunnies jumping and nibbling, squirrels rapidly and deftly finding nuts, their black eyes gleaming—and he would be overcome with an unbearable sadness.

The *problem* of Baby Winkie dying—the way it seemed both possible and impossible to him. It had seemed that Baby Winkie was life itself to him—love itself—and how could that die? He sought and couldn't find answers, just as he sought and couldn't find Baby Winkie a hundred times each day. The limbo of loving-not-finding, the repeated turn toward the absent one. It seemed to deepen and trouble the already uneasy limbo of Winkie's very existence, suspended as it was between bear and toy, spirit and matter, humanity and the natural world. He no longer knew in what direction even to wish.

One afternoon while walking in the forest, the little bear considered entering another dimension, and indeed in the sad, golden dusk slanting along the path, he soon began to flicker, turning briefly harsh and trapezoidal under the naked trees. But it hurt just as much as his own dimension, maybe more, and anyway he knew immediately that neither was this where Baby Winkie could be found. Returning to his former shape, Winkie retraced his steps to the cabin.

The limbo of loving-not-finding

* * *

He should be gathering acorns for the winter, as he had done so a year before with Baby Winkie, still an infant, clinging to his back. But the hermit's creaky shelves were stacked to the rafters with cheap canned goods, enough for the bear to get through any number of seasons. A year before, Winkie would have disdained using a can opener, but why stand on ceremony now? He let himself revert to the human ways he'd once so resolutely left behind—table and chair, soft bed, blankets, warmth, and SpaghettiOs. As when he was a lifeless plaything, often angry and sad, Winkie lived now more like a little man than a bear. A dirty little man, that is, for he let the empty cans pile up in a corner of the cabin, he never washed the spoons or made the bed, he left all the professor's books, clothes, guns, and papers in a mad jumble on the shelves, the floor, the table, and he let the rats and birds scamper in and out all day, leaving their droppings everywhere. He began watching the hermit's TV late into the night—it pulled in one channel, which showed mainly ads for exercise equipment—and he slept late. He lay on the dirty, wrinkled blankets each morning, surveyed the cabin's growing disarray, and said to himself, "Good."

Weeks. In the distance, the same bird. Keening. Each day Winkie went to the window and watched the last of the leaves fall.

Then at last the leaves were all gone and the keening stopped.

Mechanically, without thinking, Winkie began to clean. The cabin without filth and disorder would be a terrible and empty thing, he knew, but he couldn't stop. His back hurt as he scrubbed and carried and reached and bent. In a pile of books and papers he came upon the videotapes labeled "Baby Winkie in Captivity." He'd noticed them before, and though he realized now that he was, in fact, looking for something, these weren't it. His child in captivity wasn't what he wanted to see. He considered burning the tapes but decided that wasn't right either. He climbed on a chair and shoved them onto the highest shelf, muttering, "Put away. Put away." It was then, looking back down to steady himself, that he spotted Baby Winkie's memoirs, a thick yellow pad stuffed between the desk and the window. He climbed down, lay over the edge of the desktop, and grasped the pad of paper in his cotton paw. The pages were cool and wrinkled with ink, and he had a dizzy sensation akin to a merry-go-round slowing as one laid hold of the brass ring.

He pulled the papers out of their hiding place and smoothed them out carefully on the desk. He sat cross-legged before them. He began to read.

There were dozens of stories with dozens of characters, but in each the personality of the narrator was the same. He experienced an uncanny combination of privilege, discovery, and fate. He didn't want the journals to end. For when he turned to the last ink-scribbled page, and the butterflies were pulled one by one from the jar, he understood once again and in a new way that his own life with Baby Winkie was over. He had failed to save her. His tears fell on the lined, yellow pad.

A blankness. Winkie gazed out the window. It was dark now and it wasn't even raining. It was doing nothing outside.

But it was that very night that he had the Dream: Baby Winkie floating there before him; the fluttering infinity of her gaze; "Think back"; and her fading away for good.

Winkie really did awaken then, and he was left with the exact same sadness, bewilderment, and pride in his child as the first time she had disappeared. He realized these were now his feelings for Baby Winkie; they were final. The TV was still on, flashing especially dark and light in a sequence meant to convey excitement to the buying public. He switched it off. He saw even deeper despair as a possibility, let himself teeter awhile in the darkness. He tried to understand what his child's words meant. He slept again and dreamed again.

This was part 2 of the same dream. Figures of his own long life as a toy appeared to him, all the other children he'd cared for, and their two families, each waving good-bye with an excruciating combination of eyes and hands that prodded him with the keenest loss and regret. He hadn't thought about any of them in many years—Ruth as a girl, her sister, her brother, her parents; and then, later, Ruth's own family, the children one by one, Carol, Helen, Paul, Ken, and finally Cliff, each of whom had arrived with such loving, unflinching eyes, each of whom had grown up and left the bear behind. Yet in the dream it was Winkie leaving them behind—he was riding away from them on a huge white showboat, whose banjo band sounded down the ripples of the wide, brown green river. He was a dancing bear in spats and a white top hat, doing his act on the deck for no particular crowd, while all those people and children waved good-bye to him from the muddy shore.

He hadn't thought about any of them in years, and maybe that was the worst of it, that you could forget so completely what you'd lost.

Hugs, secrets, stories, games, crayons, tinsel, gifts, tears, spankings, betrayals, doggies, nicknames, hands, nuzzling, two-plus-two, kisses, fireworks, wagons, walks. These eddied away on the flat water behind the great paddle wheel of the riverboat, which merrily went, "Toot-toot," and rumbled in a way that was neither reassuring nor sinister, simply inevitable, beneath Winkie's dancing feet.

Twitching in the bed, he woke up.

It was early morning. He went outside to relieve himself. Squatting by the stream, Winkie bitterly recalled the pleasure such simple acts once gave him. He looked around the forest that he still loved: high trees, the singing of sparrows, yellow sunlight between the hundreds of empty branches. He let his mind come to a halt and for a moment the world and its pleasures poured in once again.

He knew now, from the second part of his dream, that by "Think back" the apparition of his child didn't mean recent events but more distant ones. Waving good-bye from the riverboat was only the start of remembering the other children he'd known. In his new life with Baby Winkie he had never wanted to look back—there had seemed no need to think of it, his many years as a plaything—but he realized now that the long past, too, was full of love and pain and that therefore those years, too, were a part of him. Even if they were long lost.

Continuing on his way, pondering his time before Baby Winkie, the old bear became suddenly aware of how small he was under the huge, overarching trees. He looked down at his own rounded shadow amid those of so many dormant twigs, and he wanted to cry again. It would be no consolation to trace from the beginning all the forgotten steps that had led him to this lonely place. But evidently it was his duty and so he resolved to try. He offered himself a reprieve until sundown, and then that night Winkie gave himself over to remembering his life—fitfully and in snatches at first, settling at last on that sad, happy, angry time when he was called Marie.

His capture, of course, interrupted him, but the memories re-sumed on his way to jail. So it was in the middle of Ruth's child-hood, as it were, that Winkie became a prisoner. Months would pass before he turned to remembering again, on the very eve of his court date. So, too, it was in the middle of Cliff's boyhood, as it were, that Winkie's trial began.

Part Three

*"And there is no object so soft but it makes a hub
for the wheel'd universe."*
—*Walt* Whitman, "Song of Myself"

The People
vs.
Winkie

The army general pointed with a laser pen at the poster-size photograph. "This is a satellite photograph of what we believe to be a sophisticated bioweapons laboratory where, according to scattered intelligence reports, more of these 'killer bears' are being created." He moved the light in circles around one blurry rectangle and then another. "Here. Here. And here," said the general commandingly.

"I understand," said the prosecutor in a hushed, worried tone. "Now, by 'killer bears,' you don't mean bears in the usual sense, do you?"

The general chuckled gravely. "No. That's just what we call them—because of the superficial resemblance to bears."

"But there's nothing warm and fuzzy about them, is there?"

"No, indeed. On the contrary, they are nothing less than an army of supercombatants, trained to maim and kill." The general revealed his next chart. "And created, we believe, by a scientific process we don't yet understand, but which might well involve the use of stolen children, combined with DNA from a local animal, such as a snake or rodent or, just as likely, a drug-resistant microorganism, such as smallpox or anthrax."

"Here. Here. And here," said the general commandingly.

The chart showed a line drawing of a little girl in a pink dress on the left, a thick black arrow labeled "DNA" in the middle, pointing to a naked Winkie-like creature on the right. The courtroom gasped.

"Thank you, that's all too clear," said the prosecutor. "No further questions."

"So far, so, um, good," Unwin whispered to the bear, as he riffled through a mound of overstuffed manila folders. "The jury saw, saw, saw right through all of that. Nothing to worry about, Mr. Winkie."

In fact, it was impossible to gauge the reaction of the jury, because the eight men and six women were hidden behind a curtain. In a key pretrial motion, the prosecution had successfully argued that, due to the extreme danger posed by the defendant's network of terror, the identities of jury members must remain secret. Winkie gazed now with apprehension at the high, blue expanse of fabric as it billowed slightly in an indoor breeze. It seemed then as if the curtain itself were passing judgment on him—hating him for what he was accused of, ignoring him, punishing him with drapy silence.

"Mr. Unwin?" said the judge impatiently.

Unwin continued searching through his piles of papers, folders, and computer discs. That morning the prosecution had suddenly honored his long-standing request for the release of evidence by turning over approximately 10,000 typewritten pages and 213 compact discs. In the interest of speedy justice for a case of national significance, the defense's plea for a continuance was denied, and the many stacks of testimony, lab reports, and other documents now surrounded the lawyer and his client like a messy nest. Unwin fluttered from stack to stack, his lank hair falling in his eyes.

"Sir, do you intend to cross-examine this witness or not?" the judge demanded.

There was only the scrabbling sound of the defense attorney shuffling pages.

"Here we go," said the prosecutor, rolling his eyes.

"Ah," muttered Unwin, and he began busily perusing a thick report he'd just found, grunting, lost in thought.

The judge dangled his gavel between two fingers. "Counselor . . . *Counselor*—"

Oblivious to all but the page he held near his nose, Unwin lifted one hand above his head in a shushing gesture and continued reading.

The judge looked so angry that Winkie started tugging on his lawyer's sleeve, but he paid no attention. His eyes moved rapidly across the page. "Huh, huh, uh-huh . . . What? Oh. Hm, uh-huh . . . Oh, my God! Huh. Ah . . . Huh . . . "

Several witnesses went by before Unwin even raised his little eyes from the tableful of evidence. Testimony floated past the lonely bear as if in a dream where one can only watch and do nothing. When the chief detective was called, however, the man gave Winkie such an intense look of hatred that the bear began urgently tugging his lawyer's sleeve again.

"Jesus—*what?*" Unwin snapped.

Winkie pointed in alarm, but the chief's murderous gaze had already lapsed. He looked especially calm and handsome now, as he stood very tall near the flag and spoke his oath of truth in the same booming voice the bear had first heard coming from a helicopter.

Even Unwin began to pay attention. Under the prosecutor's questioning, the chief recounted the many years spent tracking down the defendant, and the circumstances of his arrest at last. "I knew from the first moment I saw him—through the binoculars— that he was our man."

Unwin shot up. "Your Honor, um, whatever, whatever this agent believed, it, it, it, it has no bearing, no bearing whatso- ever, on, on—"

"Overrruled." Crack.

"Thank you, Judge," said the prosecutor, shutting his eyes and inclining his head as if, without the court's intervention, he would submit humbly to any attack by the defense. He turned to the chief again. "And why is that, sir? How did you know you had found 'your man,' as you put it so vividly?"

"Because he matched the profile perfectly."

"And what was that profile?"

The chief held out the palm of his large hand and began tapping it with one finger, then two, then three, as he made each irrefut- able point. "A very short male with what experts call a 'Napoleon complex,' probably deformed, perhaps severely so, socially awkward, a drifter, paranoid, totally isolated from family and friends, unmar- ried, of course, and incapable of normal, healthy sexual relations with the opposite sex, relations that could lead to the birth of nor- mal, loving children and a normal, healthy, fulfilling family life."

After months of interrogation, Winkie had grown inured to most of the chief's outlandish charges, but he did very much want to object that he had, in fact, given birth to a beautiful, happy child . . .

"But how—how could such a person even *exist*?" asked the prosecutor. "How could anyone *go on* like that?"

"Again, this is a not a normal individual." Many in the court- room murmured their agreement, and the chief grimaced with disgust. "To make up for these physical and emotional defects, such a personality will, inevitably, resort to criminal activity—especially the construction of bombs, which make him feel all powerful—like God himself."

"Terrible. Just terrible," remarked the prosecutor, shaking his head.

Unwin appeared about to object but subsided, his eye suddenly attracted by some phrase in yet another document.

"How long have you been an agent with the Federal Bureau of Investigation?" the prosecutor asked the witness.

"Twenty-eight years, sir." His thick head of hair glowed silvery beneath the overhead lighting.

"And have you ever seen a case like this?" the prosecutor asked.

"Never." The chief shook his large head sagely. "Never in all my experience have I encountered so dangerous a criminal—nor so subtle a criminal mind."

"And I think we can safely say that the experience on which you base that opinion is vast?"

The chief looked almost boyish as he dropped his chin in modest assent.

Unwin handed the chief a thick bound volume. In his endless and seemingly random riffling of pages, the lawyer had nevertheless managed to sift out a key FBI document produced not long before the bear's arrest. "Will the witness, um, um, um, please read for us, page, page, page—*page one thousand fifty-seven, the beginning of the last paragraph?*" he asked, barely able to contain the excitement of his impending coup.

"According to various reports from the field, the so-called 'mad bomber' is believed to be . . . ," mumbled the chief.

"Yes, that's it!" Unwin interjected. "Please! Do, do, *do* go on!" He made a feverish rolling gesture with both hands.

The chief frowned. "The mad bomber is believed to be, *ahem*, approximately six feet tall, age forty-five to fifty-five, overweight, of average appearance, with blue eyes, glasses, and graying hair and beard."

"And—the sketch?" Unwin prompted. "Don't, um, forget the sketch!"

The chief held up a police drawing of an angry human face wearing sunglasses and a hooded sweatshirt. Smudged and angular, the face was like none Winkie had ever seen and more frightening than even the judge himself.

"Well, and does this, um, this *rendering*, or the description you so, so, so kindly read for us just now, *resemble* the defendant on trial here today?"

The chief avoided his questioner's gaze. "Well, not precisely . . ."

"*Indeed*, wouldn't you say—NOT AT ALL?!" Unwin shouted, his cheeks and forehead literally flush with victory. The witness made no answer, but Unwin couldn't leave it at that. Triumphs such as this had come so infrequently in his career that he didn't want the moment to end. "Thank you very much *indeed*, sir. That will *indeed* do nicely. No further questions *indeed*. That will *indeed*—"

Crack! Crack! "Mr. Unwin," the judge boomed, "*indeed*, if you don't sit down *now*—"

Amid general laughter, Unwin scurried back to his seat. Winkie glanced uneasily at the blank, blue curtain and back to his lawyer, whose overexcited face couldn't seem to decide between victory and shame. "Oh, yes, we've got them by the you-knows now," Unwin whispered.

However, for the previous twenty minutes, the prosecutor's twelve assistants (who sat in a row behind him) had been madly searching through this particular document on their twelve laptops, and thanks to Assistant Number Twelve's avid data-ferreting, the prosecutor was able to come back now with one more question for the chief detective:

"What else, sir, does the report say about this criminal—on page seven hundred forty-seven, footnote fifty-six, paragraph four?"

Wearily the chief flipped through the heavy report, but then suddenly his face lit up. "Ah. Shall I read it?" he asked.

"Please."

The chief spoke the words slowly and clearly: "Both the description and the composite sketch of the mad bomber must be taken with a healthy grain of salt, for this wily criminal is also believed to be a *master of disguise.*"

All eyes turned now to the bear—eyes so inquisitive and accusing that Winkie felt as though his appearance *was* shifting, here and now, against his will, to any number of configurations—little or tall, animal or human, scary or cute—faster and faster until he was nothing but the blurred symbols of a slot machine, spinning past.

2.

Winkie stared up at the unchanging circular eye of the overhead light, which gazed back down in a way that seemed almost to pity the bear. By now he'd given up on searching the events of his life for some kind of relief—a pattern, a lesson forgotten, a morsel of hope—and instead he simply watched his mind go blank. It was perhaps 3 A.M. The bunk seemed to drop away and he was floating, yet crushed, in the stale air that had grown so heavy with all the words spoken against him that day in court. Despite the unbearable itching, he resolved each night as he lay down not to scratch, not even to move, and he usually succeeded for a time. But now, he let himself wonder, what if he *couldn't* move? The sawdust in his limbs seemed to be soaked in poison syrup, a punishment he deserved simply because it seemed so fitting. Whatever terrible new dream had begun today with the trial, this terrible sensation now was the same dream and, moreover, the worst part of it.

From below, in the shade of his bunk, came the ragged buzz of his cell mate Darryl's troubled snoring, which began every night precisely at this hour and always startled Winkie to the world as it was rather than as he feared it. He began to scratch again—a different, more mundane kind of penance. He focused on the left side of his belly, timing his movements to Darryl's breaths, which always sounded like a mountain lion growling from a cave but which actually, like Darryl himself, were harmless.

Though the hulking prisoner had been chosen by the authorities to torment the bear, he'd instead taken an immediate liking to Winkie, for there was nothing he missed more in jail than his stuffed animals. Darryl was serving a life sentence for shoplifting. He wasn't adjusting well to incarceration. Following his last rebellion he had been given newer, stronger sedatives, but in fact it was the little bear's presence that most soothed him. Though the chief detective complained repeatedly that Darryl wasn't doing his "job" and should be replaced with a more dangerous inmate, the guards were so relieved not to have to clean his shit from the walls and their uniforms that they left him where he was.

"Darryl and I get along just fine," sighed the bear, as if that were consolation for anything. The two of them were kept in isolation, a prison of two with Deputy Walter their sole jailor. Time was strange here. They were allowed no visitors, save Unwin. Darryl slept nineteen and a half hours a day and otherwise sat cross-legged on his bunk silently filling in the pages of one of the coloring books his grandmother left for him each week. Sometimes when the shouts and screams of some riot drifted here from the main cell block, he picked up Winkie and roughly cuddled him. Sometimes he pressed upon the bear an orange and purple striped Yosemite Sam, Darryl's favorite. Sometimes he even shared a slimy white capsule or two that he'd managed to hide in his cheek until Walter had left; the bitter substance inside made Winkie's eyes droop pleasantly and the itching stop for maybe half an hour.

Proceeding with his claws to the mangier right side of his belly, the little bear allowed himself to be appalled that his life had come to this. It wasn't a new thought. But sometimes, like tonight, the sense of every painful memory being carried at last to its lurid conclusion took on the strangely satisfying force of doom. He wished he could literally rub his own nose in it. And so, if this was indeed his final destination, he asked himself—as he always asked when he reached this point, as if the question could save him—what had he learned from his life?

"One," he answered himself, unflinching, almost wishing for the blow: "Love will be punished. Two . . ."

But he didn't know yet what Two was.

3.

The prosecutor rose and cleared his throat. "Your Honor, because of the severe danger posed to prosecution witnesses, not to mention their families, by the international terror and crime ring that the defendant commands and, we believe, continues to command from his cell, many of those witnesses will be represented to this court by trained actors."

A furious Unwin began to protest. "Um—um—um—um—"

"To further protect witnesses' identities," the prosecutor continued, "and so as not to prejudice the jury, we will not divulge which are actors and which are the witnesses themselves. In some cases," he added very quickly, "actors will represent witnesses who, for various reasons, aren't otherwise available to testify."

By now even Unwin's bony hands had gone red with agitation. "Your Honor, this is—Your Honor, I cannot—Your Honor, surely you must—"

Three cracks of the gavel. "Overruled, overruled, overruled. Mr. Unwin, these constant interruptions must cease, or I will replace *you* with an actor." Crack. "At least then we'd have someone who could spit the words out."

The courtroom burst into wild hilarity, with sprinkles of applause. Unwin sank down into his chair. Winkie looked daggers at the judge.

"The people call Jane Cotter!"

A slight young woman in a black dress, black stockings, and frilly white apron and cap took the stand. For a moment Winkie pretended she was Françoise, even though the uniform wasn't much like hers; as in a dream, she had come to testify on his behalf, in altered garb, at a time least expected—but of course it wasn't Françoise, and Winkie's heart sank back to its accustomed despair.

"I am employed as a chambermaid in the Savoy Hotel," Miss Cotter said very quietly, in a lilting Irish accent. "I remember Mr. Winkie staying at the hotel in March 1893." She cleared her throat nervously.

As he had explained to his assistants that morning, the prosecutor hoped to make legal history by playing on the jury's emotions in ways that had never been attempted before. Unwin half rose to object, but the judge shook his gavel at him, so he subsided back down in his chair and began scribbling furiously on his pad.

Miss Cotter continued: "I found it necessary to call the attention of the housekeeper to the condition of Mr. Winkie's bed." She cleared her throat again. "The sheets were stained in . . . in a peculiar way."

A murmur in the courtroom. Even Unwin stopped scribbling for a moment, and Winkie wished he could hide under the blanket in his cell.

"Go on," said the prosecutor.

"On the third morning of his stay," Miss Cotter said, "about eleven o'clock, Mr. Winkie rang the bell for the housemaid. On answering the bell, I met Mr. Winkie in the doorway and he told me he wanted a fire in his room." She swallowed. "There I saw a boy of eighteen or nineteen years of age with dark close-cropped hair and a sallow complexion."

Another murmur.

"No further questions. Our nation thanks you for coming forward, Miss Cotter."

"Um . . . Your Honor, a moment . . . A moment . . . Um . . . Um . . . Your Honor, a moment . . . Um . . . Um . . ."

"Mr. Unwin, if you do not begin your cross-examination in ten seconds—"

"Yes, oh yes, all right—" But as he moved toward the witness box, he knocked over several piles of folders, CDs, and diskettes.

"Leave it!" the judge snapped, as Unwin stooped to retrieve them. By now this had happened so many times that it didn't even inspire laughter. In the deadly silence Unwin managed to straighten his body only halfway before addressing the witness.

"Miss Cotter—how old are you?"

"Objection. Your Honor, what possible bearing—" began the prosecutor, but the witness had already answered, "Twenty-four."

The judge actually seemed interested for a moment. "I'll allow it."

"Twenty-four years old," Unwin repeated. By now he was stand-

ing up straight. "OK. And yet you say you saw the defendant in
1893?"

"Yes," she answered.

"More than one hundred years ago?"

"Yes. So?"

Unwin lifted his hands in lawyerly wonder. "So, Miss Cotter,
how is that possible?"

"Objection!" came the shout again. "Miss Cotter is not an expert on the laws of time and space."

The judge pondered a moment but quickly caught himself. "Sustained," he said flatly.

If possible, Unwin looked more stunned now than ever. "Well then,
well then, I have nothing, nothing, nothing further!" he cried.

Crack! "The defense will please refrain from his theatrics or be
held in contempt."

Unwin sat down muttering. It was a key defeat, for it cleared
the way for the next several months of testimony.

"Mr. Winkie was the person who seduced and compelled me
into the snares of witchcraft," said Witness C, whose name was
withheld "for security reasons." He was a short stocky man who,
like Witnesses A and B, was sweating profusely in a black wool
coat and black wool breaches, buckled boots, and a tall black hat.
"He promised me fine clothes for doing it. He brought poppets to
me, and thorns to stick into those poppets, for the afflicting of other
people; and he exhorted me, with the rest of the crew, to bewitch
all of America, but be sure to do it gradually, if we would prevail
in what we did."

Winkie bristled: he would never stick thorns into a poppet or
any other toy.

"America thanks you for your bravery in testifying," said the prosecutor.

"Your Honor—" Unwin sighed, rolling his eyes.

The judge swatted the air once.

"And what has happened to you since you came forward?" the prosecutor gently asked the witness.

"Ever since I confessed having been a horrible witch, I have been myself terribly tortured by the devils and other witches, and therein undergone the pains of many deaths for my confession."

Though Winkie had certainly imagined torturing many people in his life, he was sure he'd never actually done it. But what if just thinking about it was enough?

Howard Morgan, a teenager with thick brilliantined hair, had just taken the oath. He pulled at his starched collar and bow tie. The prosecutor blew dust from an old textbook and carried it to the witness stand.

Mr. Morgan, did you study under Professor Winkie?

Yes, sir.

(Holding up the textbook) Did you study this book, General Science?

Yes, sir.

How did Professor Winkie teach that book to you? I mean by that did he ask you questions and you answered them or did he give you lectures, or both? Did he ever undertake to teach you anything about evolution?

Yes, sir.

Just state in your own words, Howard, what he taught you and when it was.

It was along about the 2nd of April.

Of this year?

Yes, sir; of this year.

(Unwin began to protest that the defendant had been in jail all of this year but the judge said that was a matter of fact, which the jury would decide. The witness continued:)

He said that the earth was once a hot molten mass too hot for plant or animal life to exist upon it; in the sea the earth cooled off; there was a little germ of a one-cell organism formed, and this organism kept evolving until it got to be a pretty good-sized animal, and then came on to be a land animal and it kept on evolving, and from this was man.

(Winkie was fascinated but wondered how his own existence might fit into the scheme.)

I ask you further, Howard, how did he classify man with reference to other animals; what did he say about them?

Well, the book and he both classified man along with cats and dogs, cows, horses, monkeys, lions, horses and all that.

What did he say they were?

Mammals.

(Nearly everyone in the courtroom appeared deeply offended. Winkie, however, knew what a mammal was and felt happy to be one.)

Classified them along with dogs, cats, horses, monkeys and cows?

Yes, sir.

Nothing further.

The prosecution often scheduled its most colorful witnesses for the afternoon, to keep the court interested. Shortly after lunch, a rotund but delicately featured man, with precise goatee and large, clever eyes, came floating down the center aisle in a red damask gown and red velvet bonnet, both trimmed in ermine. Thirty-three mother-of-pearl buttons down his front signified the thirty-three years of Christ's life.

"Pope Urban the Eighth," he said in elegantly accented English, when asked to state his name. "Formerly Cardinal Maffeo Barberini," he added, with a slight bow. His long, white hand appeared particularly graceful atop the Bible as he swore to tell the truth.

"Your Holiness," said the prosecutor, having first knelt and kissed the scarlet hem of his robe. "Please now tell us the defendant's crimes against the Holy Faith."

Urban smiled deferentially. "He holds as true the false doctrine, taught by some, that the sun is the center of the world and immovable and that the earth is not the center and moves." There was a murmur of alarm among the spectators. The pope smiled again, almost apologetically. "Expressly contrary to the divine and Holy Scripture, this doctrine is calculated to injure our faith."

The prosecutor pressed one hand to his heart. "Our *faith?*"

Urban closed his eyes and gravely nodded. The spectators gripped more tightly the plastic arms of their chairs.

The world and everything in it is a miracle, thought Winkie, but wearily, that night in his cell. He had just taken one of Darryl's capsules. Looking once again up into the pale green glow of the ceiling light, which so far had never blinked once, he imagined the starry sky, also unblinking, which night after night he and Baby Winkie used to watch traverse the grand and velvet distance of the horizons. A slow, vast, beautiful spin—why?

As if in answer, the circular bulb began to blind him. Winkie clicked shut his eyes. His own faith in life had indeed been shaken, and he wondered if the pope had been right—if he himself had injured that faith and had even meant to do so.

The little bear sighed and tried to sleep. In the green-lit cube that was his home now, Darryl snored.

4.

Each day the prosecution introduced some new charge against the bear, while certain crimes, like random numbers in a game of chance, tended to come up again and again. From the testimony of Alfred Wood, formerly a clerk, currently not in any occupation: After dinner I went with Mr. Winkie to Sixteen Tite Street. There was nobody in the house to my knowledge. Mr. Winkie let himself in with a latchkey. We went up to a bedroom where we had hock and seltzer. Here an act of grossest indecency occurred. Mr. Winkie used his influence to induce me to consent. He made me nearly drunk. [Testimony censored.] Afterward I lay on the sofa with him. It was a long time, however, before I would allow him to actually do the act of indecency.

Prosecution: *Surely you are to be commended for resisting him as long as you did.*

(Unwin objected that this wasn't a question and was overruled. "Grossest indecency," Winkie murmured to himself, as the next witness was brought in, Charles Parker, age twenty-one, a valet:) *Where did you first meet Mr. Winkie?*

Alfred Taylor took us to a restaurant in Rupert Street. We were shown upstairs to a private room, in which there was a dinner table laid. After a while Winkie came in and I was formally introduced. I had never seen him before, but I had heard of him. We dined about eight o'clock. We all sat down to dinner, Winkie sitting on my left.

Was the dinner a good dinner?

Yes. The table was lighted with red-shaded candles. We had plenty of champagne with our dinner and brandy and coffee afterward. We all partook of it. Winkie paid for the dinner.

(Though he couldn't recall the incident, Winkie felt satisfaction in having treated the other guests.)

And then?

Subsequently Winkie said to me, "This is the boy for me! Will you go to the Savoy Hotel with me?" I consented, and Winkie drove me in a cab to the hotel. At the Savoy we went first to Winkie's sitting room on the second floor.

More drink was offered you there?

Yes, we had liqueurs. Winkie then asked me to go into his bedroom with him.

Let us know what occurred there.

He committed the act of sodomy upon me.

(A stunned silence in the courtroom. Winkie wrote on his lawyer's pad, "What's sodomy?" Unwin blushed.)

Go on, please.

I was asked by Winkie to imagine that I was a woman and that he was my lover. I had to keep up this illusion. I used to sit on his knees and he used to [censored] as a man might amuse himself with a girl. Winkie insisted on this filthy make-believe being kept up.

("Filthy make-believe," Winkie repeated to himself, still trying to understand. "Make-believe filth . . .")

Nothing more with this witness.

The young man nervously straightened the collar of his tunic, which was white linen with black trim in a Greek key pattern. "The defendant is a clever speaker," he warned, narrowing his eyes, "and you must be careful not to let him deceive you, for he can make the weaker argument seem the stronger." Winkie furrowed his brow. "He believes neither the sun nor the moon to be gods, like other men. He says that the sun is a stone, and the moon earth. And he corrupts the young by teaching them not to believe in the gods the state believes in but in other new divinities instead."

New divinities sounded good to the bear, but there was a general murmur of disapproval.

"You have spoken well, Meletus, son of Meletus of Pitthos," said the prosecutor. "No further questions."

The witness shook back his long black hair with satisfaction. All eyes turned to the defense.

"Um . . . Um . . . A moment . . . ," said Unwin, searching through his piles of notes.

Winkie continued gazing in puzzlement at the witness, trying to remember ever meeting him. Their eyes locked for a moment. Meletus looked away.

"Mr. Unwin—" sighed the judge.

"Your Honor, again, um, again—maybe I'm crazy, but um, I don't see any of this in the pretrial testimony . . ."

The prosecutor chuckled indulgently. "If you look again, Mr. Unwin, I think you'll see that this witness was deposed on the same day as the Oracle at Delphi."

"Delphi . . ." Unwin pulled another sheaf of papers from a folder on the floor. "Delphi . . . Delphi . . ."

This particular exchange might have been written off as simply another low point among many for the bear's troubled defense. However, as commentators would note later, the prosecution had committed a major error in mentioning Delphi. For by some miracle, Unwin now actually laid hands on that particular document—one among literally thousands that the state had filed only that morning.

"Aha!" Unwin shouted.

The judge rolled his eyes; the prosecutor shook his head; behind the curtain, some of the jurors tittered. But with unusual focus the defense attorney strode toward the witness and thrust the paper into his hands.

"Mr. Meletus, please read this deposition aloud. For the benefit of the court."

The witness hesitated, stroking his thin beard.

"Mr. Meletus, again, I ask you to please read for us the sacred words of the oracle."

The witness cleared his throat. His voice was low, but the words were perfectly distinct:

"Of all men living, Winkie most wise."

The courtroom fell into an uproar.

It was a significant victory for the defense, but by the time order was restored (the court had to be cleared and a two-hour recess called), Meletus's admission seemed all but forgotten. The prosecutor was ready with three of his most important witnesses.

"The people now call the Afflicted Girls," he boomed. Cries of horror rippled through the courtroom, for these witnesses' shocking claims had been reported on extensively in the media. "But first, the defendant must be strongly enjoined not to look upon them until instructed to do so, for as you shall see, if he should glance their way but once, they shall fall into their fits."

"Very well," said the judge.

"Your Honor—" said Unwin.

"Sit down, Mr. Unwin. Whatever it is—overruled." He banged his gavel. "Bring in the witnesses, and the defendant shall lower his eyes until instructed otherwise."

A stout bailiff stood in front of Winkie as he stared down at the Formica brown of the table.

The rest of the courtroom watched then in eager silence as slowly down the aisle came two girls of twelve and one of about seventeen, each wearing a white bonnet and long black dress with starched white collar. They settled together into three battered metal folding chairs that had been placed next to the witness box.

"Ann Putnam, Abigail Williams, and Elizabeth Hubbard, do you solemnly swear . . ."

When they had lowered their right hands, the prosecutor commanded gravely, "The accused will now please look upon these witnesses."

To Winkie's surprise and chagrin, as soon as he glanced at them, all three girls fell to the beige floor writhing and moaning. "Whish, Whish, Whish!" said Williams, stretching her arms as if to fly. "I won't, I won't, I won't sign the devil's book!" shouted Putnam, who got up and began running around the courtroom. "Goodwife Nurse," cried Hubbard, pointing. "Do you not see her? Why, there she stands!"

The bailiff aimed his pistol toward the window, but nothing was there.

"Your Honor, please!" said Unwin, half shouting. "Clearly they cannot testify in this condition."

"And who do you suppose *put* them in such a state?" countered the prosecutor.

"I certainly don't know," said Unwin. And here he made one of his unfortunate jokes, wildly throwing up his hands in theatrical disgust: "Maybe the *devil* did it."

The judge looked at him sternly. "How comes the devil so loathe to have any testimony born against your client?"

This cast Unwin into more than usual confusion. Putnam continued running to and fro, while Williams and Hubbard thrashed on the polished floor, their long dresses spread out around them like black pools. Winkie was frightened.

"Judge," the prosecutor loudly affirmed, "if the accused be allowed to look upon them no longer, and if he should only then touch them but once, their fits will surely cease."

"Proceed."

The bailiff now roughly tied a handkerchief around Winkie's head, covering his eyes. In turn, each of the three struggling, raving girls was brought to him, he was made to touch her hand with his right paw, and each time—much to everyone's relief, including the bear's—the struggling and raving stopped. Suddenly the courtroom was silent.

"So we see that by his touch," said the prosecutor, "the venomous and malignant particles, that were ejected from the defendant's eye, do, by this means, return to the body whence they came, and so leave the afflicted persons pure and whole." He wheeled around to face the jury curtain and called to them, "What further proof need you?"

Winkie's sleepless glance roved this way and that across the nine-by-nine-foot ceiling. The stuffing of his head was throbbing, and the Afflicted Girls seemed to cry out within the sound of Darryl's rasping breaths. "Whish! Whish! Whish!" If there had been a mirror in the cell, the bear would have looked into it to see if his own gaze really was so harmful and, if so, then surely to harm himself with it, too, for that was only just.

Winkie had always let his angry gaze fall wherever it might and never stopped himself from hating, but if he could somehow make three poor girls collapse in agony with a mere look, without even wanting to, then how many other, more terrible ills might he have caused in his life? He had seen his own child harmed, and every child he'd ever known, from Ruth to Cliff, and now these scenes flickered before his memory with a new and searing might. For what if it was the very witnessing that had caused them?

He clicked his terrible eyes shut and began to cry.

When he opened them again, after what had seemed like years of sorrow, he was surprised to see Darryl's wide, blotchy face hovering near his pillow, peering at him with bewildered concern. Winkie hadn't noticed that the snoring had stopped. He thought to look away, remembering the evil of his glance, but realized in the same instant that Darryl was, evidently, unfazed.

"Don't cry," said the hulk slowly, his huge, tired eyes rimmed with red. They stared at each other awhile longer and then, with drugged gentleness, Darryl patted Winkie's forehead once and returned to bed.

The bear was almost consoled.

"And there appeared another wonder in heaven," said the man in the brown burlap caftan. The prosecution had cannily saved John the Apostle for last. He stared straight ahead, wide-eyed, apparently seeing only the spiritual realm. His feet were bare and his beard was white and voluminous. "And behold a great red Winkie, having seven heads and ten horns, and seven crowns upon his heads. And his tail drew the third part of the stars of heaven, and did cast them to the earth. And there was a war in heaven: Michael and his angels fought against the Winkie; and the Winkie fought and his own angels, and prevailed not; neither was their place found any more in heaven. And the great Winkie was cast out, that old bear, called the Devil, and Satan, which deceiveth the whole world: He was cast out into the earth, and his angels were cast out with him."

The courtroom burst into applause, with shouts of, "Yeah!" The apostle couldn't resist waving to the crowd.

"Your witness, Mr. Unwin."

The defense lawyer sat rubbing his temples. The trial had been going on for more than seventeen months, and in all that time he'd scarcely slept. "No questions," he sighed.

Winkie looked at the apostle in wonder as he slowly stepped down from the witness box and hobbled away. Once again the bear felt strangely compelled by the testimony against him, for he really did feel like he'd been cast out into the earth.

But who, then, he wondered, were his angels?

Winkie

vs.

the People

1.

"Mr. Winkie, I hope I may speak, um, frankly, and therefore I frankly must urge you, urge you most frankly, to testify on your own behalf."

Winkie shook his head. It seemed that his whole being rebelled against speaking before his accusers, and now he couldn't even bring himself to say the word *no* to his own lawyer. He shook his head once.

Unwin began pacing back and forth in the tiny cell, clutching his head. "But really, but how, but what, but goddamn it—"

Darryl, who had been coloring quietly in his bunk, looked up to see if the lawyer was annoying his friend. "Mr. Bear?" he asked, his two giant fists at the ready.

Unwin froze midstep, but Winkie made a calming gesture with both paws and Darryl returned reluctantly to his crayons.

Sighing, the lawyer sat down again in his folding chair. "All right, Mr. Winkie, if that's how you want it, but, but, but, again, as your defense begins tomorrow, I must . . ."

Winkie closed his eyes and stopped to admire once again the Spartan beauty of his silence with respect to the authorities.

Somehow it didn't please him the way it used to, but he told himself it was perfect and he mustn't waver.

"Orange," Darryl murmured. Unwin had trailed off and there was now only the nonsound of waxy color giving itself to the page.

A night of sleepless defiance had left the bear sour and headachy, but as he was led into court that morning, he thought maybe he glimpsed, through the legs of the crowd, a smiling radiance he dared not hope to find. Agents Mike and Mary Sue and Deputy Walter seemed to huddle around him longer than usual as they unlocked the three, tangled chains that connected his shackles to each of their own wrists. But when at last he was lifted up to his seat and his guards had stepped aside, Winkie turned to see Françoise waving and beaming at him from the front row. Next to her sat a voluptuous woman with thick, dark hair falling around her shoulders who was also smiling, and to whom Françoise gestured with her eyes so that Winkie would know this was Mariana. Lifting one paw a few inches, which was as far as it would go, the bear thought he might weep—to see that Françoise was safe; to find her there on his side.

He faced forward and Unwin whispered, "Good morning, Mr. Winkie, how are you, good, I see you've spotted Miss Fouad, that's fine, but please, no more waving, I'm very nervous and I don't want you to give them any excuse today, any excuse at all, to, to, to restrain you any further, not now when we need to be focused, I mean really really really focused, on your defense, so please, please, please, Mr. Winkie, I beg you, restrain yourself."

Winkie didn't know what to do now but look sad.

"No long faces either! You must project confidence, Mr. Winkie! We *both* must. God knows it's hard enough for me, I don't want to have to worry about you, too!"

Winkie glared at him.

"All right, I'm, I'm, I'm sorry, um, um, um, never mind. Please!" Winkie nodded once in pardon, and Unwin proceeded to tell, with growing excitement, the story of Françoise's release. "It really is wonderful. Classic. It really goes to show. You see, Miss Fouad's, um, um, you know, *friend* is also a cleaning woman, I mean, person, cleaning *person*, anyway, anyway, as I was saying—she doesn't work at the hospital; rather, and quite fortuitously indeed, she cleans an old building downtown that houses the, um, you know, the Gay and Lesbian Community Center and, moreover, moreover, Legal Aid, the ACLU, and PETA."

Winkie looked at him with bewilderment.

"You know, the ACLU?" said Unwin, lifting both hands. He sighed. "I, I, I can't explain it all to you now and anyway, anyway, it doesn't matter. The important thing is they all got involved, each for their own reasons, of course, and the hospital workers union, too, and, well—suffice to say." He spread his hands and repeated with finality, "*Suffice . . . to . . . say.*"

Winkie waited for more, but Unwin busied himself once again with his mounds of folders, discs, and papers. The bear tugged at his sleeve.

"Mr. Winkie, the trial is about to begin, and I really . . ."

Seeing Françoise's name on one of Unwin's documents, the bear began pointing to it urgently.

"What? I just *told* you—all charges dropped. Except one, um, here, I'll show you . . ." He unearthed the morning newspaper. "Practicing medicine without a license. She pled guilty to treating your gunshot wounds. Five-hundred-dollar fine, which PETA paid. OK?"

Winkie tried to unknit his brow and brighten his eyes, as if he understood.

Unwin had already resumed straightening and restraightening his various stacks. What he didn't tell his client was that only just that morning, on the steps of the courthouse, he had refused, quite impulsively, the help of all the organizations he'd just mentioned.

"No doubt about it, I'm very nervous this morning, *very* nervous," he began muttering, "I don't know why, well, of *course* I know why, ha-ha, that's obvious, more than obvious, but so what if it's obvious, even if it's the most obvious thing in the goddamn world, I'm still nervous and I wish I wasn't, I wish, I just wish . . ."

"All rise."

Like a flock of large birds the spectators moved swiftly to their places as the judge paraded in looking even more distracted and annoyed than usual. He sat, and the ceremonial rumble of the jury and the spectators taking their own seats sounded especially ominous, the silence that followed especially full of portent. Sighing deeply and rolling his eyes, the judge said, "If Mr. Unwin will please call his first witness."

"If it please the court," interrupted the prosecutor.

The judge looked at him over his reading glasses. "Yes?"

The prosecutor stood up, and half turned to address not only the bench but the entire courtroom. "The people move that this trial be ended now and the defendant be executed immediately."

Shouts of "Yeah!"

The judge wearily began banging his gavel but the yelling only grew louder. Winkie turned to find Françoise, who gazed back at him with wide, fearful eyes. "Your—Your honor—Your—Your—" Unwin was stammering. Several men tried to rush the defense table, but the bailiffs pushed them back. Winkie pressed himself flat against his chair. "Get him!" "String him up!" "Woo!" At last one of the bailiffs shot his pistol in the air, and the yelling and whistling ceased. Dust and pieces of light fixture rained down as people took their seats again.

"I—surely you—this travesty—we must—mistrial!" Unwin cried.

As usual, the judge ignored him. "Mr. Prosecutor," he said, glancing uneasily in the direction of the press, "this is a most un-usual request . . ."

The prosecutor rose. "Your Honor, if the accused is allowed to mount a defense, he will simply take it as an opportunity to spread more of his lies or, worse, to send secret, coded messages to his network of terrorist sleeper cells!"

Unwin began stammering again and there was another cre-scendo of murmuring in the crowd.

"Hush, goddamn it," said the judge. Crack! He ran his hands over his face, trying to think.

For the judge had that morning received a certain fax. There was no return address or phone number, which meant it came from his contact in the U.S. Attorney General's office. Scrawled in thick marker, it said: "Fouad acquittal expected to result in greater press scrutiny of whole Winkie 'affair.' Must maintain appearance of justice. PS: You never received this."

But evidently the prosecution had *actually* never received it. Or was the judge's own fax a mistake? Or even a trick? Or perhaps the prosecution's request just now was intended as some kind of drama in which he, the judge, could bravely act the part of fair-ness? Certainly that would go over well at any confirmation hear-ing that might be coming up . . .

"Mr. Prosecutor, while I certainly share your concerns," he began, speaking slowly and carefully, "as well as your disgust for this defendant, I mean, for the crimes he is accused of, and while I will certainly consider stopping these proceedings at any point if I feel Mr. Winkie is using his defense merely as a mouthpiece for terrorism"—he looked sternly at the bear and was startled to see the answering rage in his face—"still, I must, by the laws of this great and gentle land, allow this trial to go forward. Mr. Unwin—" He winced at the thought of listening to this man day after day for God knew how long. "Your first witness?"

After several attempts to speak, Unwin did then manage to move once again for a mistrial, but the request was denied, and after a short recess for the judge to imbibe more of his heartburn medication, Winkie's defense began.

"Penelope Brackle!" barked the bailiff.

Mrs. Brackle was a large, round woman with orange red hair, wearing teddy bear earrings, a teddy bear watch, a plaid skirt dappled with yellow teddy bears, a sky blue blouse in a pattern of smaller bears, and a matching teddy bear tam-o'-shanter. Winkie's glass eyes widened. She seemed like some kind of wizard of toyland, cloaked in the talismans of her particular magic. Even her purse displayed a field of bears, and she wore a huge teddy bear broach, gold with two glittering ruby red stones for eyes.

Unwin asked Mrs. Brackle to please tell the court her occupation.

"Stuffed bear expert and collector," she said firmly.

The prosecution stood. "Your Honor, really . . ." He rolled his eyes and lifted his hands to heaven. "Relevance?" His favorite assistant, Number Twelve, chuckled indulgently.

"It's it's it's quite quite quite relevant," Unwin sputtered.

"Approach," said the judge, and the two lawyers went to the bench. Winkie couldn't hear what they were murmuring, only the tail end of the judge's words—"Well, if Mr. Unwin is determined to make a complete *fool* of himself, he may certainly do so with the full blessing of this court." Crack.

Winkie didn't see why an expert on teddy bears should be seen as foolish, and he scowled at the judge all the more.

"Now, Mrs. Mrs. Mrs. . . . Brackle," said Unwin. "Please list for us your credentials."

"I am a past president of the American Society of Teddy Bear Collectors and have contributed dozens of articles to *Teddy Bear Review* and other arctophile journals. Currently I publish a monthly newsletter, *Bears Anonymous*, and my own collection includes more than three thousand bears from America, England, Germany, France, and Australia."

Winkie was impressed.

"And were you, um, able to examine, um, the defendant?" Unwin asked.

"The prosecution wouldn't allow it, so I looked at the police photos that you sent, and the X-ray."

"Good. Good. Excellent." Unwin began pacing up and down. "And what did you conclude?"

She smiled broadly. "This is a very rare bear."

Unwin stopped pacing. "Rare?"

"Very rare indeed!"

Despite everything, and for the first time in more than a year, Winkie found himself feeling proud. The unfamiliar sensation almost hurt his chest.

"But the defendant *is* a teddy bear?" asked Unwin.

"Oh, yes, most definitely. Most definitely!"

Winkie basked in Mrs. Brackle's admiring glance.

"And how, um, how can you determine that?" asked Unwin, beginning to pace again.

"Everything about him says 'teddy bear,'" she answered. "Everything. Might I show you?"

Unwin stopped and turned to the judge. "May she explain using the defendant?"

Wearily the judge nodded, and one of the bailiffs lifted Winkie up and seated him again squarely on the sill of the witness box. Any embarrassment the bear might have felt was allayed by Mrs. Brackle's firm yet warm touch, which confirmed he was in the presence of a true specialist.

"As you can see, the fur is blond mohair," she said, briskly stroking his furry ears this way and that, "typical of a bear made in the first half of the twentieth century. And the stuffing," she added, giving his middle an expert but gentle squeeze, "is definitely excelsior."

"Excelsior?" asked Unwin.

"Very fine sawdust. Again, excelsior stuffing is one hundred percent teddy bear."

Winkie beamed.

"Go on, go on," said Unwin.

She moved his arms this way and that. "The limbs are jointed, another distinct teddy bear trait. He has the large ears characteristic of a British bear," she continued, tugging at them gently, "and I can see that the right one has been torn off and reattached."

Winkie shuddered to remember that day, decades ago, when Cindy the dog got ahold of him. Mrs. Brackle wasn't only a wizard but a fortune-teller.

"And and and were you able to identify the manufacturer?"

"Well," she chuckled, "that took some doing. The arms are slender and slightly curved, with long paw pads in a spoon shape, as was common with the Hugmee bears from Chiltern Toys in England. But the legs also are slender, which doesn't match the

Hugmee profile. The pads were probably felt, but the cloth is so worn that it's impossible to tell for sure, and the claws are nearly worn away as well."

No human could be more thoroughly in sympathy with what it meant to be a Winkie. Indeed, the rest of the courtroom seemed mesmerized as well by Mrs. Brackle's confident and enthusiastic expertise.

"I can feel a squeaker, or rather the remains of it, which I had noticed in the X-ray," she continued, gently probing the place on Winkie's back that once squeaked when pressed. "This places him among the many novelty bears produced during the 1920s—another clue to his provenance. But of course—" She chuckled, holding her hand to her mouth—"Of course I've forgotten to mention the most remarkable thing of all about him—I mean, truly extraordinary."

Unwin smiled. "And what is that, Mrs. Brackle?"

"Why, the eyes, of course."

She leaned forward and gently grasped the bear's shoulders. "May I?" she asked, and Winkie nodded. He had complete confidence in her. "Just relax," she said, like a very good doctor, and she tilted him backward until his two glass orbs automatically rolled shut with their distinctive click-click. Then she tilted him upright again and they clicked open.

Mrs. Brackle giggled delightedly. "Marvelous, aren't they? Just marvelous. I mean, we've all seen eyes of this sort on baby dolls—they were first introduced in 1922—the Bye-lo Baby. Her eyes closed in 'sleep,' that is, when you laid her down. Of course it's very common now, but back then it was quite an innovation—part of a whole explosion in mass-produced consumer goods for children, which has continued to this day. Anyway, I'd read accounts of Bye-lo-like eyes being incorporated into a teddy bear, but apparently very few of these bears were made, so I'd never actually *seen* one and I wasn't even convinced they actually existed—until now, of course." She sighed with great satisfaction. "May I present to you, ladies and gentlemen of the court, from the Wholesale Toy Factory in North London, patented in 1921—" She gestured grandly toward Winkie—"The Blinka Rolling-Eyed Bear."

The courtroom murmured, the press scribbled, and Winkie blinked back tears.

"Winkie, Blinka, Winkie, Blinka," he murmured. The courtroom faded, its crowd and its questions, and he seemed to float down into his own essence.

A very rare bear. Very rare indeed! But still and always a bear. Mohair. Excelsior. Extraordinary, remarkable, marvelous. Why, the eyes, of course. The bear is rare but exists. Patented in 1921. The Blinka exists.

Not a Hugmee—a Blinka. Not just a Winkie—a Winkie the Blinka. Most definitely! Winkie the Blinka. Winkie the Blinka the Rolling-Eyed Bear.

"If the court would please remove the defendant from the witness box," said the prosecutor disdainfully, and Winkie was whisked back to his seat.

"Bye-bye," Mrs. Brackle called after him.

The prosecutor turned to her and brusquely asked, "Ma'am, please tell us again your area of expertise."

"Teddy bears and toys."

"Ah. That's certainly a very important field of inquiry." The courtroom chuckled. Mrs. Brackle frowned. Winkie fumed. "And do you know anything about genetic engineering?"

"What?"

"You know—the ability to combine the genetic material from two or more species in order to create a new individual exhibiting new traits—such as large ears, or mohairlike fur? Do you know anything about that?"

"No."

Unwin half rose. "Your, Your, Honor, I fail to see the rel—the rel—"

The judge gave a single twirl of his hand.

"And are you familiar," continued the prosecutor, scarcely missing a beat, "with the many and various genetic defects and mutations, such as extreme dwarfism, hermaphroditism, and other, far more ghastly phenomena such as clothlike skin, the complete absence of internal organs, and eyeballs hard as glass?"

Mrs. Brackle adjusted her teddy bear scarf. "No."

"And have you studied chromosomal damage and other ill effects from the use of illegal drugs such as LSD, ecstasy, coke, crack, heroine, or methamphetamines?"

"No."

"Well then, how about the latest breakthroughs in plastic and reconstructive surgery and how those breakthroughs might be adapted by unscrupulous physicians for criminal purposes?"

"No."

"Ritual scarification and other appearance-altering rites?"

"No."

"And can you identify the horrible disfiguring effects of certain rare infectious agents, including and especially sexually transmitted diseases, which are all too prevalent in various remote regions of the globe?"

Mrs. Brackle's hands fluttered nervously. "Oh my, no."

"Or the horrible disfiguring effects of exposure to radiation or chemical or biological weapons—effects that can go beyond the average person's wildest imagination?"

"No."

The prosecutor sighed loudly. "Mrs. Brackle, do you have *any* scientific or medical expertise of *any* kind?"

The witness cleared her throat. "No. But I *am* most certainly an expert on teddy bears, and—"

"No further questions."

"Animism is the belief that, um, sentient spirits inhabit plants and other inanimate objects," said the next expert, a gray-haired man in a baggy gray suit who, except for his silver spectacles, looked very much like Charles Unwin and who was, in fact, Unwin's identical twin brother, Edwin. He was an assistant professor of anthropology at a nearby university.

"Tell us, um, more, Mr. Unwin," said Unwin.

Not only Winkie but the entire courtroom was amazed that there were two of them in the world. It was like watching someone conduct an interview with himself.

"*Ahem,*" said Unwin.

"*Ahem,*" said Edwin. "Animism has been called, um, the seed of religion, and is believed to originate in how we interpret our dreams."

"Our dreams?"

"As Hobbes proposed in *Leviathan*, the original notion of the soul stems from, quote, 'ignorance of how to distinguish Dreams and other strong Fancies from Vision and Sense,' unquote. Or as, as, as Edward Clodd put it in his seminal 1921 monograph, *Animism*, the so-called savage believes that, quote, 'there is within himself something which quits the body during sleep, and does the things of which he dreams.' Unquote. It follows, then, that animals have souls, and even plants and other natural objects, such as rocks or rivers."

"Why is that?"

"Well, just as the sleeper doesn't move while his dreaming self might traverse continents, so too, so too, the motionless rock or tree must contain a similar spirit fully capable of movement and will."

At these words Winkie experienced a great sense of relief, as if he had just been regranted motion and speech.

"And this belief is very ancient?" asked Charles Unwin, raising his eyebrows. "Surely no one believes it now?"

Again Winkie grew anxious.

"Yes, um, very ancient—animism is one of the oldest, if not *the* oldest, religious or, um, metaphysical system known to humankind. But its basic elements inform all religions, old and new, and, in any case, in any case, it would be wrong, terribly wrong, at least in my view, to call any religious belief, quote, primitive or, quote, outmoded. There are certainly plenty of intelligent people in the world today who believe in animism, or something like it, and not just, just so-called primitive peoples."

Winkie felt vindicated once more, but the prosecutor rose to object. "Your Honor, are we supposed to sit here and listen as this witness tells us that one religion is as good as another?"

Scattered applause in the courtroom. The judge looked disdainfully at the two Unwins, as if they were rapidly multiplying vermin. "The witness will refrain from pursuing his radical, relativist agenda in my courtroom. We are here to establish *facts*."

"Certainly, oh yes, *facts*, of course," said Charles and Edwin in flustered, sarcastic, perfect unison. Then, as one they blushed to have spoken exactly the same words, just as they used to do so often as children.

Charles shut his eyes and tried to concentrate. "So, primitive or not," he said at last, "absurd or sublime, can the notion of animism apply to man-made objects as well?"

"*Ahem.* Yes. Oh, yes. Before I was, um, interrupted, I was about to mention the Findhorn Community, founded in Sussex in the late 1950s, as a modern example of people who claim to to to have communicated with, quote, 'etheric' forms or bodies—such as the ruling spirits of carrots, broccoli, and other vegetables, whose advice they sought regarding cultivation, or the Mole King, whom they humbly requested to forbid his subjects from ravaging their garden."

Winkie wondered why so many of the spectators were giggling. Hadn't everyone seen the Mole King?

"Apparently such prayers worked quite well, by the way," Edwin continued, his chin thrust resolutely forward. "The original Findhorn garden was, by all accounts, quite extraordinary— not only did they eliminate, um, moles, but they raised fruits and vegetables of more than twice normal size, with no fertilizers, and they were able to make their flowers bloom in the middle of winter. In short, um, they did the impossible." Edwin had begun gesturing extravagantly with his hands, as if directing a symphony of ideas. "You see, the residents of Findhorn believe that spirits inhabit everything on the earth—animal, vegetable, or mineral— and that this whole host of metaphysical beings is ready and waiting to help us. It certainly is a very appealing idea. And I must say that the sincerity with which it's put forth is surprisingly, um, compelling."

Whispering, then low, derisive chuckling emitted from the prosecutor and his favorite assistant. Number Twelve then nervously replaced a stray hair in her bun, biting her lip.

"So, under such a belief system," said Charles, trying to maintain his composure, "could, for instance, a, a, a *teddy bear* also be inhabited by such a spirit?"

The prosecutor shook his head as if trying to fend off a swarm of gnats. "Your Honor, I won't even dignify this line of questioning with an objection!"

The two Unwins turned from pink to reddish purple. They could almost have been twin five-year-olds, standing their ground in the school yard. "Well then, well then, well then," Charles said, "the witness may then, then, then, go ahead and answer the question!" He faced his twin. "Mr. Unwin—please—for the record—could a Blinka Rolling-Eyed Bear be inhabited by such a spirit?"

Edwin stared defiantly at the courtroom. "I don't, I don't, I don't see why not. Findhorn's founders wrote that, quote, quote, quote, 'Machines, too, respond to human love and care,' unquote. And they were known to say thank you to their garden tools and home appliances. Which is to say, this is a philosophy of unbounded, universal kindness. And who are we to say they're, quote unquote, wrong?"

The agitated question hung in the air a moment. "Thank you," said Charles.

The judge smiled at the prosecutor, who waved his puffy, freckled hand. "I have nothing whatsoever to ask this quote unquote witness. I only request that we have no more Unwins participating in this trial. One was enough."

A wave of laughter. Opening his mouth to speak, but not speaking, Edwin stepped down, while Charles, too, opened his mouth in vain. Yet something inside Winkie was vibrating as gloriously as a bell. First his body had been affirmed today, and now his soul. He wanted to ponder the day's testimony for a long time, and he actually looked forward to getting back to his cell tonight, when he hoped he could repeat it all back to himself as Darryl quietly colored . . .

But just then his lawyer barked, "The defense calls, um, um— Clifford Chase!"

* * *

Winkie's eyes widened and he began tugging Unwin's sleeve in disbelief. He shook his head vigorously, no!

But really the bear was caught between yes and no—between the unbidden, headlong joy at the thought of seeing Cliff again, and the equally unbidden slap of this boy's betrayal, so long ago but suddenly as fresh as the instant.

"Now, now, now, Mr. Winkie," said Unwin, casting a nervous glance toward the judge, "I can see that you don't like this, but as we, as we, as we discussed, this is the only witness who has come forward who, who, who—"

In fact, Unwin had so often imagined discussing Clifford Chase with his client that he had neglected actually to mention him or his offer to testify. If Winkie had been better prepared, his affection for this figure from the past might have at least tempered his bad memories. As it was, the various injustices he'd suffered under this boy and his whole family seemed to merge now with the wrongs he'd both suffered and seen over the past year and a half, starting with the abduction of his child . . . So that today as Chase came down the aisle, Winkie saw not a friendly witness but something more like one of his persecutors. Ignoring Unwin's whispered arguments to the contrary, the bear folded his paws tightly and slumped back in his chair, so that his eyes barely came above the defense table.

Meanwhile Chase, a thin, sandy-haired man in his forties, was being sworn in. ". . . the truth, the whole truth and nothing but the truth, so help me God." As he sat down, he glanced expectantly toward Winkie, but the bear stared ahead in fury at Unwin's books and papers.

The defense attorney asked the witness to state his relationship to the accused, and thus the questioning proceeded. As Unwin had meant to tell his client, Chase was one of only a handful of people who could attest to the bear's previous life as a stuffed animal. The prosecution had been able, without much trouble, to exclude the testimony of Ruth Chase and other family members as irrelevant and/or prejudicial. But Unwin had urged the youngest son to be in court today anyway, just in case, and much to the lawyer's surprise, the people did not object to his being called. (In fact, the judge and the prosecutor had conferred during the morning recess, agreeing that such a concession would make a favorable impression on the media—with minimal harm to the people's case.)

Under Unwin's halting questioning—and despite the defendant's obvious dismay—Chase was reasonably persuasive, bolstering the defense claim that Winkie was most certainly a toy, not a terrorist, and accounting for his whereabouts from Christmas 1925 up until about a year before the bear's arrest, when he disappeared from the home of Ruth and David Chase. "We assumed then that Winkie, I mean Mr. Winkie, the defendant, had been misplaced," Chase recalled. "My mother said, 'Oh, he'll turn up.' But he never did, and now of course it's clear that he ran off. My mother discovered a broken window at about the same time she noticed that Mr. Winkie was missing, and in retrospect it seems likely that that was how he escaped."

"Objection. Speculation."

"Sustained. The witness will stick to facts and refrain from drawing conclusions." Crack.

Unwin rolled his eyes and resumed:

"Mr. Chase, to your knowledge—to your *knowledge*—had the defendant gone missing at any other time before then?"

"No."

"And that, that, that would include the ten years beginning in 1993?"

"Yes."

"So, so, so, during a period when Mr. Winkie is accused of con-structing and mailing, um, three hundred forty-seven letter bombs, he was, to your knowledge, actually where?"

"At my parents' house, on a shelf in my old bedroom, by the window."

"And what was he doing there?"

"He was sitting—motionless."

On this and other key points, Chase spoke softly yet firmly and, by all accounts, made a decent impression on the jury. However, as the prosecution no doubt had expected, his credibility suffered badly on cross-examination.

Paging through documents, evidently medical records, the prosecutor asked, "Mr. Chase, are you depressed?"

Chase nervously pushed his glasses up his nose. "Not particu-larly. Not at the moment."

"Because you take medication for this condition? In fact, more than one medication?"

"Yes."

"So you suffer from a mental illness?"

Unwin began to object but the judge barked, "The witness will answer."

"Yes," said Chase. "I guess so."

"You guess so." The prosecutor brought his fingers to both temples, as if trying to decide what to ask such a witness next. "OK, well then, let's just suppose—" (Waving his arms crazily) "for the sake of argument, just for the sake of argument—that Mr. Winkie, the defendant, is indeed the same person as the Winkie you knew and loved as a child. Let's just suppose." (Shrugging) "How do you conclude that he's a good bear? Did he ever talk to you?"

"Well, but—"

"Mr. Chase, please. Answer the question. Did he ever talk to you? Did he ever say, for example, 'I am a very good bear'?"

(Sadly) "No."

"Well then, perhaps there were acts of goodness or courage on his part that you witnessed? Perhaps he rescued you, or some other child, from a burning building?"

From behind the curtain, the jury chuckled.

"No . . . But he often let me hug him. And he listened to me."

"Ah, he listened. And how do you know that? Did he nod his head? Did he repeat back to you what you had just said? Did he perhaps speak appropriate words of comfort, or give you advice?"

"Well, of course not."

"Of course not. Exactly. Of course not. In fact, you never saw him do, or say, anything at all, did you, Mr. Chase?"

". . ."

"I'll take that as a no." (Theatrical sigh) "So, I must ask you again, Mr. Chase, how do you know he's a good bear?"

"Um. By the way he looked at me."

All eyes turned now to the defendant, who sat there scowling, his pupils crooked and wild above a snout mended with coarse thread to a shapeless nub, his face worn nearly furless except for the ragged, uncombed bits on his too-huge ears. Laughter rippled through the courtroom.

"I see what you mean, Mr. Chase."

More laughter. "Defendant looks *terrible,*" whispered a helpful bailiff to the jury, not wanting them to miss the joke. Unwin objected but the prosecutor simply retracted his last statement. "Proceed," said the judge.

"You were about to say something, Mr. Chase? Don't let me interrupt."

"I didn't care how he looked . . . I loved him anyway. I was a child, and he was mine."

At this the bear himself shifted fully sideways in his chair, sighing forcefully, folding his arms again in silent, angry protest.

"In fact, whether he was once your toy, as you believe, or he wasn't, as so many other witnesses maintain, you know nothing at all about the defendant, do you?"

Chase hung his head and didn't answer. The prosecutor smiled to himself.

"No further questions."

By most accounts, the day's testimony did little to sway the jury toward acquittal and may even have bolstered the prosecution's case. Yet somehow, in his busy fog of self-doubt, and certainly without realizing it, Unwin had intuited something of far deeper importance while devising his defense strategy—not what might persuade the jury but, rather, what the little bear himself needed to hear. For despite the shock and pain of Cliff's testimony, Winkie left the courtroom that day a different creature.

At first it scarcely seemed so to him. As the police van sped away and the shouts of the courthouse receded, the day's events came back to Winkie in a jumble—Françoise's smile . . . "I present to you: the Blinka Rolling-Eyed Bear" . . . "Machines, too, respond to human love and care" . . . "He was a strange bear, but I think he was a good bear, and I still believe that" . . . "In fact . . . you know nothing at all about the defendant, do you?" ". . ." But though that final exchange had seemed so upsetting at the time, so utterly unwelcome to his mangy ears, it now appeared strangely equal to all the others. It wasn't that he forgave Cliff (that was for Cliff to do or not do) but that his time with Cliff was simply another fact of his existence. The notion was vast, yet light and ineffable as a feather. Rumbling along in the darkness, the bear lost himself in puzzling over it . . .

Suddenly the doors of the van were flung open, and Winkie beheld with the freshness of a dream the familiar floodlit entrance of the jail, Deputy Walter in silhouette against the blue-green, rapidly stuttering light, motioning for him to descend. It wasn't in any way a good moment, yet Winkie let it be absolutely clear to him. Click-click. That was when he decided, without really knowing why, yet knowing definitely: The next morning he would tell Unwin that he had changed his mind: He would testify, after all.

2.

"Good night, Mr. Bear," said Darryl in his flat way, handing him a torn-out page showing a rose, whose many petals he had carefully colored red, orange, pink, and purple, with black leaves. Darryl had never given Winkie anything before, nor had the bear noticed any flowers in his coloring books, but here was one, and it was a present just for him. "Thank you," Winkie said, sniffing the picture, pretending the crayon smell was like roses. He laid the page fondly next to his pillow, pulled the scratchy blanket to his chin, and, for the first time in more than a year, fell immediately into a deep sleep.

He looked out to sea and spied in the distance a gray rat with its long pinkish rat tail running gingerly along the waves—a feat that the little animal achieved, Winkie saw, not by faith but by rapidly wiggling its vile rasp of a tail on the surface of the water. He wondered how this worked and how long the little rodent could keep it up. Was this some new kind of rat with new abilities, or was it just a regular rat who tried too hard? Soon the gray furry thing made it to a small outcropping in the middle of the flat sea. It was a bird then. The dream noticed no transformation, sudden or gradual: The rat was simply a bird, as if it had always been one—black with a clean, white head, a seabird.

Meanwhile the dream had become a nature show, whose narrator sonorously announced, "Now he can fly off." And indeed to Winkie's relief the seabird pushed off from the rock—the hard surface it had needed all along—and silently took wing. The bear woke.

The cell's white walls remained unchanged, and the peace of sleep seemed utterly lost. Though the bird part might have been encouraging, Winkie felt only revulsion for the rest of the dream. He wanted nothing to do with that rat skittering across the water. Why dream such a thing—and today of all days, the day he was to testify? It was disgusting, and by dreaming it he was only burrowing further into his own disgust and despair. Miserable and alone, Winkie sniffed the antiseptic walls of the jail, and he thought of the angry faces shouting at him day after day both inside and outside the courthouse: "Shame!" Suddenly it didn't seem to matter what Penelope Brackle or Edwin Unwin or anyone might say about him. He, Winkie, was nothing more than a disgusting rat that made use of its long rat tail in a disgusting and perplexing miracle of self-levitation. Such a creature could never be classified, nor its means of locomotion. It could never be understood by anyone, least of all itself, and so it had tried to hide its true nature by turning into a lovely seabird. But Winkie knew all along what the creature really was. He couldn't help knowing it.

"Ick," he said, which made him think of Cliff. It was strange yesterday to see him not just grown up but middle-aged and yet to find that his own sentiments toward this person were exactly the same as they had been that fateful day in the hurricane forty years ago.

The self-loathing, too, was exactly the same. "Ick, ick, ick." He didn't see how he'd ever overcome that pall on his soul—how he'd managed to blink and throw the book and climb through the window and jump to the lawn and on and on until his most recent resolve, just last night in the van, to testify on his own behalf.

"I am my own bear," he tried to tell himself.

Never since he'd come to life had Winkie gone back on any decision, nor would he now; he would carry out his intention just as he had promised himself last night—but he was wrenched by doubt. It was in this state that the bear tugged on Unwin's jacket that morning and, still finding his mouth unwilling to make even a sound, fell back on old ways and pantomimed his wish to testify. To his oath, too, Winkie could only nod, and then reluctantly he climbed onto the chair in the witness box and waited, with the utmost anxiety, for his lawyer's first question.

The bear's sudden change of heart had taken Unwin by surprise, and he hadn't prepared more than a rough mental list of the questions he would need to ask. But there were no other witnesses to call, his stammered pleas for even a brief recess were denied, and so it was now or never. Unwin took a deep breath, closed his eyes, and tried to enter the trancelike state that he seemed to require in order to interview his client with any success.

"Was it a gradual accumulation like snow," he began, "which all at once breaks a branch and comes crashing down, or was it more like a lightning bolt, Mr. Winkie, that made you decide to tell your story today?"

Glancing nervously at all the eyes fixed on him, Winkie swallowed and pointed to his left.

"Snow that breaks a branch. Good," said Unwin. "And was the accumulation a gradual realization of who you are and what formed you, for better or worse, or was it a slow understanding of the need to fight for your freedom?"

Winkie almost began to think this wouldn't be so difficult after all. He pointed to his left and then his right.

"Both. Good." Unwin breathed in and out slowly. "And when you make such a decision, does the moving forward feel like trudging through hot, dry sand or like crossing a busy street in brilliant sunshine?"

Winkie shrugged.

"Sometimes trudging, sometimes—"

"Your Honor," cried the prosecutor, holding his head in his hands as if in pain, "this is the *strangest* line of questioning I have ever heard in any courtroom anywhere."

Up to this point the spectators had been fascinated simply to see the little bear sitting in the witness box and had listened with unusual attention. But the objection brought a ripple of chuckles.

"Well, well, I, I certainly," Unwin said, "certainly don't, don't, don't think quote unquote *strange* is grounds for, for, um—"

"Sustained." Crack. "Mr. Unwin will please stop leading the witness."

The defense attorney looked like he was about to cry but shut his eyes again and took several more deep breaths, which Winkie in his own nervousness mimicked. Sigh, sigh, sigh . . .

"Your Honor, is this witness going to testify or not?" asked the prosecutor.

Crack!

Both Winkie and Unwin jumped.

"Mr. Unwin," barked the judge, "if your client does not provide this court with his own testimony—not ridiculous phrases put into his mouth by his so-called *attorney*—I will hold both of you in contempt and this trial will be ended at once!"

Murmurs of approval throughout the courtoom. Winkie shuddered.

"Certainly, certainly," Unwin stammered, shaking back his gray bangs with several violent jerks of the head. "Mr. Winkie," he began, trying to resume slowly and calmly, but speeding up immediately, "um, please explain to the court, in your own words, as the judge has asked, explain to everyone gathered here, that is, to the judge and the prosecutor and the jury sitting behind that curtain there, that is, to the best of your ability, that is to say, please explain the events leading up to your, um, unfortunate arrest and incarceration, which was more than a year ago now, please, thank you."

Winkie wished now that he had practiced conversing, at least a little, during his time in jail. He had never spoken to anyone in his whole life except Baby Winkie, yet now he was expected to bring forth answers and explanations in front of a sea of strangers. He tried to decipher Unwin's question, but as soon as he had, fact after fact began flooding in from the past, all in a jumble, so that he couldn't even list them all to himself, let alone choose among them. Even the soft scratching sound of the courtroom artist seemed deafening.

"Just start at the beginning," Unwin prompted, as gently as he could, but sounding as impatient as ever. "And think carefully."

Winkie compressed his brow, trying to simplify the torrent in his head. Several minutes went by. Then, with a hopeful face, he tried: "A E I O U."

Though the sounds had felt strange in his throat, it had seemed like a good answer. But Winkie saw the prosecutor exchange smirks with his favorite assistant and several in the press area shake their heads. Unwin rubbed his eyes so feverishly that the bear thought they might pop out of their sockets. "OK, um, let's try again," the

Even the soft scratching sound of the courtroom artist seemed deafening.

Houlihan's
Hartsfield-Jackson Airport Atr
Atlanta, GA

1109 Cecila C

Tbl 709/1   Chk 366   Gst 1
              Sep14'10 04:30PM

**** Seat 1 ****
    1 Woodbr. Caber.   6.70
    1 GorgonzolaBurger   10.89
    1 Add Caesar   3.89
Tax   1.50 Total   22.98
              ***** All *****

    Subtotal   21.48
    Tax   1.50
05:10PM Total   22.98

Gratuity Not Included.

Thank you for visiting us
and please come again
www.cintl.com   1-866-203-5480
Customer Comments?

lawyer said, sighing. "OK. Mr. Winkie, please explain to the court, in your own words, to everyone gathered here . . ."

Hearing the question repeated, virtually word for word, wasn't very helpful, especially not in that tone of voice. But Winkie tried to put the right expression of certitude on his face, concentrated, and boldly said: "If, but, why, surely, notwithstanding, so."

Unwin sighed loudly. "So, so, so—what? *What?*"

The bear blinked at his tone but was determined to answer more quickly this time. "And so it was, and so it happened, and so it came to pass," he asserted. "Therefore I say unto you."

Surely this was irrefutable, Winkie thought, but Unwin asked, "'I say unto you' *what?* What came to pass?"

Winkie concentrated again. His mouth was just forming the *L* of *Light* when the prosecutor cried out, "Your Honor!" He held up his plump palms in a grand shrug.

"I quite agree," said the judge. Crack! "Mr. Unwin, I say unto you again that if your client doesn't start making sense, it shall come to pass that—" Crack! Crack! Crack!

The courtroom's guffaws seemed strangely distant to the bear as he turned from the scowling judge to the grinning prosecutor to the blushing, sputtering Unwin. Feeling especially small and friendless, Winkie blurted out, "Once upon a time there was a bear!"

The laughter ceased and all eyes turned to him.

"Good!" said Unwin, less irritably, and he began making rolling gestures with both hands. "Please! Please, go on!"

But this confused the bear more than ever. Once again he thought he'd finished with the question, but Unwin continued looking at him, imploringly, his hands slowing to a halt in the air. Winkie lifted his own paws in a shrug, jingling his chains. "The End," he tried.

There was more tittering and Unwin began rubbing his eyes again. "No," he moaned. "No . . ."

Winkie glared at him. "Objects. Food. Rooms," he said defiantly. "Dust and shame and unending boredom. And so the old bear struck out for a new world!"

Unwin perked up a little. "Keep going. What do you mean by a 'new world'?"

Winkie frowned and rolled his eyes. Why did he even bother? A new world was a new world. What else could you say about it? Yet he knew he had to try. "What the bear wanted. What the bear did," he answered. "What the bear saw and ate and understood."

He never knew what might interest Unwin, and now the lawyer's restless blue eyes slowed and settled on Winkie in genuine curiosity. He didn't seem to know what to ask next, yet he didn't seem to mind, either, and in that moment of calm the bear suddenly had a new inkling of what he wanted to say. The courtroom was quiet as he closed his eyes and spoke into the darkness. "By and by it came to pass that a little bear went to wander the world. Bushes bloomed and berried, while light came down and went back up again. He had a baby." Winkie panted a few breaths to rest, for speaking like this was nearly as difficult as giving birth. "There were two little bears then, large and small. They didn't know why, but each day cloth and stuffing looked and found its own. The trees breathed and hundreds of clouds went by, even when they slept. Rain or snow came down in lines or sometimes swirls, just to please them. The afternoons grew. Songs were sung. Then the big mean Blob-Man came yelling, and stole the baby away." Winkie held back tears. "Once upon a time there was a sad and lonely bear. He lived in a hovel. 'Come out with your hands up!' Tingle and noise, bright and quiver. The bear fell slowly down." Winkie rubbed sniffle from his nose and tried to concentrate again. "There once was a sad bear all alone. He lived in a cage, and he remembered everything. The End."

* * *

There were a few confused titters, but otherwise no one made a sound. The spectators might have been surprised by their own sympathy, but it didn't seem to stop them from listening.

"And who is that bear?" asked Unwin, gentle-voiced again.

What a stupid question, Winkie thought, it couldn't be more obvious—and yet, thinking of the answer made him want to cry again. Why should that be?

"Me," he said at last.

Unwin paused a moment before asking, "Can you tell us about your child?"

"I . . . ," Winkie began, and this word, too, seemed to wound him. But he knew with the wisdom of all his experiences that he had to keep going, no matter how much it hurt. "I turned to look and her eyes looked back," he continued. "It was Baby Winkie: her eyes, her fur, her ears, and again her eyes. They looked back at me."

Again there was silence.

"And who is the 'Blob-Man'?" Unwin quietly asked.

"The one who stole Baby Winkie!" the bear cried, wondering how his lawyer could have missed this point, too.

"I know—I mean, was this the man?" Unwin asked, returning from the defense table with a photograph of the old hermit. "Him?"

Winkie startled backward at the sight of that awful face, as if the photograph itself could harm him. "Yes," he said, nodding, and quickly handed the picture back.

"Let it be stipulated that the witness has identified this photograph of—"

"Of a GREAT AMERICAN HERO, murdered in COLD BLOOD by the DEFENDANT!" yelled the prosecutor. "Your Honor, this is an OUTRAGE. You cannot permit this SLAN-DER to continue!"

It was indeed a risky topic for Unwin to have taken on. Several members of the press were yelling, "Here! Here!" for they had never referred to the hermit as anything other than "the kindly old man of the forest." Six different books by that title would be arriving in supermarkets and bookstores soon, and polls showed that the public felt even more positively about the old hermit than they felt negatively about Winkie—yet Unwin pressed on.

"I submit that not only is the hermit a kidnapper," he shouted, "but nothing less than the mad bomber himself!"

In a trial marked by repeated disturbances, the mayhem that followed this assertion was surely the worst. "Christ, not again," muttered one of the bailiffs. With his billy club he pushed back a phalanx of journalists trying to rush the defendant. Unwin ducked and the prosecutor swung. Eggs and tomatoes whizzed by in every direction. Even Françoise and Mariana were wrestling with a uniformed policeman, while the lights flickered and the judge cried, "Order!" again and again. Winkie cowered at the back of the witness box, and as the noise crescendoed to a steady roar, he was about to start bellowing, "*Heenh! Heenh! Heenh*"—he could already hear the primal cries echoing in his head—but instead, much to his surprise, his back straightened and his mouth began speaking loudly and deliberately, as if to the wind and rain from high atop a promontory:

"Not so long ago I came to life. Maybe my inmost soul knows how, but I don't. I was watered by love, and eventually I sprouted.

For years, children had looked into my eyes. For years I was hugged, carried, dragged around. Wishes were everywhere. My own took their place in that deep, sparkly ocean. And when one by one the children and their wishes had all ebbed away, yet my own remained: Then I came to life. Why, why, why? Am I my own? The miracle is bigger than me, I know, but the loneliness feels even bigger."

Unwin and the prosecutor, a wrestling ball, tumbled past the witness stand. The bailiffs beat at the screaming crowd. But the more Winkie spoke, the calmer he became.

"My wish now is to be free again. I ask for it—I don't even know why. There's no point, you'll just say no, but if only I could be let out into the world, my story might begin again, and there could be more wishing for me and also more to give. People have always loved me. Why? So many times and worst of all when I lost my child, my eyes wanted to click shut forever—yet somehow I still had love to give, and always have. Why, why, why? Despite it all. Why was I created, and why do I love? What is it about me that survives? Despite it all, despite it all: It's my heart: I can't help it."

As Winkie paused to think a moment, a stray reporter lunged toward him with gnarled hands ready to strangle, but Deputy Walter tackled him. They struggled on the floor. And in the wild, lolling hatred of his attacker's eyes, Winkie suddenly understood the dream he'd had that morning, and he wanted to shout it to the world.

"A rat coasts on water," he said. "Small waves, the rat's wake and the horizon gleaming. The hated thing even hates itself but skims along the small waves anyway. Rat turns to bird, but really it's both, and always was and always will be. So.

"The flat sea and luminous sky. Light folds in on itself, out again, glittery shards fall together, with small clicks, to make the next thing you see. Even for a hated thing, light unfolds again, breaks, little waves break and seem to speak, the circle of jeweled light folds and unfolds again, and eyes click shut on tears: Could a rat-bird go free?"

Winkie sighed. "In the dream and in remembrance of the dream, inside and outside, a hated thing might be let go, might fly off, might weep, and then the wider world could unfold again in small clicks, beautiful shard-clicks, eye-clicks—a flower opening, and a bear dives in, listens, sniffs, and in sniffing, looking, and hearing, dives in—the rose in the coloring book, the rose of the world and of hope. A beloved thing. Eyes open click upon click, first dark, then light, like gliding through an archway into sunshine: This is, and always has been, the life I was given. Thank you."

Winkie opened his eyes again to behold the raging courtroom and was amazed to see one person as still and calm as himself. It was someone who had always scowled and smirked at him, but now she stood in the front row just staring, lost in thought, while others exchanged blows on either side of her.

It was the prosecutor's favorite assistant, Number Twelve, and she had heard every word that Winkie had said. For despite every fact and argument that her boss had so vehemently put forth against the bear, she had allowed herself to wonder, on occasion, if the hated defendant might not be so guilty after all (just as she sometimes wondered if the prosecutor really loved her and, over the past few weeks, if he was seeing someone else). Her special friend had tolerated no doubts about the case among his staff, whose loyalty was legendary, and she herself had agreed whole-heartedly, not only in the office but also many times in their hotel room, that a criminal as terrible as Winkie must be vanquished by whatever means necessary. But today, hearing the little bear speak for the first time, this sensitive young woman who had never challenged any authority was thrown first into terrible confusion and then, just as Winkie had fallen silent, into the sudden rapture of a new and surprising clarity: She no longer just doubted the bear's guilt; rather, she was convinced of his innocence—and, more important, of the need for her to act, even if it meant losing everything.

"Rat-bird," she repeated, thinking of both the defendant and herself. "Despite it all." She was strangely at peace, yet full of questions. "Why must I stand alone? Is every choice an act of grief? Is every life a story and every story one of survival? Doesn't that prove there's hope for anyone? And how might this be verified?" She scarcely noticed the brawl that continued full tilt all around her but saw now that Winkie himself was looking at her, with sad, questioning eyes. They held an uncanny pathos for her, those shiny brown glass orbs—something pure and unmediated—and she marveled that she hadn't seen it until now. She remembered herself as a child, holding her dolly in the darkness and pondering the infinite. She seemed almost to be dreaming, and dreamily she asked herself, "What if you give a point of view to something that can't have one?"

3.

When at last the yelling had died down and everyone had brushed the egg and tomato bits from their shoulders and taken their seats again, Number Twelve remained standing, her bun half-askew from an altercation that had passed near her. The judge looked at her with twinkly curiosity, wondering with some pleasure if something was up between her and the prosecutor. Number Eleven tried to pull her back down into her chair, but she shook him off.

"Your Honor," she said, her voice weak yet eerily penetrating, "it is my solemn duty to report the suppression of key evidence in this case—by the office of the prosecution."

Unwin and the press snapped to attention. Assistants One through Eleven gasped. The prosecutor gazed at Twelve for a long moment of amazement, as if she had just turned into, say, a giant salamander. Then he said to her, quietly but commandingly, in the manner that he always used with her in private: "Judy, sit down."

She began to cry but stood her ground.

The judge had no time to enjoy the prosecutor's shock, for his mind was busy trying to decide what was expected of him. Had some kind of warning, or instructions, not reached him this morning? Fax machines could be so unreliable; sometimes they ran out of paper and you didn't notice . . . "This is a very serious charge for a young lady to be making," he ventured.

Judy wiped the tears from one cheek. "I know," she said.

"And it seems to have *upset* you," the judge added.

"Yes, she's very, very, very upset," put in the prosecutor. "In fact, she's gone completely mad. We worried this might happen—the stress of the trial, you see."

The other assistants nodded as one, but Judy was steadfast. The judge fidgeted, wondering what tack to try next, while Unwin, as baffled as everyone else, refrained from speaking just yet. Assistant Number Three handed the prosecutor a slip of paper, from which he began to read:

"Your Honor, given the unusual volume of evidence involved in this case, it wouldn't be impossible that some materials, materials of no consequence, of course, of no consequence whatsoever, could have been *lost* or *overlooked* by this office, but certainly I welcome the opportunity to correct the error, if indeed there was one, and . . ." He flipped over the paper, found nothing, and began gesturing angrily at Number Three.

"It wasn't an error," said Judy. "It was deliberate."

Shock and murmuring.

Unwin moved for dismissal but was predictably overruled. A large truckload of additional evidence was turned over that very afternoon, and the defense was given until the next morning to sift through it all. Françoise and Mariana went over to Unwin's office to help, where the boxes overflowed into the building's lobby and out into the parking lot. It was past three in the morning before Mariana discovered the most important body of evidence, that is, seventeen boxes containing the entire contents of the hermit's cabin—including dozens of notebooks and videotapes in which the madman boasted of sending mail bombs to dozens of his enemies across the country and, furthermore, admitted kidnapping the strange, mesmerizing creature called Baby Winkie.

These materials exonerated the bear completely, of course, but the judge received instructions to let the trial continue. It did so for another three weeks, as Unwin played every videotape and read each notebook aloud for the jury's benefit. Judy had been fired and was being investigated herself for obstruction of justice. The prosecutor maintained his firm belief in Winkie's guilt, calling the new evidence nothing more than a blip, but op-ed pieces began to appear, here and there, in cautious support of the defendant. The Free Winkie Campaign, founded by two students of Edwin Unwin, took fire and spread to other college campuses. Their colorful signs and banners soon outnumbered those of the anti-Winkie forces gathered outside the courthouse. Still, as the trial neared its close, the outcome was far from clear.

The prosecution's closing argument was brief and effective:

"Ladies and gentlemen of the jury, your duty is clear, and your choice is simple. For what hangs in the balance here today is nothing less than the American Way of Life." He looked up at the ceiling, apparently blinking back tears. Many in the press section were also visibly moved. They held up their tape recorders with one hand and dabbed at their eyes with the other. "Therefore," the prosecutor continued at last, "I say to you now: If there is a chance—even the *slightest chance*—that this defendant is guilty of *even one* of these terrible crimes, then you *must* convict him. For in doing so, you will surely *save lives*. Thank you."

From somewhere in the jury box came the sound of quiet whimpering.

"And what if he's guilty of other crimes!" shouted someone from the back of the courtroom. It was the chief detective, who after months of silence could bear no more. "Crimes of which we have, as yet, no knowledge! Crimes that could be even worse than what he's accused of now! Crimes he could have done countless times!" Two bailiffs began dragging him to the exit. "Will all of you simply stand by and *do nothing*? Could you *live* with yourselves? Could you look your *children* in the eye?" As he was yanked through the door, the chief saw the judge frowning and wagging an index finger at him, in discreet warning. "You and your damn faxes!" the FBI man shouted back, just as the double doors were closing. "If you're not careful, that Satan-midget will go free!—"

The judge rubbed his forehead and tried to compose himself. What could he have meant by 'faxes'? he practiced saying, in his

head, to an imaginary investigator. He cleared his throat and tried
to look stern. "Mr. Unwin? Your closing argument. Please!"

"Your Honor, for reasons that are, um, obvious, once again I
must ask for a mistrial."

The judge touched his ears as if in pain. "Not that *word* again.
Mr. Unwin, the jury didn't even hear him."

The defense attorney sputtered his astonishment at this
assertion.

"Oh, all right, I'll fix it." The judge faced the curtain and spoke
in a rapid monotone: "The-jury-will-please-disregard-that-
unfortunate-outburst-from-a-law-enforcement-officer-which-has-
been-stricken-from-the-record-thank-you." He sighed and turned
back to Unwin. "Proceed."

Now, Unwin had always had the greatest difficulty with closing arguments. In fact, as he had confessed to Winkie that same
morning, nothing in the world made him more nervous, and none
of his recent triumphs in this case seemed to make any difference.
If anything, his anxiety was worse than usual. He took several deep
breaths. Once again the crucial moment had come, and though
he tried and tried, he simply could not compose himself.

"Ladies and, um, gentlemen of the, the, the, the," Unwin said.
"This is, is, is, is—is not— This case is not, is not, is not about—"
He began shuffling through his notes. "My client, Mr. Winkie, is,
is, is, is, is, is, is, is . . ."

Françoise and Mariana stared at their shoes. Winkie watched
Unwin's whole body shift one way and then another, as he passed
from one stutter to the next. "When, when, when—if, if, if—
surely, surely, surely . . ." But though the bear knew his future was
at stake, he couldn't help but feel that these syllables made a rare
kind of sense, that his lawyer was speaking a truth about him that

no other utterance could have. It wasn't to be deciphered or interpreted; it was as simple and straightforward as birdsong. "We are here today, we are here, we are, we—" The bear leaned forward, as if toward a warbling shadow in a bush. He didn't want to miss a note.

The rest of the courtroom, however, was growing ever more agitated. Many would call the Winkie closing one of the most painful performances in the history of the legal profession. After more than twenty minutes, Unwin managed at last to speak just one complete sentence: "My, my, my client, surely then, surely, surely then, is, um, um, innocent—innocent!"

At that, the judge banged his gavel once and quickly said, "Thank you, counsel."

Unwin seemed to shake himself from a nightmare. "What?—"

"Thank you," the judge firmly repeated. He looked around the rest of the courtroom, which gazed back at him with grateful relief. "All right, then, if there isn't anything else, we'll proceed to final instructions for the jury."

"No, but I—I—"

Crack!

4.

The police van came to a halt, and the doors burst open: sunlight, flashbulbs, a wall of bodies screaming behind the barricade. "Free Winkie!" they yelled. "Kill Winkie!" they yelled.

The jury had deliberated more than two weeks. Past the cameras and the mob the little bear was led up the too-bright steps, down the dim hallway, and into the windowless anteroom where they always had to wait until the judge was ready.

The little room was an oval but otherwise perfectly nondescript—white walls, Formica table, metal chairs with black vinyl cushions. Here it was utterly silent, and neither Deputy Walter nor Agents Mike and Mary Sue nor the bailiffs spoke a word. Even Charles Unwin sat in complete silence, chewing his nails. The hemmed-in air was neither warm nor cool. Winkie's shackles cut his ankles but he didn't bother to twitch. He stared ahead. He didn't know how long it would be before the judge and the jury were ready for him.

He tried to think good thoughts. He hadn't known that his life would come down to this—a quest for hope. Long ago, on that fateful afternoon when Baby Winkie was born, it had seemed to the bear that at last he'd found hope forever. Now it appeared to be his quest forever.

One of the guards cleared his throat, and the small purgatorial room was quiet again. Winkie seemed to see hope flickering before him then, like a big, bright coin spinning in the blank, oval space between the walls—the ghost of a coin, turning slowly, appearing and disappearing in the air a few feet in front of his eyes. If it turned sideways, you couldn't see it; or like the moon you saw half of it, or a quarter, a sliver, whatever, or even all of it, briefly, round and golden. And the dazed air in which that spirit-coin spun was palpable as fog; hope hid in these particles or showed itself, turning, flickering; and that bright, elusive shape seemed to make the air the air, the room the room, the moment the moment. Winkie watched. As in a dream, there had to be a rule, and the rule in this case was that you couldn't reach out and touch the hope before you, no more than Lot could look back. Not that the bear even had a choice. Hope spun; Winkie watched it. It shown between the particles of the present, or it didn't; he simply watched it.

"Ladies and gentlemen of the jury, in the matter of the People versus Winkie, have you reached a verdict?"

Even the question seemed to hang in the air a moment. Winkie gazed at the blue curtain puckering slightly in a draft.

"No, Your Honor."

The bear drew his chin back in surprise, and the courtroom began chattering wildly. The judge banged his gavel until silence reigned again.

"Am I to understand that you are hopelessly deadlocked?" he asked.

"Yes, Your Honor." The voice could have been male or it could have been female; Winkie couldn't tell. "We have been unable to reach a verdict."

The judge looked very annoyed. "On all nine thousand six hundred seventy-eight counts?"

There was the brief sound of papers shuffling. "Nine thousand six hundred and seventy-eight. Yes."

The judge sighed. "So be it!" Crack! Crack!

The gavel rang with its usual finality, as if the bear's fate would never be decided. A young reporter ran out of the courtroom yelling, "Hung jury!" Everyone began talking at once. Winkie was still trying to understand what had happened when Unwin lifted him from his seat. "We did it!" he cried, hugging him tightly. "I, I, I can't believe it! Congratulations, Mr. Winkie!"

The bear felt his lawyer's tears of joy plopping on the top of his head. He hardly dared ask, but he had to know for sure. "I'm . . . free?"

Unwin pulled back. "Um, not exactly . . . " He laughed in embarrassment and set the bear down again. "But, but, but—well—well . . ."

Winkie turned to find Françoise and Mariana in the crowd, but they looked almost as confused as he was. Françoise waved and tried to smile. Others were jeering at him; maybe they always would.

"Order!" the judge was shouting, as usual. Gavel, gavel, gavel. "Mr. Prosecutor—will the people be seeking a new trial?"

Winkie's ears stiffened with alarm. He began tugging Unwin's sleeve, but the lawyer was shaking someone's hand and paid no attention. At length the courtroom settled down and the judge repeated his question.

"We *most certainly* request a new trial!" came the prosecutor's resounding reply. "And we request that the defendant remain in custody, *without bail!*"

Winkie—revolutionary of family life and of the very laws of nature and narrative—was not yet free. The bear gulped, Unwin stammered his protest, and the wrangling began all over again.

A Teddy Bear
in the World

Winkie wandered through the vast marketplace, taking in the extraordinary sights—camels, limousines, donkey carts filled with beat-up furniture, baskets of spices, bins of cassette tapes, women carrying huge trays of freshly baked pita atop their veiled heads. Amid such bustle and variety, no one even noticed—or no one cared—that Winkie wasn't a man but an old, stuffed bear.

This was fortunate, because he wasn't supposed to be here. Though he'd been granted bail after all, and the Free Winkie Committee had gladly paid it, Winkie still wasn't allowed to leave the United States. So Françoise took him along to Cairo in her carry-on bag. She was here visiting her mother, who had had a minor stroke.

Winkie wore a sky blue caftan and a small, maroon fez perched between his ears. Though Françoise spent mornings with her mother at the hospital, her afternoons were free, and she walked alongside the bear now in a flowered headscarf, speaking with animation, gesturing in chopping motions with her long, brown hands.

"It is a mere contrivance for tourists," she said. She was talking about the weekly performance by the whirling dervishes at the ancient mausoleum. "It is totally, totally fake."

Winkie liked how Françoise said the ts in "to-tal-ly," her accent having grown stronger here, but he nevertheless was looking forward to seeing the dervishes tonight. In fact, he was relieved not to have to expect authenticity. He lifted his two cotton paws in an attitude of come-what-may. "The faker, the better," he said.

Immediately the little bear feared he might have offended her, but Françoise laughed out loud. "Then I must see them as well!" she answered. It seemed they were becoming better and better friends.

In the tall windows of the Khan al-Khalili sparkled hundreds of tiny perfume bottles in ornate shapes and iridescent hues, edged with gold or silver. They were tiny as doll vases and topped like minarets. The blue-dark alleys wound and intersected in a maze, giving way to shops of silver, brass, or inlaid wood. Each was stacked to the ceiling with goods—jewelry, rugs and woven things, chess sets, and obelisks of stone. Evening approached. Winkie could hear the call to prayer blaring from a high loudspeaker, plaintive and overamplified.

So here he was. It would be a miracle and a surprise for him to be anywhere now instead of jail. But to find himself in this bustling city full of surprises, a place more than equal to his own sense of wonder: It was a gift of fate, and that in itself was another small miracle. People were everywhere. The marketplace went on and on. He and Françoise made their way past bolts of fabric, racks of plaid short-sleeve shirts, and used jeans with decorative stitching, then stalls piled with old radios, stereo speakers, avocado green princess phones. A slender woman shrouded entirely in white glided by as if in a dream, carrying on her head the largest and greenest lettuce the bear had ever seen. Just then he happened to glance to his right and saw through an open doorway hundreds of men prone in white and blue gowns like his own, the intricate singing of evening prayers drifting over that stillness. Winkie paused a moment, holding Françoise's hand in silence; then the two were jostled and moved forward again. "A beautiful sight," whispered Françoise, "but the mullah of that particular mosque is a rabid fundamentalist."

Soon, by a route that Winkie never could have retraced, they came upon the spice market. As Françoise began to argue in Arabic with a portly merchant, the old tan bear stood on tiptoe sniffing a pyramid of bright orange powder mounded taller than himself. It was an odor he'd never encountered before, dusky, woody, and pungent. Being entirely new to him, it could suggest no particular memory, and yet it made him think of Baby Winkie. For it was so fresh, and so unprecedented—he breathed in again the orange sharpness—that it evoked the possibility of all new experience and therefore of all memory.

From now on, Winkie thought, whenever he encountered it, this particular scent—a subtle fireball in the nose—would always bring back this particular moment when he had thought of his child, a moment that of course would be lost anyway, like all moments. Gazing now at the other pyramids of color, oblivious to Françoise's shouts at the turbaned spice seller, Winkie began thinking of all the steps both chosen and chanced that had brought him to this time and place—all that he'd learned, everyone he'd loved—and felt momentarily at peace with his own nostalgia. Today Françoise had reminded him that he didn't have to go back to America and stand trial again if he didn't want to, and the bear allowed himself to enjoy, for now, the fact that he hadn't yet decided what to do.

Françoise and the merchant came to an agreement, money was exchanged, and she and Winkie left the market carrying several small, fragrant packages wrapped in speckled gray paper. Passing between crumbling buildings the color of pale sand, the two reached yet another busy street. Cars, trucks, and taxis vroomed past. In the cab from the airport, Winkie had noticed that there didn't seem to be traffic signals anywhere in the city, or they were broken so often that no one paid any attention, or maybe everyone would have ignored them anyway. The bear hesitated at the curb. Battered vans brimming with passengers barreled past, and the slender, dark young men hanging out the windows laughed and pointed at a small group of European tourists who were, like Winkie, afraid to cross.

"You just have to let them know you exist," said Françoise. As Winkie watched, she murmured a prayer, set her foot down onto the dusty pavement, and simply moved forward into the fray. She had waited for only the slightest lull, and now the many autos, vans, and scooters slowed, stopped, or went around her. No one even honked. From the other side of the street, Françoise smiled and called back to the bear: "Not too slow, not too fast. Like this." She pantomimed the attitude of assurance that she had only just demonstrated—head bent in a certain way, arms relaxed yet determined at her sides.

Winkie, too, then placed his coarsely stitched foot in the road and made his way to the other side without incident. From then on, whenever he did so, it was a small and thrilling act of faith, and the slowing and parting of the cars and trucks and especially the countless beat-up little taxis enacted a minor miracle. The many vehicles seemed implacable, caring nothing for anyone or anything besides their destinations, yet somehow they made way for him, a little bear, and each time Winkie crossed he felt as though he had waded into the very flood stream of life and paradox.

"You just have to let them know you exist."

Acknowledgments

I'm grateful to my editor, Lauren Wein, for her remarkable sense of both structure and nuance and her unfailing belief in this book; to my agent, Maria Massie, for her expert guidance and unwavering support; and to Gabrielle Glancy, Wayne Kostenbaum, Robert Marshall, and Lisa Cohen for their inspired suggestions and insights through repeated readings. Thanks also to David Rakoff, Kevin Bentley, Catherine Kudlick, Carol Chase, Helen Chase, Noelle Hannon, Brian Kiteley, Barbara Feinberg, Bruce Ramsay, Ralph Sassone, Erin Hayes, Maggie Meehan, Michelle Memran, Bernard Cooper, and Frederic Tuten for their astute comments on all or part of the manuscript. For research help and/or stimulating conversation, I'm indebted to Sharon Novickas, Mike and Jean Kudlick, Ann Ruark, Katherine Dieckmann, Fatima Shaik, David Gates, Etel Adnan, and Simone Fattal.

Special thanks to Christopher Lione for art direction and Photoshop wizardry for the image of Winkie in "Egypt" and to John Kureck for the backdrop photo of the pyramids and his advice and help on all of the images. I'm grateful as well to Tai Dang, David Gavzy, and Barry Howard at *Newsweek* for processing, printing, and scanning; to American Medical Imaging in Brooklyn for the X-ray of Winkie; and to Gretchen Mergenthaler for designing the book's cover and Claire Howorth for handling publicity.

Thanks to Brian Kiteley for inviting me to read at the University of Denver at a crucial juncture; to Blue Mountain Center and the New York Foundation for the Arts for their support while I was working on this project; to Ken Weine, Roy Brunett, Karen Wheeler, and Diana Pearson at *Newsweek* for giving me time off to write; and to Paul Lisicky and Aldo Alvarez of *Blithe House Quarterly* and Robin Lippincott and Ellen Balber of *bananafish* for publishing chapters from this book early on (in somewhat different form).

Finally, my love and gratitude to Ruth Chase, 1915–2006, who gave me her teddy bear and her playfulness, and who held Winkie next to the rose.